The Realms Series

Book One

Wonderland

Emory R. Frie

For Sydney, who is mad in the best way possible.
All the best people are, after all.

Time is drowning,
Hearts are burning,
Heads are rolling,
Nothing can save you now,
Tick tock, tick tock;

Creatures talking,
Weak are rising,
White Queen's nearing,
Nothing can save you now,
Tick tock, tick tock;

Cards are bleeding,
Crowns are sweating,
Tea is spilling,
Nothing can save you now,
Tick tock, tick tock;

Red Queen, here's your warning,
Wonderland's raging,
Alice is coming,
Highness, time is drowning,
And nothing can save you now,
Tick tock, tick tock, tick tock...

-The Mad Hatter

Chapter One

Alice

It was a dreary day in an unknown town in England. The sky was grey and gloomy rain fell from the heavens. On the streets, everything was perfectly normal. Everyone went about their daily business, hunched under umbrellas and big hats in their attempt to stay dry. Automobiles drove down the stone paved street, so slow that the water hardly stirred when they teetered over particularly large puddles.

That day was hardly memorable to many people in that English town. But it wasn't their fault. After all, how could they have known?

None of this, however, was known to Alice. She knew as much about the town and the people as they knew about her. Within the next few weeks, however, nearly everyone in that town would know about her. But all they'd know would be a lie. They probably wouldn't even think she was real. But she was. She was all too real.

Even if Alice knew about the rain, or the people, or the small unknown town, she probably couldn't have cared less. For her life was about to change. Not for the better, mind you. At least, at the time, that's what it felt like to Alice.

She was led by two burly men deep underground. The sight might have been comical if it weren't for the circumstances. They really didn't need to hold her arms so firmly as they walked down that dark passageway. Alice wouldn't have resisted. She would have come with them somewhat willingly. Even if she had put up a fight, it would've been easy to drag her if necessary.

Alice was seventeen years old and of average height, though she seemed thin and small then. Her hair, usually blonde and full, now hung down her back tangled and limp. Blue eyes were cast down to the ground, seemingly drained of all sense of life. The usual twinkle of curiosity was lost. She didn't wear an expression of pride or joy, but an expression of loss and sorrow. It was as if she didn't care what happened to her.

Alice had that air about her of being forced to age far beyond her years. She had seen things most would never believe. That's why she was there now.

It was her father who sent her there. He'd turned her in, believing that she was losing her mind. Her father didn't approve of imagination. He didn't approve of anything Alice did for that matter. When Alice turned up again after being missing for months and started telling all sorts of stories about the adventures she had that were, in his mind, quite preposterous, he didn't know what else to do.

That's when he heard about the Facility.

Perhaps it was once called something more official, something with an acronym to shorten its name. But to the people sent there, it was merely called the Facility. There wasn't anything official about it.

All of this was what led to where Alice was then.

She felt the slight slant of the floor and knew that they were going lower underground. The tunnel was dark and dingy. An eerie, greenish glow illuminated from the overhanging lights. At least it wasn't high above ground. Alice didn't mind holes, just heights.

Alice never looked up into the faces of her escorts. But if she did, she would've found their beefy faces covered with scars. One even had an eye patch over an empty socket. And if the two guards looked down at Alice, they would've seen a wilted, rather pale girl clad in a wrinkled, faded dress.

They stopped short of a tall black door at the end of the long passageway. One of the guards pounded the door thrice. Alice winced with each deafening noise as they echoed through the tunnel.

The door opened with a long groan, a shabby old man holding it open. He stared up at the girl with beady eyes as she walked by, guard at each side.

The new tunnel they entered was brighter than the last, but in its own gloomy way. All sides were painted grey, the walls lined with doors. Only a small barred window decorated each door like a prison. Weeping brushed past Alice's ears as they walked down the hall. Afraid of what she might see, she dared not look through the windows. Cries were hardly ever sounded without reason. In a place like that, the reasons couldn't be anything less than horrific.

Seconds seemed to drag on for hours. With each heavy footfall, Alice's heart dropped a little lower. Finally reaching the lift at the end of the hall, the three stepped in, the lift shifting a bit as they entered. Before Alice even had the thought to run away, the doors closed and the shaft creaked as they descended farther down.

Alice thought she might cry, but the tears never came. Her eyes seemed to say that they'd done enough crying already to last a lifetime. It was as if all sense had left her and she was merely a ghost. She wasn't afraid. She didn't feel any emotion at all, really.

The lift stopped abruptly and the doors eased open. Alice and her companions entered a big room that reminded her, in a dark sense, of a courtroom she'd been in long ago. There were no windows, as they were underground, and a long table stretched across the floor. Three chairs sat on the opposite side. Another was empty, waiting for her. The other three chairs were already occupied by two men and one woman, all of which with an appearance of strong severity.

"Please sit," a bald man stated, his mouth moistened with the words.

She didn't protest and silently obeyed, slipping into the uncomfortable chair. Looking down at her hands folded in her lap, Alice knew that she ought to be scared. Most would've been petrified in that kind of situation. But she wasn't. She'd faced much worse than this.

The woman shuffled through her papers before staring menacingly over her half-moon spectacles. "Your name is Alice Pleasance Liddell, correct?"

"Yes," Alice answered in a weak voice. It was not weak for fear, mind you, but for the lack of use in quite some time.

"Miss Liddell, you are here because you have been professing that you have visited a... *fantasy* land, is that right?"

"It wasn't fantasy," Alice persisted, lifting her head to face her prosecutors.

"Just answer the question, Miss Liddell." The woman's cold grey eyes pierced into her.

"Yes," she muttered, her head hanging down once more.

"And your father was concerned about this childish proposition…"

"It's not childish!" Alice raised her voice.

"You will keep your temper, Miss Liddell, or there *will* be consequences!" The woman stared down her long, beaky nose at her.

"Miss Liddell," the sleek haired man spoke up. "Have you ever had any such problems before?"

Her fury was building up inside her. It was all she could do to contain it as she said flatly, "I *don't* have any problems."

"Please, just answer the question, Miss Liddell."

"No."

"We have been told otherwise," he countered. "Your father reported that a similar incident occurred seven years ago after your sister, Lorna, ran away from home."

She said nothing, simply sinking lower into her seat at the mention of her sister.

It didn't take long for the inquiries to continue. "We have reason to believe that you went missing a few months back. Is that correct?" His voice was sickly smooth.

"Yes."

"In addition to the time you disappeared seven years ago?"

How could they understand such disappearances were completely unrelated? But of course they couldn't. All they cared about was where she claimed to go.

"Yes," she answered.

"And where, may I ask, did you go when you went missing?"

There it was. The question they'd all been dying to ask. Still, the oily man was taunting her, Alice knew it.

She didn't respond, much to their dissatisfaction.

"Where did you go?" the woman asked, harsh and unyielding.

Still, Alice did not respond.

"Where did you go?" the bald man boomed, saliva flying from his lips.

Alice's voice was barely a whisper when she answered.

"What? Speak up, Miss Liddell!"

Blue eyes flashed when she lifted them to face those hypocritical doubters. For a moment, the familiar life flew into her eyes just as it'd done when she fell down the rabbit hole, when she'd passed through the looking glass.

"Wonderland."

Chapter Two

Curiously Familiar Stranger

Alice was flung ruthlessly into her cell, landing hard on the floor. The heavy iron door swung shut behind her. Its sound echoed in her soul.

Alice didn't move. She didn't speak. An utter mortifying ache filled her gut from her bold proclamation. She'd never planned on actually telling them where she'd gone. She couldn't help it. Something had taken over her.

But she knew exactly what had taken over her: her old self. She thought the old Alice was dead, but she was simply trapped inside of her, screaming and shouting to be free of the sorrowful prison she'd put herself in. Alice was trapped inside of herself. And for a moment, just one moment, the old Alice had set herself free.

What had given her the key? Was it the mention of Lorna? Her father? Was it the taunting, the questions, the memories? Or did Wonderland really have that much of a hold on her? She supposed it didn't matter, though. She couldn't get back to Wonderland, just like she couldn't get Lorna back, or convince Father she was sane, or save her friends. She couldn't even save herself.

A realization came over her suddenly. She didn't know when she'd ever get out of that Facility, nor even if she could get out. Fear washed over her as she lay in a crumpled heap. She was imprisoned… again. Tears glistened in her eyes.

"Hello?" a voice sounded from a corner in the dark room.

Alice skittered back in surprise, eyes searching for the voice's source.

"Oh, I'm sorry," the voice apologized. "I didn't mean to frighten you."

"No, it's just…" her voice trailed off.

"You thought you were alone," the voice guessed.

Alice nodded.

"I understand. I probably should've come out of the corner to introduce myself before I spoke. But, you see, I was a bit surprised myself. I didn't know I was getting a new roommate today."

A figure crawled out of the darkness and into the eerie light. The voice's source turned out to be a girl roughly fifteen years of age according to most observances. But appearances could be deceitful. She had curly brown hair pulled back in a loose ponytail by a frayed bow. Though she was small and seemed frail, she wasn't timid. Her eyes said otherwise; big and brown, filled with wonder and adventure. She wore a blue dress, or at least it used to be blue. Now, it was faded and wrinkled, hardly the kind of garment for a girl such as this.

The girl smiled warmly at Alice. "Hello."

The corners of her mouth twitched into a small smile as she said quietly, "Hello."

"What's your name?"

"Alice Pleasance Liddell," she replied as she'd been taught to do. "What's yours?"

"Wendy Moira Angela Darling," was her response.

Alice looked curiously at her. "I've heard that name before."

"I would expect so!" Wendy laughed to herself. "You heard it from a book, I'd bet, or at theatre."

"You were named after a character?"

"No. The character was named after me."

Though still confused, Alice changed the subject, "Where are we exactly?"

"Well, I like to call it the Fantasy and Magic Maintenance Facility, but it's a bit lengthy, so most just call it the Facility or an asylum."

She didn't like the word *asylum*. Asylums were for mad people, *prisons* for mad people. But Fantasy and Magic Maintenance... Alice shook her head. "I don't understand."

Wendy sighed and tried to explain better, "You see, the people running this place don't like the idea of magic ruining their perfect little world. If they hear that someone's spreading rumors about any oddities, they'll do almost anything to get the rumors to stop. If the rumors don't stop, they find the source and whisk the culprits here."

"But why?"

Wendy shifted into a more comfortable position. "They think of magic and similar abnormalities as poison. They think that those who believe in it are pests. They try to *knock some sense into us*, so to speak. They wish to stomp out our knowledge of the truth. They think of us as different, that we're poisoning their *perfect* world. They call what we went through a problem, an experience, a dream... but we know that it's much more than that."

15

Alice wasn't sure how she liked the phrase of *they* versus *we*. Who were *they*? Who were *we*?

"Does anyone ever get out?"

"Only if the problem is fixed. If you've proven to them that you no longer believe that where you went or what you did or who you met was no more than just a dream, then you're let go. But they'll try to break you. Not until you're successfully broken will you have any chance of freedom."

"How long have you been here?"

Wendy shrugged. "I'd say a little over a year."

Questions raged through Alice like a flood. "You said that the character *Wendy* in a book and play was named after you. What do you mean by that? How is that possible?"

"There are many people in the world just waiting to twist a story to fit their interests. Our stories are too unbelievable not to be twisted," Wendy explained. "Nearly everyone here has a book based off of us and our stories. But the thing is, people don't always want the truth, they just want what sounds right. For example, it is true that I went to Neverland, and quite a lot of the story is true, but it doesn't end right. I never stopped going to Neverland. Captain Hook is very much alive. And why would Peter take me away only for spring cleaning? I'm not a maid!"

"So, it is true, then? There really is a Neverland?"

Wendy smiled at Alice's enthusiasm. "Yes, but trust me, the stories aren't completely truthful. I don't know why they made so many changes. Peter is very much real, but the book makes him sound like a small, conceited boy. They made Neverland sound like nearly everything was a great game, when it wasn't. And I already told you about the ending mistakes."

"Well, what is the truth, then?" Alice asked, excited that there were others like her. She wasn't the only one who'd traveled to a fantastic new world filled with magic and wonder. It made her feel less crazy.

"Alright; let's see, where should I start?" She began, but the story was always inside her, a life of its own, ready to be released. "Blind Man's Bluff was teeming with pirates, all with at least an ounce of bloodthirst in their hearts. Captain Hook led them, the most vengeful and cruel of them all, striking respectful and quaking fear into any and all who faced him. They were always on the hunt for Peter. Hook had a nasty hunger for the death of his sworn nemesis ever since the feud between Lost Boy and pirate began. Somehow, due to the way Neverland connected with Peter Pan, the pirates could never seem to find the Lost Boys' hideout in all the ageless years they searched. That didn't stop them from trying, though.

"The Panther Tribe inhabited Flying Eagle Peninsula just above the white faced cliffs. The Chief was readying his daughter, Tiger Lily, to head the tribe when the time came. Unlike the pirates, the tribe was able to find the Lost Boys' hideout and often raided camp for supplies in the dead of night. They didn't like wasting their time with Peter and the Lost Boys much, though. No, they much preferred going after the pirates.

"Mermaids lurked in the island's lagoon, trapped there like a prison. They're deadly creatures. With their bewitching beauty and hypnotizing songs, it was all a perfect trap to lure their victims. What's worse was the lagoon's waters were so reflective that nothing underneath the surface could be detected. But once underwater, things could be seen all too clearly. Many pirates, tribesmen, and Lost Boys were lost to the mermaids. They almost got me once. Lucky Peter was there.

"On Neverpeak Mountain lived a great dragon with pearly green scales that blended with the crystal mountain rock. I never saw her much, only a few times. She mostly kept to herself. Dangerous and fearsome, she didn't like it when someone ventured onto her mountain. The Lost Boys made certain not to hunt on the dragon's territory.

"Ghosts haunted Skull Rock. Only on the occasional adventure did I see them. They were mostly pirate ghosts, but others showed themselves every so often. They could be deadly and manipulative, but Skull Rock still made for a great hiding place for captured treasure.

"The fairies were the only other creatures I can think of that weren't deadly. Not really anyway. They were friendly and charming, though a bit shy. Most never ventured far from Pixie Hollow. I don't know why the book made Tinker Bell so jealous. Perhaps she was at first, but she became a good friend, especially when I was surrounded by boys.

"There were lots of Lost Boys, too—all different ages. Nothing was better than a good game or adventure to them. They were good sports when Peter brought me and my brothers there. They respected him and looked up to him. The Lost Boys and Peter taught me many things: how to fight, how to fly, how to truly live. I loved it in Neverland, despite the constant danger. But it was so much better than being told to grow up constantly at home."

"What made you come back?" Alice asked.

"It wasn't that simple," Wendy admitted. "I love my family, my brothers, my parents. The first time I went to Neverland, I took John and Michael with me. But even though many don't like to admit it, Neverland makes you… forget if you're not careful. The older you are and the farther from the island you are, the more memories come back. After a while, my brothers were beginning to forget our parents. Unfortunately, I was too. So we came back to England, and truth be told, I never let them come with me again. I could remember things easier, but I couldn't stand it if little Michael forgot what a mother was, or if John questioned if he had a father."

"But you kept going to Neverland?"

"I couldn't stay away. Peter visited me a lot, and I'd return with him every so often, which was how…" She sighed as if so many things resulted in her returns to Neverland.

Alice tried to find the right question for what she wanted to know. "But why did you come back… this time?"

Wendy's eyes flashed with hatred, the name sounding like a curse, "Hook. He kidnapped me when no one expected it, took me back to England. I'm not sure what he would've done, but I escaped and fled to London where I was found and taken home. But once here, I couldn't fly anymore. I can't fly unless I have my happy thoughts; that's the trick to flying. But I left them back in Neverland with Peter. I haven't been to Neverland or seen Peter since."

Alice sat stunned for a moment before bringing up the courage to ask, "Why did Hook take you back to England?"

Wendy looked down at her hands folded in her lap. "Because I'm Peter's weakness. I don't know why Hook didn't just kill me. It would've been the perfect revenge."

A pause passed between them, one girl filled with memories, the other filled with questions. But none of those broke the silence.

All Alice could manage was a soft, pathetic, "I'm sorry."

"Don't be. It's not your fault," Wendy assured, forcing a smile. "Anyway, we should get some rest. I'm sure everyone will want to meet you."

"What do you mean?" she asked. Was this about *them* or *us*?

"Well, everyone who's not broken, at least," Wendy corrected herself, grinning.

Chapter Three

We, the Unbroken

Perhaps it was because of the interrogation that Alice dreamed of the first time she was in Wonderland. It was all a search for something, but had she known she'd been searching for herself there?

First, it was the rabbit, the white one with the pink eyes and a button down waistcoat. She didn't know why, but she knew that somehow that rabbit would lead her to a better place, one without a drunken father or a hole where Lorna used to be. A world of her own. How could the child know even before she fell down the rabbit hole?

Down, down, down…

"Obviously, you can't go that way."

It was a boy, red hair stuck up in all directions, his form similar to a potato. A potato with carrot hair. He looked at her stupidly, or rather, a bit smugly.

"Going down wouldn't make any sense, does it Dum?" questioned a second boy of exact proportions and features.

"No, Dee, there's nothing sensible about any of it!" replied his brother. "There can't be any question; she'd have to have gone through.*"*

"Only thing that makes a lick of sensibility."

Why did they throw that word around: sensible? There wasn't anything sensible about this place!

Music tapped her on the shoulder, drawing her attention. It came in color, like smoky rainbows clouding about her in jolly melody. It parted like a curtain to reveal the never ending table of tea and cakes, pots whistling, butter swishing, all in maddening rhythm to the music's color.

"I was wondering when you'd come by!" cried the new boy wearing a hat that hung lopsided on his head. It was much too big for him. He had to push the thing up constantly so it wouldn't fall over his eyes.

"Is it your unbirthday, too?" questioned another tea party guest: a rabbit. But he was the wrong color, a cinnamon brown where as she sought sugar white.

"I suppose it is," she responded, utterly confused by the whole ordeal. "But it's hard to tell; I haven't felt like myself recently."

"Whyyyyy?" The droning voice made her sleepy. She rubbed her eyes, but when she opened them, the tea party was gone. A caterpillar stood before her, staring through moon shaped spectacles with perplexing wisdom.

"Well, it's all so confusing, you see," she tried to explain. "I like it here, but I believe I've become entirely different since I fell down the rabbit hole. Am I still the same Alice? Or have I become a better or worse one?"

"Yes," was the caterpillar's reply.

"Yes, to what?"

"It doesn't matter."

She wanted to inquire further, but she was distracted. Laughter surrounded her, echoing from all places at once. She could've sworn she was laughing herself but for that her mouth wasn't open.

"Who's there?" she shouted.

Still, more laughter in giggles and hoots, snorts and chortles. It was all kinds of laughter at once, yet all one *voice. A smile shimmered to being above her, like a crescent moon with teeth.*

"Do you know the way back?" she asked the smile.

"Back?" it replied. "Why would you go back? It's silly, isn't it? Going backwards? Forwards, sideways, left, right, up, or down, those are best ways to move, but never back."

"But I have to go home now, you see," she explained. "I have to wait for my sister. She's coming back, you know!"

"Never back, never back!" the smile persisted, a shadow seeming to form around it. "People don't like going back, even if they must. I don't like going back! And I'm not people! But I look back, sometimes, every so often, just to make sure I'm not leaving anything important behind. Like my tail! I can never be sure when I leave my tail behind me by mistake."

A door opened. Was it there before? But it didn't lead her home.

Roses, roses, painting white roses strawberry red. And tarts! Who took the tarts? Did Underlanders take the Duchess' tarts?

The Queen of Hearts...

"Alice."

Alice's eyes snapped open. It took her a moment to remember where she was. It was so dark she barely saw Wendy's silhouette looking down at her.

"What is it?" Alice groaned, rubbing her stiff back.

Wendy hushed her. "We have to be quiet; don't want to wake anyone."

Alice watched Wendy's dark form sneak off. Curiosity overcame confusion as it always did for her as she crawled after the girl. She watched as Wendy moved aside her small, flat bed and dug her fingers into thin cracks in the wall to pull out a section of concrete. A tunnel was exposed, large enough for a small someone to go through.

Through the rabbit hole, the thought echoed in Alice's mind.

Wendy tossed her brown curls as she whipped her head back. "You first."

Alice didn't say anything, just sat there dumbly. Was this a trap? Was the Facility trying to pull some scheme to trick her?

"Come on, Alice," Wendy beckoned. "There's nothing dangerous. I'll be right behind you, but we've got to hurry."

She obeyed silently, curiosity overcoming her once again. Crawling into the tunnel, Alice got down on hands and knees so as not to hit her head. It was a tight fit, but she could still move. A vague nostalgia pounded in her chest, like a distant memory dying to be free. The old Alice was screaming, banging in her cage. She wished to be free, but Alice wouldn't let her. She didn't want feelings to rise again before she could stop them.

Alice wiggled farther in, making room for her new friend. Concrete grinded as the wall was fitted back into place. Pitch blackness swam around them, suffocating the tunnel.

"Keep going," Wendy whispered behind her.

Alice turned back to the endless darkness and crawled along the tunnel, Wendy closely following. The peculiar smell of age, dust, and dirt churned well with the musty air. This was an old tunnel; much too old for it to be dug out by Wendy. But Alice had already determined that Wendy only discovered the tunnel.

Something touched her foot, and Alice jumped, hitting her head on the tunnel ceiling. She muffled a startled cry as her hand flew to her throbbing scalp. It didn't take long to register that it'd been only Wendy.

"Sorry, that's my fault," Wendy apologized. "We're nearly there."

Sure enough, the end of the tunnel swelled before them before long. Alice placed her hands on the barrier, pushing and pulling, expecting the dead end was a secret door.

"There's a trapdoor above you," Wendy hinted.

Slightly embarrassed, Alice got on her knees to better position herself. Pushing up on the aged wood above her head, it gave way. Light streamed in aggressively.

She stood up, blinking in the sudden brightness. As her eyes adjusted, she could make out two figures moving towards her. Hands grasped her arms and pulled her out of the tunnel. They released her when her feet found the floor. Pulse racing in preparation for danger, Alice instinctively backed up until her heel thumped against a wall.

Two boys helped Wendy out of the tunnel. Alice didn't know what to say or do or even think. Her head buzzed with questions. When was her head never buzzing with questions?

"Thanks, boys." Wendy grinned.

"The pleasure is ours," one boy teased, giving an extravagant bow.

Wendy laughed. "Jack, must you always be so modest?"

Jack was a tall, eighteen-year-old boy with short, brown waves that swept lightly over his brow. Dark blue eyes glittered under thick eyebrows. A big grin spread over his face that suited him well with deep dimples caving in past the corners of his mouth. Freckles dotted his nose, adding to his fun character. A faded green shirt hung over his shoulders, too large to properly fit him. His jeans were torn at the knees and frayed along the ankles.

The other boy—his name yet to be revealed—was better built and slightly shorter than Jack. A chiseled chin made him look older than his nineteen years. A long white scar ran along his jaw, standing out amongst his sharp complexion. He had lemon blond hair cut short to his head and icy blue eyes that sent a chill up Alice's spine. Whereas Jack's shirt was too large for him, this boy's seemed too snug. The grey fabric pulled tight over his muscular torso, only loosening slightly over the abs. His jeans were worn, but the threads held together better than Jack's.

"Who's your friend, Wendy?" His voice was deep when he spoke. A tinge of some rough accent played about his tongue.

"I was going to do introductions once Red got here," Wendy admitted.

"Do what when I got here?"

Alice twitched at the sound of the new voice.

From a secret door in the wall emerged an eighteen-year-old girl. Long black hair fell down her back with slightly rough texture. Her eyes were a brilliant bottle green and they flashed with the unmistakable glint of secrets. Every step was made with edge and purpose. An air about her hinted she was a tough mystery to solve. Alice could already tell this girl was dangerous if on her bad side. She wore a dress that might've once been scarlet. But like most everything in that Facility, it'd become faded and dull.

"Who's this?" Her voice was strong and steady, much like her.

"Well, now that you're all here," Wendy introduced, "everyone, this is Alice. She's my new roommate; just got in yesterday."

Alice blushed as everyone looked at her.

"Alice, this is everyone." Wendy gestured.

Jack leaned close to whisper, "I think you have to be a little more specific."

"I know that!" she said, pushing him away teasingly. "I was just getting there. Alright, this is Jack Caldwell, *the* Jack from *Jack and the Beanstalk*. However, his real story consists of a kingdom of giants, narrow escapes during his adventures, and the death of a close friend. The giants killed her and captured her brother before Jack could make it out. He was caught by the Facility before he could go back to execute a rescue mission."

Jack gave a weak smile, the memory obviously painful. But Alice saw it, the spark of revenge in his eyes before he could hide it. She'd seen it before. Dare she say she was even familiar with it herself.

"This," Wendy indicated the other boy, "is Kai Ødegård. The story based off him is known as *The Snow Queen*, but his true story's a bit more tragic. Kai wasn't kidnapped by the Snow Queen; his best friend Gerda was. Kai managed to follow her through the portal she'd used to a frostbitten world, enduring many hardships once there. When he finally made it to the Snow Queen's castle, he was tricked and barely escaped with his life when he fell into some kind of portal back to this world. Kai was searching for another way back when he brought the Facility's attention. As you can see, they managed to obtain him before he found a way back."

Kai's icy eyes were cast on the ground, obviously not wanting to make eye contact with anyone. His fingers traced his scar in habit, his brow knit together in aggravation.

He's a man in love, Alice thought.

"And last, but not least," Wendy said, motioning to the black haired girl, "this is Rubina Ellen Daim—better known as Red—from *Little Red Riding Hood*. A wolf chased her into another realm where she discovered him to be both man and beast. He'd been hired to hunt Red down and take her to his employer. She was hunted for a long time before she had a terrible incident... but she doesn't like to talk about that. Anyway, it resulted in her falling back into this world where she continued to run until the Facility took her in. Red says that the wolf, Fang, is still out there hunting her. She doesn't know who wants her or why."

The glint of secrets flashed in Red's eyes as the memory returned. What was she hiding?

"And then there's me! But I've already told you my story. My trips to Neverland took a toll on me, and it was obvious that I wasn't growing up physically at any normal rate. My parents began lying about my age, and even claimed that John and Michael were my older brothers when they surpassed me and began families of their own. Rumors spread with flavors of growing disorders. But the last time I made it back, my records were revealed to authorities when they took me home. The Facility found me, ended up kidnapping me when my parents refused to send me with them. From what I've heard, Mother and Father are still looking for me. I miss them terribly, though they'd thought my head was full of fantasies when I tried to explain why I wasn't growing."

How old was she? It had to be considerably more than fifteen to draw much attention. It only added to the multitude of questions in Alice's head.

"And here we are," Wendy concluded her introduction of the unbroken.

Of course, all curious Alice had to say were questions.

"And where are we exactly?" she asked.

"Honestly?" Jack spoke up. "We don't know."

"What do you mean?"

"We've only known about this place for about… two or three months, maybe?" Red responded.

"Wendy discovered the secret passageways," Kai informed. "They lead from each of our cells to this room."

"We think it must be a forgotten storage room," Wendy commented.

Alice looked around. It did seem like a forgotten storage room. There was an assortment of chairs and some old furniture. Boxes were stacked here and there in piles. But she felt a strange warning in her gut. There was no door, which was odd, and no window either. Did they really believe this was just some spare room?

"Now that you know about us," Wendy interrupted her thoughts, "maybe you could tell us a little about yourself, your experience, and how you got here?"

Alice took a deep breath. She'd never really talked about it to anyone, not since she told her father. When she was little, she told anyone who would listen about her adventures in Wonderland. But it was different when a ten-year-old told such fantastical stories with certainty than it was when a nearly grown girl told them. It wasn't sensible.

You're mad, Alice, her father had insisted.

He was right.

So for the second time in twenty-four hours, the old Alice was allowed to speak.

Alice began softly, like a child afraid of being scolded, "Alright, I suppose there's no other way to put it. Two times I have gone to Wonderland, a place where so many curious things happen and can be found. Flowers talk there and sing strange songs only flowers can sing. Some animals have souls like people, probably more human in some sense than we are. Other strange creatures inhabited there; mome raths swarming in the depths of the Tulgey Wood, slithy toves grazing in the Mimsy Meadows, jubjub birds nesting in the Diamond Mountains, and borogoves scampering through the Sugar Desert.

"I met many of my closest friends there: The Tweedle Twins who were the most positive loyal men I've ever known; the Cheshire Cat couldn't stay on the same train of thought for long if he tried; the White Queen was more of a sister to me than anything; the White Rabbit always claimed everyone was late because he had a knack for arriving anywhere precisely on time; and…" The words came easier now, but this name was hard to say, "The Mad Hatter, Remus, he always found a way to make the impossible possible and stood by me 'til the end.

"Wonderland was ruled by the Queen of Hearts last I journeyed there. Everyone's terrified of her. I suppose I should say *nearly* everyone's afraid of her. She took pleasure in causing people pain if they didn't do as she wished. Her favorite form of torture was to rip beating hearts out with her bare hands. Her victims still lived on but with no emotion and hardly any soul. Her second favorite was to show what she called *mercy* by cutting off one's head. Only the Duchess rivaled her in cruelty.

"I don't know why, but last time I was there the Queen of Hearts wanted me. She was constantly after me. Before too long, she managed to capture me, but Remus set up a small army to save me from whatever fate I had. They attacked the castle. That was my last night in Wonderland. I saw the Queen of Hearts rip out Remus' heart right before I stumbled back into this world.

"My father didn't believe me when I told him what happened. He thought I was going insane and I was speaking rubbish. Somehow he contacted the Facility and sent me here. *They say I'm mad.*" Alice couldn't help but give a huff of humorless laughter at the irony. "That's my story, the reason I'm here. It's my tragedy."

Silence hung heavy as everyone processed Alice's words. No one tried to comfort her, for they knew there was no comfort for such matters. It wasn't hard for them to comprehend it. They'd all gone through loss and pain and despair. Most everyone lost someone they loved or cared about. That's what bonded them together; they understood.

They related and empathized. They knew they weren't crazy, despite what everyone else might've thought.

This understanding started their lifelong friendship.

It was getting late. A distant bell chimed thrice in the silence.

"We need to get going," Red stated. "We don't want to be missed."

They quietly nodded.

Red started off, but turned back to say, "It was nice meeting you, Alice," before she disappeared behind the hidden door.

"See you later, Wendy, Alice," Jack said as he and Kai climbed up a stack of boxes and into a hole in the ceiling.

Alice followed Wendy into the secret passageway under the floor. The two crawled down in silence and were soon back inside their cell. The wall was put where it belonged, and Wendy's bed was back in its place. They simultaneously crawled into their hard, flat beds and pulled thin, threadbare blankets over their tired bodies. Alice didn't close her eyes, though. Thoughts and memories kept racing through her mind.

Wendy's voice, soft and gentle, asked, "You and Remus were more than just friends, weren't you?"

Alice felt a tear slip down her cheek. "Yes."

She heard Wendy sigh before questioning, "You said that Remus was a *mad* hatter. Was he really mad?"

Alice found herself smiling through her trailing tears.

"Everyone's mad in Wonderland."

Chapter Four

Dreaming Memories

Week One was attempting to reason.

Perhaps the Facility members were confused and ever more convinced of her madness when Alice laughed every time they used the word *sensible*. They asked her questions. She answered in complete, maddening seriousness. It was even more frustrating when she began reverse interrogation, daring to ask *them* questions like a toddler.

"Why am I here?" she'd ask.

"Because your father is concerned of your sanity," the poor fellow would respond.

"Why?" Alice pestered.

"Because you claim to have gone to a nonexistent land with frog footmen, and rabbits, and bread-and-butterflies," he explained, a dryness in the back of his throat.

"Aren't there footmen here?" she'd question. "And frogs?"

"Well, yes," he'd stutter, "but they're never one in the same."

"Why not?"

"Because it's not sensible."

Alice snickered.

"What about butterflies?" she'd continue. "Those are here too, I'm sure."

"Yes, but never on bread!"

"Now you sound mad. Who would ever want just plain butter? Butter without bread is like a tea party without tea. It's an impossibly possible impossibility!"

Sweat beaded his brow like dewdrops. "I believe we've gone off topic, Miss Liddell…"

"And what about rabbits?" she interrupted. "Surely you're not denying their existence, too."

"Of course not, but *real* rabbits don't talk or carry pocket watches or sip tea!" he'd exclaim. "It's just not sensible!"

She chuckled.

"Miss Liddell," he'd groan, "this is all impossible! Don't you understand that? It's impossible!"

Her expression was all seriousness, as if he'd hit a nerve. "Impossible…?" she'd say slowly, eyes shining. "Impossible is just a word."

Week Two took a less than civil approach.

"For the last time, Miss Liddell," the stern woman ordered. She was fittingly dubbed Mrs. Bones, her skin quite nearly opaque, not a single scrap of fat in her body. "Where were you during this summer's disappearance? Don't lie to me this time!"

"I never lied to you," Alice retorted.

The woman briskly struck Alice across the face. Alice inhaled through her teeth, but didn't cry out. She spat blood at Mrs. Bones' feet. It speckled like rose petals.

"How *dare* you talk back to me!" Mrs. Bones shouted, her grey eyes burning with stiff cruelty. "Now, I will ask you one last time, Miss Liddell. *Where* were you during this summer's disappearance?"

Alice turned her eyes up with bitter intensity. A rebellious sneer twitching her nose; it was probably mistaken for madness. "*Wonderland.*"

Her head snapped back as another blow struck her face. Blood trickled down her cheek and she tasted the sourness of it in her mouth. The side of her face smarted into cardboard painful to the touch. Mrs. Bones stood ridged, breathing deeply through her tiny nose. Her lips pierced tightly together in a thin line, a fine finish to the skull image.

The skull turned sharply to the guard standing by the door. "This isn't going to work. Put Miss Liddell back in her cell. We will treat her just as the other stubborn ones from now on... until she breaks."

The guard nodded. He took Alice firmly by the arm with his beefy hands. She winced when he grabbed a sore spot: a sickly yellow bruise she'd accommodated during a pervious interrogation. Roughly the guard led her out of the room, Mrs. Bones' cold eyes following them out the door.

Soon Alice was thrust into her cell, as was tradition, and the heavy iron door locked shut behind her. Even after two weeks, she still held her own in the brutal interrogations and tortures. Most would've been halfway broken by then in that Facility, but not Alice. Her body was beaten and covered in black bruises and agitated cuts, yet she still endured. She'd suffered much worse than that in the past.

Wendy wasn't in the cell. Alice didn't concern herself though. Wendy's interrogations sometimes went longer. The Facility went harder on Wendy than on her, since Alice was still the new one. She had a feeling, though, that was going to change soon. It was just as Mrs. Bones said: Alice was indeed one of the stubborn ones. She wouldn't give up easily. She wouldn't give up at all.

A slot at the bottom of the door opened with a click. A shriveled mousy hand pushed in a dirty bowl of water and an old rag before disappearing again quickly. The slot shut. Alice picked up the rag, finding an extra morsel of bread and cheese folded inside.

"Thank you, Gus," Alice whispered to the vanished mouse-like hand.

She divided the small loaf and little wedge of cheese. Gulfing down half of the spared rations, she saved the rest for Wendy. After finishing the meager meal, she soaked the rag in the lukewarm water and pressed it to the wounds on her face. Cardboard skin turned tender instantaneously.

Her ears pricked at the sound of approaching footsteps. She quickly hid Wendy's morsels in the pocket of her skirts instinctively. No need to beg for more trouble than she already had. She didn't want Gus ratted out either, for that matter.

Alice quickly scrambled to the side as Wendy was ruthlessly thrown into the cell beside her. What a painful tradition. The door slammed shut and the bolt locked into place with a rusty groan.

When Wendy looked up the swollen eye and split lip was plain. Her hands were severely bruised, her knuckles raw and bloody. She seemed much smaller in that moment.

Alice took out the bread and cheese from her pocket and gave them to Wendy. "Gus snuck this in."

Wendy sighed appreciatively, gobbling down the food. "God bless him! Despite all the trouble he could get into, he still helps us."

"Here." Alice handed her the rag and bowl.

"Thanks." Wendy took them. "Mrs. Prig decided to use the rod today. It wasn't that bad. Better than the whip. Who'd you get?"

"Mrs. Bones."

"Again? Ouch! She has a boney hand, that one. At least you didn't get Mister Rune. He's the worst, so I've heard. Kai and Red had her a few times. He's only used for special occasions, especially for those who've been caught trying to escape."

Escape. The word vibrated in the air.

"Is it possible?" Alice blurted out.

"Is what possible?"

"To escape; is it possible?" The question constantly nagged the back of Alice's brain ever since she'd arrived.

Wendy smiled, much too bright a look for a girl with a black eye and blood in her teeth. "Why do you think Kai and Red got Mister Rune for a while? Getting out is the easy part. It's staying out that's nearly impossible. The Facility hunts you down fast. They have eyes and ears practically everywhere... *in this world*."

First, Alice's heart fell to her toes. She'd hoped it would be possible to leave and never return. But she supposed that if it was easy, most everyone would've escaped by then. Perhaps, then, if escape was to be possible, some impossibilities were required.

"Have you tried to escape?" Alice asked.

A sparkle shone bright in Wendy's eyes. "I've never stopped trying. I just haven't been caught, yet."

They went to sleep early that night so they could visit the others later. Alice closed her eyes and fell asleep almost immediately. Her dreams were restless. The memories resurfaced. It was like she was living it again.

She sat in the Queen's dungeons. Overwhelming darkness pushed on all sides. Silence lay heavily in the air. Nightmares were never too far away. What would become of her? What would the Queen of Hearts do to her?

Commotion sounded, like ringing diamonds and crashing pans.

She stood and pressed her face against the barred door. What was happening? She heard a voice, her name, pounding footfalls.

"REMUS!" she screamed. "REMUS!"

"ALICE!"

"REMUS!" She banged against her cell door. It rattled on its hinges.

A scramble of feet reached her cell. "Alice," Remus said. Blue eyes grabbed her and never averted. "It's going to be alright."

She held his hands between the bars. Tears slipped down her cheeks, hopes that managed to leak out like stars.

Tweedle-Dee ran up behind him, taller now, gangly. Had he not eaten since her first visit to Wonderland? "I've got it, Remus."

"Right; Alice," Remus urged, "back away from the door."

She nodded. His hands received a last squeeze before she retreated to the back of the cell. Dee threw a handful of powder at the door's hinges. It stuck and sparked. A deafening clatter of metal, and the door fell. She too fell into Remus' arms, taking in their security.

"We've got to go, Hatter," Dee ushered.

Remus took her hand and together they ran out.

The three of them dashed out of the dungeons, joined by Tweedle-Dum, who was just as tall and gangly as his brother, and the White Rabbit, his waistcoat especially dusty. The group was intercepted in the Great Hall by the Queen's cards—the title dubbed to the soldiers by the natives. But a battle was already underway.

There was the White Queen hurling balls of light at the soldiers, causing them to collapse to the ground like dominos... or better described as a stack of playing cards. The Cheshire Cat appeared and disappeared in different places, causing great confusion among the enemy. He dropped objects on their heads.

Remus continued to drag her through the chaos. Pins and needles flew from his hands aimed at approaching soldiers. They collapsed in pain from the poison on the strange weapons.

"WE'VE GOT HER!" Remus shouted. "FALL BACK!"

The small army surged for the doors to escape. But the very doors that would lead them to safety opened and out stepped the Queen of Hearts in all of her evil and cruelty. More of her cards flooded in behind her, causing the rescue party to falter back.

Utter chaos broke. Screams bounced off the walls, battle cries jabbed the air, diamond blades screeched unnaturally. Deep, dark red collected in pools on the sleek floor.

Remus turned to the twins. "You two, get her to safety."

"No," she retorted. "I want to stay and fight. I won't retreat when all of you are in danger!"

Blue eyes grabbed her again, urgent, pained. "You're more important than you think you are, Alice."

He brushed her cheek gingerly and gave her that crazy smile of his. A twinge of safe familiarity in all that horror. Then he thrust her to the twins, who dragged her away despite her struggles. Loyal men were hard to fight off.

Remus turned away and raised his sword. She struggled frantically as the twins heaved her across the room. But she saw it all. Remus was after the Queen of Hearts. He threw his sword back in momentum for the blow, but the Queen raised her finger and the sword flew out of Remus' hands. A thick poisonous needle the size of a dagger appeared in his fist. He tried to send her a heavy blow, but she knocked his arm aside. The Queen whacked another thrust away again and again.

The crowd cleared just enough for her to see it.

The Queen plunged her hand into Remus' chest. A blood curdling yell blasted from his mouth.

It was a blow to her stomach. Shock overtook her. She couldn't do anything.

An evil smile rested on the Queen's face. Withdrawing her hand, the Queen of Hearts held the Mad Hatter's beating heart in her fist. He fell back, a body crumpled to the floor.

"NO!" she screamed.

Emotion and desperation came rushing back. She struggled against the twin's arms. They shoved her away.

She was going to crash into the mirror... The collision never came. Her body plunged through the glass, a cold wave of ice water then nothing. She knelt in the forest behind her father's house.

Looking around, she recognized where she was instantly. Pain and sorrow as she'd never felt before filled her to overflowing. Launching into a flood of tears, she screamed Remus' name over and over again as if that would return him to her, or better yet return her to him. She didn't want to believe what she'd witnessed. The shock still weighed heavy on her...

"Alice," a voice whispered loudly in her ear, "Alice!"

Alice opened her eyes. She breathed mightily, instantly aware she was drenched in cold sweat. Tears spilled steadily down her cheeks. Wendy leaned over her, concern on her face.

"Are you alright?" Wendy asked.

Alice took a while to answer, "Yeah. Yeah, I'm alright."

"You kept saying his name in your sleep," Wendy informed, "Remus' name."

Alice tried to swallow the lump in her throat. "Yeah, I was... living it again: my last time in Wonderland."

"If you don't want to go tonight, I'm sure everyone will understand..."

"No. No, I'll... I'll be fine," Alice insisted. Her hesitation and repetitions suggested otherwise.

She quickly got up, mopping her forehead with the back of her hand. The two girls made their way down the secret tunnel quickly. Soon, they were in the forgotten storage room with the others. As was typically the case, questions were asked. Alice asked most of them.

"Is there any news on Goldie?" Wendy inquired after everyone found some kind of seat to rest on.

"Who's Goldie?" Alice asked.

"Gladys Locks, but everyone calls her Goldie," Jack explained. "She's one of the younger ones here; hasn't taken her experience very well."

"She has nightmares," Wendy added, "screams in her sleep. Goldie is extremely paranoid ever since she ran into a family of talking bears. So, is there any news?"

"They let her go," Red informed. "She broke this morning."

"Oh. It's probably the best for her. I think she needed to move on with that, seeing what she went through and how young she is," Wendy commented.

Alice couldn't help but think how old she'd been when she first went to Wonderland. Ten years old. She ran into a lot more than just talking bears. Why didn't it bother her then? What made her different from this Goldie Locks girl?

Perhaps she's more sensible than I was, Alice thought.

Red supplied the next topic by announcing, "Guess what I heard?"

"We're all going to be freed tomorrow?" Jack guessed.

All eyes looked at Jack with at least a fraction of annoyance. Things like that didn't really happen, and it wasn't typical to joke about something like that. Freedom was a sensitive subject when no one expected it any time soon. But this was Jack. He had a habit of joking about most everything.

He shrugged. "What? It was just a guess."

Wendy rolled her eyes before turning back to Red. "What is it?"

"A new book's coming in. The Facility is running it through similarities with the case, seeing if it's an adequate match."

"Another book?" groaned Jack.

Red hit him. "They're our only means of entertainment in this place."

"Spare us our meager pleasures," Wendy added with a smile.

Adequate match? Alice wondered.

"Who is it about this time?" Kai asked, straight to the point.

A smile itched at Red's mouth. "Let's just say the book's called *Alice's Adventures in Wonderland.*"

All heads turned to Alice.

A pit formed in her stomach. "How is that possible? And what do you mean by an *adequate match*? Did someone find out about me before the Facility? I never talked to anyone else…"

"Alice!" Wendy cut in to explain, "What Red meant was that the Facility found a story, whether it's been around for years or simply days, that closely matches your own. They like to use it as a method to prove we're lying or make us think we're crazy."

"But… wait, *years?*" Her mind raced, but different questions replaced that one. "How could anyone write a book about me? My story is certainly not book worthy and I'm absolutely positive that I didn't have the classic *happily ever after.*"

"The authors tied to the Facility don't care about what *really* happened. All they care about is the idea. They twist our stories to suit their fancy, then they sell it. All of us have dealt with it." Jack grinned as he explained, "Sometimes, we get a good laugh at how naive the stories are."

"But how could they do such a thing?" Alice protested. "Don't they have any respect?"

Kai shrugged, answering with a forlorn truth, "It's just what they do, turn our tragedies into their fantasies."

It was the first time she noticed the chain bearing a ring under his shirt.

Chapter Five
Impossibly Possible Freedom

It was a few weeks later when the book came in. *Alice's Adventures in Wonderland* was thrust into Alice and Wendy's cell after a morning of brutal interrogation. Brushing out the pages to press neatly together again, Alice inspected the jacket. Red cover, black spine, and gold etchings. A circle in the front featured a girl who could pass for Alice at ten, holding a pig in a bonnet. The back circled a cat's head with more of a smirk than a smile. She didn't recognize the author's name, so she knew she hadn't told him anything. But what confused her more was the publication date.

That's impossible, she thought. *I wasn't even born then.*

Her mother, perhaps, would've been better suited for the child's role in the book. Not Alice. It'd be impossible.

Never the less, she made herself as comfortable as she could and poured herself into the book. She'd always prided herself in being a fast reader. It was one of the attributes her father was actually impressed with. Even as it was a children's book, it wasn't a surprise that Alice whipped through it before the day was over.

The ending was what did it. No, the story never said Lorna's name, but Alice knew no other biological sister. Her eyes stung and her throat tightened. If only she really had woken up in the lap of her sister. But it seemed happy endings only occurred in the confines of a book. Alice never woke up from her supposed dreams of Wonderland. Even if she did, Lorna wouldn't have been there to brush the leaves off her face. That too was a mere fairytale.

After Alice finished, she tossed it aside. Though later she would suppose that it was a clever story, truly a similar one to the truth. But the thought of Lorna made her agitated. That was too personal a detail to mess with. Now, all she could see were the mistakes.

It wasn't the truth.

The truth was too painful.

All at once, Alice found herself choking with laughter. What nonsense! It was the most nonsense she'd had in weeks! That bound collection of impracticalities may not have been the impossible she was waiting for, but it fed her laughter. It fueled her madness. It made her forget all about the new bruises from that morning's torture session with Mrs. Prig.

She hadn't had Mrs. Bones since last week.

"Was it anything like what really happened?" Wendy asked, lowering her book: dark green with gold illustrations and borders, titled *Peter and Wendy*.

"No," Alice found herself laughing harder, even as she knew what she said wasn't entirely true, "not at all! It was hardly anything like it!"

"I can see you're handling it quite well." Wendy chuckled a little.

Her face hid behind her book again. Why she was even reading the book was a mystery. After all, Wendy had the whole thing memorized cover to cover from hours upon hours of rereading the same words. Perhaps it was one way to feel close to the worlds they loved, reading the stories that were only a shadow of reality. It was better than nothing.

Maybe Alice too would have her own retold tale memorized. There wouldn't be much else entertainment, unless the interrogations counted.

Alice continued to laugh, unable to stop. Finally, she calmed down, though her smile remained. It felt good. It'd been so long since the last time she really laughed. But the absence of it made thoughts rush back. She realized how Remus would've responded to such lack of mirth. Given his way, Alice should never stop laughing and smiling.

"Don't ever lose your smile," he once told her. *"Don't ever let anything take away the joy from your laugh. You never know when the taste of laughter on the tongue or the scent of happiness in the air might save one's life."*

A warm glow bloomed in her heart. It swelled at the thought of Remus. At first, Alice thought she might cry. But then she thought she'd laugh again. She didn't do either, just sat staring into empty space. A soft smile manipulated her lips.

Alice looked over at Wendy, who still held the book up to her nose, but she wasn't reading. Shiny brown eyes stared blankly at the words on the pages. Again, Wendy looked much younger, much smaller than she really was. Alice felt the urge to say something.

"Tell me about Peter," were the words that popped out. She regretted them instantly. Wendy set her book aside as Alice quickly added, "Only if you want to!"

"I don't mind," Wendy insisted, a smile growing on her face. "What do you wish to know first?"

"How did you meet?" Alice inquired.

"The first time he came to my window was because of his Shadow. It was hiding in my room; Peter was trying to find it."

"How could a shadow hide in your room?" she interrupted, even though she thought it a stupid question as soon as she said it. After all, why should she question? She believed in rabbits in waistcoats and smiling cats.

Wendy shrugged. "It's how Peter's shadow works. The Shadow is a tie to Neverland of sorts. In a way, it's a creature of its own, yet it's not..." She sighed, trying to explain, "The Shadow is part of Peter, but at the same time is a part of Neverland. It's both in one, and thus its own. Does that make any sense?"

"Hardly, but don't mind me! Just keep going with the story."

She laughed. "Anyway, it was a game they used to play when they visited this world. I was maybe around eleven or twelve when the Shadow decided to hide in my bedroom. Peter saw where it went, so he was searching frantically in my room. The commotion woke me. But I didn't panic for some reason. Maybe I had a feeling I knew him. Maybe it's because Nana never stirred or my brothers didn't wake. Maybe I was just too shocked when I saw him fly.

"I was afraid he'd wake up the boys, so I was quick to draw his attention. He didn't seem surprised by my presence, but he did ask if I'd help find his Shadow. Of course at first I thought this a peculiar question; but if a boy could fly, why couldn't a shadow hide? I found it in one of my dresser drawers. Shadow attached itself to Peter once discovered. I liked him instantly.

"We became fast friends. He told me all about Neverland and his many adventures, and I told him stories of my own. He was curious and interested in everything I had to say, as I was in what he said. He visited me nearly every night, bringing Tinker Bell with him every now and then. I'd relate some of Peter's stories to John and Michael, who quickly adapted them to their playing. That went on for a few months before he finally took us to Neverland."

"What's he like?" Alice asked next, "Peter Pan?"

She didn't know the face Wendy saw, but she recognized the look of a girl in love. How to describe what the heart saw? Impossible. All that could be done was scrap together personas and characteristics to formulate a partially complete puzzle of the boy.

"Peter loved to have fun," Wendy brought the first piece of his character. "He and the Lost Boys were always playing some kind of game when they weren't busy. But Peter was also responsible, more so after I knew him longer. He was like the Lost Boys' big brother. As leader, he took his responsibility seriously. The Lost Boys respected him, looked up to him, and Peter never took advantage of that. He always put them first. He wouldn't eat unless he knew there was enough food to go around. When there wasn't, he'd claim his own meal was simply invisible, like a game. He took time to teach the Lost Boys whatever they needed to know. He trained them, comforted them, played with them, saved them… I learned more from him than I ever did at home."

"Was he the only one who could fly?"

"Only a few others could fly, mostly the boys who'd been there longest. They'd have to keep their happy thoughts close, though."

"Happy thoughts?"

"Like talismans or tokens. They remind you of your happiest self, even if you don't remember what made you happiest," Wendy explained with a touch of pity in her tone. "I was able to fly, too, after some practice. But like I said before, I'd left my happy thoughts behind in Neverland with Peter."

Alice wanted to ask what Wendy's happy thoughts were, but she decided to ask something else, "How'd you fall in love with him?"

She didn't blush, but her smile deepened, her face brightened. That's true love. It's not embarrassing. It's complete, all the happiness, all the pain, all the love.

"Before long, we'd grown closer than I've ever been with anyone," she explained. "For me, it was gradual. He was my best friend. I found I was in love with him before I could help it. But I didn't make much of it until this one day… I don't even know how long it was after we met. I know John was grown up more than I was at that point.

"I was in Neverland out scavenging for food, and found a berry patch near a ledge by the lagoon. A wet hand suddenly grabbed my foot and dragged me in! Soon, the mermaids pulled me under the surface, surrounding me. They tried to drown me. Water filled my lungs; I thought they'd succeed. Somehow I managed to break the surface several times before they took me deeper. Fortunately, Peter had seen me as he flew overhead. He dove in, kicked off the mermaids, carried me out, and we flew into the forest.

"That's when he told me that he cared about me too much. He told me how he couldn't bear it if he lost me. He said he loved me too much." She sighed, "That's when I realized how he was growing up. My trips to Neverland may have hindered my growth, but Peter's trips to the Mainland spurred his. We were growing together, however slowly."

"Did he kiss you?" asked Alice, who was all for the romantic moment, as most girls are.

Wendy's smile broadened. "Well, *I* kissed him." It vanished suddenly. "And that was my mistake. There were pirates spying the area, and that's how they found out about Peter's weakness: me. It may have taken many more years, but that's why Hook kidnapped me and took me back to England."

Alice sat motionless, wisely refraining from inquiring further.

Brown eyes stared into unseen space. Memories of Peter Pan and Neverland flashed behind them.

The lights went out, indicating dark hours in the world above ground. Alice slipped under her thin blanket, but Wendy didn't move. There was no rush; the group of five already agreed not to meet that night. They all needed to catch up on lost sleep.

Wendy still hadn't moved when Alice finally drifted off.

Alice and Wendy were led to their interrogation room for the day. How odd that they were going together. Their sessions were typically separate. But they both received an even greater shock when thrust into their room. Three others were already inside waiting for them: Red, Jack, and Kai. They gave each other confused glances as Wendy and Alice sat in the only vacant seats.

What's going on? Alice pondered. *Did the Facility find out about their meetings after hours; the tunnels between their cells?*

The door opened again and in walked a tall, brisk woman. Crisp jade eyes took in the sight of the five of them. Her ginger hair was twisted up atop her head, her white blouse was stainless, her ice blue skirt stiffly pressed. In her hands she held tightly to a clipboard. She didn't seem like the type of person who'd work in a place like the Facility. At the same time, though, she could've been running the place.

A security guard stood by the door once she walked in.

"That won't be necessary, Mister Barkley." The woman waved off the guard. Her accent was fake.

He looked slightly taken back, but grunted and walked out of the room. The heavy door slammed shut behind him. The sound was like ice breaking.

The woman walked purposefully to the middle of the room, her words flowing out rapidly as she went, "My name is Anne Christiansen and I will be working with you today. I expect immediate obedience from all five of you. Do *everything* I tell you and all will be exceptionally fine. Do I make myself clear?"

"Yes, Miss Christiansen," they all said in unison.

"Very good." Miss Christiansen gave a brief smile before her lips formed a tight line. "They are watching, so I shall give harsh criticism and instruction to each of you in turn. At the appointed time, you will all be expected to do what is necessary. Understood?"

"Yes, Miss Christiansen," they said again. They didn't really understand at all.

Miss Christiansen nodded and turned quickly to Red. "You are Rubina Daim?"

"Yes," Red's voice didn't falter.

Miss Christiansen glanced down at her clipboard. "It says here that you were brought here a year and a half ago under the assumption that you have been followed by a particular wolf-man, is that correct?"

"Yes."

"And you still believe this assumption?"

"It's not an assumption, it's the truth," Red argued, voice unwavering but it did grow sharp at the edges. "And yes, I believe every word."

"So you are telling me," Miss Christiansen's tone grew stronger, louder, "that you have never once doubted this ridiculous tale?"

"I am," Red's tone now matched Miss Christiansen's. Bottle green eyes looked defiantly up at jade ones.

"Even after all this time being locked up, you continue to believe this nonsense of a *werewolf* hunting you down like a bounty hunter?"

Miss Christiansen leaned so close that they were but centimeters apart. Red could feel cold breath on her face.

"Yes," she stated, chin jutting out.

Miss Christiansen struck Red across the face. Jack started to rise, furious, but Kai stopped him from getting up. Red turned her head back to look up at Miss Christiansen. Both shot cold glares.

"Foolish girl," Miss Christiansen hissed. "I am only going to say this once…"

But what she said next, only Red knew. Miss Christiansen dropped her voice so only Red could hear. Red's face drained of all color. The secrets in her eyes flashed wildly.

Miss Christiansen finally stood straight, steely. "Do you understand?"

Red looked vaguely and fearfully up at the woman. She nodded silently, beaten. Terror kindled among the others.

Alice furrowed her brow. What was so bad that caused Red to be so scared?

"Good." She turned on her heel to Kai. "You are Kai Ødegård, is that correct?" Her pronunciation was precise.

"Yes," Kai said, voice like grinding stone.

Miss Christiansen flipped through her papers. "It says here that you are under the belief that a girl known as Gerda Vår was kidnapped by a magical phenomenon, the Snow Queen; am I right?"

"Yes."

"Well, I have been sent here to tell you that *this is a lie*," she emphasized the last four words clearly.

"It is not a lie!" Kai shouted, his accent bubbling up thickly.

"Yes, it is," her tone stayed calm but harsh. Fake accent pushed on. "It was not real."

Bursting with rage, he stood up so quickly his chair fell over with a clatter. "Then what happened to Gerda?" Kai thundered, slipping in and out of English, "*Var är hon?* Where is she? Why can't anyone find her?"

"I do not *care* where Gerda is!" Miss Christiansen raised her voice and head to match Kai. "I could not care less about where she is! She might not even exist. She may be a figment of your *naive* imagination for all I care!"

"*Hon är verklig!* She is not a figment of my imagination. She was taken by the Snow Queen!" Kai bellowed, "SHE'S REAL!"

Miss Christiansen had tears in her eyes for some unknown reason. It was one of the many mysteries that'd be added to that day.

"You will keep your temper, Herr Ødegård, and *return* to your seat!" Miss Christiansen ordered; her shouting hid the quiver in her voice.

Kai was practically fuming, but he forcefully set his chair upright and sat down. The four legs snapped with the force. He stared loathingly up at Miss Christiansen. He hardly noticed when they switched colors for but a second before returning to their crisp shade of jade.

Miss Christiansen bent low so they saw eye to eye. "Now, you listen and you listen well…"

No one else heard what was said after. Miss Christiansen lowered her voice yet again so only he could hear. Kai's eyes widened at hearing her words and his fury seemed to disappear. His mouth formed a thin line, but not in anger.

Miss Christiansen stood straight again. "Do I make myself clear?"

Kai silently nodded as Red had done previously. The remaining three became even more confused, curious, and frightened. Alice's frown deepened.

"Good."

Miss Christiansen briskly strutted away from Kai and proceeded towards Jack, who appeared unnerved.

"You are Jack Caldwell?"

"Yes," his voice quivered only slightly.

"Mister Caldwell, it says here that you are under the impression that you climbed an enchanted beanstalk to a land with giants, correct?"

He cleared his throat. "Yes."

"Not only do you claim to have seen these giants, but you also claim that your friend, Jill Silver was murdered by them? You also claimed that her brother and your friend, Harry Silver was kidnapped by them?"

Jack's voice grew a little stronger when she tapped his emotions, "Yes."

"And you, Mister Caldwell, have deliberately chosen to disagree with reality and logic even after you have been repeatedly told otherwise?" Her tone was harsh. "Even after you know that a similar story to yours has been discovered to originate for over two hundred years?"

Jack sat straighter in stubborn dignity. "Yes!"

Miss Christiansen's mouth was next to his ear in an instant. "Listen here, Mister Caldwell. I will only tell you this once…"

And then her voice became so low that no one could hear but Jack. His reaction caused even more curiosity for Wendy and Alice. His eyes grew bright and his mouth hung open in disbelief.

Miss Christiansen stood and said, "Understood?"

Jack nodded vaguely, mouth still hung open.

"Good." And with that, Miss Christiansen turned away from Jack and stopped in front of Wendy. "Are you Wendy Darling?"

Wendy stuck out her chin. "Yes."

"And you are under the impression that you visited a land known as Neverland?"

"Yes," Wendy said confidently.

"It says here, Miss Darling," Miss Christiansen indicated her clipboard and papers, "that you loved this Neverland and never wished to leave. Why then did you return?"

Wendy sat straighter. "My family is in England. I would return for them. But as I have told the Facility before, this past time I was taken back by force."

"Yes, it says here that you believe that a Captain James Hook kidnapped you and brought you back, a highly unlikely story."

"I see no other reason why I would have been wandering the streets of London like a beggar when the police found me," Wendy said calmly. "Why would I return like that and not to my own house instantly?"

"Clearly, the only other reason why was that you never left at all!"

"Then," Wendy said, keeping her composer, "explain to me why I have not aged properly in over two decades? Feel free to correct me on the exact time, I lose track."

Miss Christiansen looked about to burst, but her voice was steady as she leaned over and said, "You will listen to me when I say this…"

And again, she lowered her voice so only the girl could hear. Wendy's eyes flashed, but other than that her expression didn't change.

Miss Christiansen stood straight. "Got it?"

Wendy stared fixedly at her. There was a slight nod.

"Good." And Miss Christiansen then turned to her last victim. "You are Alice Liddell, am I right?"

"Yes," Alice's voice was surprisingly strong even though her insides were shaking.

"And you so foolishly believe that you visited a magical land called Wonderland?"

"Yes."

"And you have come to believe this because of what reasons, might I ask?"

"Because it's the truth," Alice said, exasperated at having to repeat the same thing she'd told all other interrogators.

Miss Christiansen stooped down so that they were eye to eye. "*Where is your proof?*"

At this, Alice felt outrageous. Why would she need any proof? She didn't have to prove anything to anyone. So that's how she decided to answer, only allowing her tone a bit of edge, "I don't need proof to appease my doubters. I know what the truth is and that's all that matters to me."

Miss Christiansen was silent for what seemed to be the longest time. It was coming. The storm would break through. Alice prepared herself for it.

"Listen to me, Miss Liddell, and you listen well." She lowered her voice then and this time, Alice heard what she said: "Stick together, make haste, and do not stop. Once out, head for the edge of town. There will be a small patch of trees. You will either recognize it—in which case you must do as you did the last time—or you may accidently stumble into it. Either way, make certain *all* of you go down."

Alice was confused as Miss Christiansen stood up. One thing she was sure of: her impossible had come.

"Agreed?" the woman asked.

Stunned, Alice nodded.

"Excellent."

She walked away to the middle of the room. Jade eyes looked over the five of them, something like a warning in the gaze. *Prepare yourself,* they seemed to say.

"I assume you all know what to do. I expect immediate reaction at the correct time. I will be leaving you now. Do not wait. Make haste and everything will go fine."

Miss Christiansen walked out of the room, brisk and mysterious as the wind, leaving the door wide open.

They wouldn't see her again for a long time.

Red stood suddenly. "Come on."

"But…" Alice started.

Wendy grabbed her arm and pulled her up. Her strength was surprising. "You heard Miss Christiansen. We're breaking out."

A loud commotion sounded down the hall.

"Hurry!" Kai ushered.

The five hastened out into the hallway. The guard, Mister Barkley, was out cold on the floor. Miss Christiansen was nowhere in sight.

"This way," Red stated.

They quickened their pace as they headed for the lift, somehow squeezing in the cramped space. The shaft groaned its way up. No one budged. They were so tightly packed they were stepping on each other's toes. When the doors opened and the lift stopped, they toppled out.

"Hey! What are they doing?" a burly guard shouted in the familiar grey hallway.

"Go, go, go!" Jack shouted.

They scrambled to their feet and made for the heavy door at the end. The little old man was there at his post, twiddling his mousy hands. His beady eyes lit up when he saw the group fast approaching. Taking up an object that looked peculiarly like a paddle, he smashed the unsuspecting guard in the head in just the right spot. The guard crumpled.

The old man took out the keys and unbolted the door just in time for the five to run through.

"Thanks Gus!" Wendy called back.

"Good luck," Gus called, disappearing into a secret door to escape the scene.

All was eerie light and dark shadows up the passageway. Running up to the surface, they never broke stride at the sight of the new guard. He stepped in the way of the pursuing group of escapees, head down and arms out.

Kai dashed ahead and punched the guard right in the jaw. The guard swung out for him, but Kai dodged and rammed into his stomach. Staggering back in surprise, the guard hit his head against the wall. He went out cold, a bump forming on his head and blood trickling from his mouth.

A crack like thunder burst behind them. Five pairs of feet stopped dead in their tracks. Five pairs of eyes looked back to see more guards pouring in after them.

"Run!" Wendy cried.

They whipped around and sprinted up the rest of the way. But the door between them and freedom was locked. There was no time to get it open.

"How can we get out?" Alice asked, panting.

Red's lips formed a thin line as she raced ahead with a new found speed. One could call it *inhuman* speed. Her form shrank and she ran on all fours. Clothes melted into thick fur that covered her all over. Alice's breath coupled in shock. In the blink of an eye, where once was Red, now ran a pitch black Wolf.

The astounding shock spread through everyone. Even the guards faltered in their pursuit. The Wolf leapt for momentum and hit the door hard with her body. The poor door broke off its hinges easily and fell with a loud clang.

Though in awe, the other four escapees ran after the Wolf. Light enfolded them and they were blinking in the sunshine. They were out! They were finally out! Alice turned her head to find the Wolf transformed into her old self again as they sprinted down the cobblestone street.

"Wow, Red!" Jack exclaimed, too impressed to be surprised.

She smiled slightly.

"This way," Alice called, turning to the edge of town.

No one argued.

People shouted in alarm, automobile horns beeped at them. It wasn't raining, but there were puddles on the ground. Droplets went flying.

The huffing of their pursuers reached their ears. No one looked back, but they knew they were still being followed.

They kept running.

Alice turned a corner and there she saw the small clump of trees in the near distance. It was just as Miss Christiansen had said. With new adrenaline, she ran faster, as did the others. Trees engulfed them. Alice took that moment to glance back at their pursuers. They weren't far off.

Her foot hit an upraised root and she pitched forward. There should've been the pain, the thud, the ground. But Alice fell. She didn't stop falling.

First were the shadows thickening around her, swarming her vision, filtering through her lungs. There was a scream somewhere above her—or below her? —that indicated the others followed her down. But the darkness was familiar and warm, like cuddling under the blankets on a cool winter night. Comfort smothered Alice's fear of heights. The yells of her friends were far off like a distant memory.

Colors blossomed around her in full bloom, inking into each other. Bursts of tangerine brought fragrances of citrus to her senses. Strokes of aquamarine swept over her like a curtain of dew. Yellow made a pleasant fizz on her tongue. Emeralds sang the music of spring. Pink tasted like sugar.

Then the darkness again like a breathable liquid that slowed her fall.

Alice's feet touched soil and she stood firmly on the ground. Cool air came rushing through her lungs, the echo of emptiness sucked to her ears like a vacuum release. There was a loud thud as her companions landed on the floor and toppled over in surprise.

"What happened?" Jack's voice groaned in the darkness.

"Is everyone here?" Red pronounced. "Jack? Kai? Wendy? Alice?"

"I'm here," Wendy moaned.

"Here," sounded Kai.

"Where exactly is *here*?" Jack asked.

"Alice, are you there?" Red called out.

"Yes," she responded quietly.

"What now?" It was Jack again.

Familiarity surged through her. Alice instinctively reached out and felt for something in the darkness. Fingers brushed silky fabric. Sweeping the curtain aside, light didn't exactly fill the room, but it appeared there. A snap that made you doubt the darkness' previous presence.

A burgundy door stood in front of her. Something was different about it. An itch in the back of her mind told her so. But Alice didn't show any surprise. She felt none. With shaking hands, she grasped the golden knob.

Kai, Wendy, Jack, and Red shuffled to their feet. Alice opened the door.

A collective gasp escaped from the others' lips when they stepped outside, but Alice said nothing.

"Where are we?" breathed Wendy.

Alice was silent. She couldn't believe it. Could it be possible? It couldn't, yet here she was standing on those very grounds. Her impossible happened. It was home. Alice was home.

"Everyone, welcome to Wonderland."

Chapter Six

Bizarre Flowers

"This is incredible," Wendy whispered.

It truly was. Colors were everywhere, more radiant and beautiful than any they'd seen in a long time. A brilliant cerulean sky hung high above, stretching endlessly into the distance. Flowers of every shade reached up past their waists, scattered in groups over the landscape. Flowers do hate to grow alone. Giant spotted toadstools ranged between the sizes of a cantaloupe to that of an apple tree. Strange trees extended far over the distance like a wall, blocking the horizon from view.

Nothing, and yet everything, seemed to have changed since last Alice stepped foot in Wonderland.

"What curious little butterflies," Red mumbled, gazing at the tan and yellow winged creatures flying about.

Alice smiled to herself. "Those are bread-and-butterflies. And that," she pointed to the other winged creature Jack was trying to touch, "is a rocking-horsefly."

As if on cue, a kaleidoscope of bread-and-butterflies clumped together on a leaf to form a small loaf of bread. The rocking-horsefly zipped around, its shape exactly like a miniature rocking horse with two long transparent wings protruding from its back. It was speedy like a dragonfly. Except, of course, dragonflies looked much different in Wonderland.

Looking behind her, Alice expected to see the gold knobbed, red door standing open wide to let them back into the world they just stumbled out of. To her bewilderment, it wasn't there. The door vanished, taking their chance of turning back with it. But Alice wasn't disappointed. She belonged here in Wonderland. She never wanted to leave, not ever again.

Jack suddenly rounded on Red. "What was *that*?!"

In a snap, Red was instantly defiant. "What was what?"

"Don't start acting like nothing happened," Jack pressed. He turned to Kai. "You saw it, right? I can't be the only one!"

"I saw it," Kai admitted.

"I don't know what you're talking about!" Red persisted. Worry in her sheepish eyes betrayed her.

"Oh, come on!" Jack threw his hands in the air. "One minute we're running for our lives, the next you... you *transform* and knock the bloody door off its hinges!"

"Yeah, what was that?" Wendy asked. "Did it have anything to do with what happened before you were caught by the Facility? The thing you don't want to talk about?"

"I... I don't..." Red stammered, her defiance wavering.

"Don't deny what happened," Jack warned, eyes twinkling. "We all saw it! We just want some kind of explanation."

"Alright, fine!" Red exclaimed, fists clenched against her sides. "Yes, it does have to do with what happened before I escaped Fang."

"HA!" Jack proclaimed.

"What happened?" Alice asked, voice soft. Since she knew Red the least, her offence at not knowing this sooner was drastically less than the others'.

Bottle green eyes flashed with the memory that changed her life. Didn't Red know she could share the secret she'd kept hidden for so long? She knew she should. These were her friends. They should know.

Red took a deep breath before beginning to weave her tale, "About a year and a half ago, Fang... he found me. I tried to fight him off, but he changed to a wolf so it was impossible to outrun him. He charged and... struck." Hesitantly, she brushed her long hair off her shoulder and pealed back the dress' collar to reveal white scars of a wolf bite on the base of her neck. "He bit me during a full moon. I broke away; somehow fell through a portal that took me back. Shortly after I found out that... well, you know... the Facility caught me."

"Why didn't you tell us?" Wendy murmured.

Hesitation grew in her voice, "I can switch whenever I like, but I hate to. I don't talk about it and didn't tell you because I don't like to admit *what* I am. I didn't want any of you to look at me or think of me different. I didn't want you to see me as a monster."

"Ah, Red." Wendy gave Red a half hug. "Just because you're a wolf doesn't change who you are. None of us think of you as a monster. Right?"

"Right," it was said in unison.

"I think it's amazing! Incredible, really," Jack spoke up, dimples deep in his wide grin.

Red gave a feeble smile.

They stood silent for a moment while Wendy had her comforting arm around Red. Kai stared at his feet; Jack pushed the rocking-horsefly to make it rock back and forth in midair. Alice was still taking in the marvel of being back in Wonderland.

I'm home, she thought with both awe and dread.

"Well," Kai finally spoke up, "where to, Alice?"

Alice looked up at the purpling sky. It made the trees look blue and the grass strangely black. "We'd better find something to eat and somewhere to sleep," she commented. "Night is falling fast."

There was a small feast of honeysuckles and a sweet, milky liquid from buttercups before they found a patch of tall flowers near a huge toadstool, deciding to rest there for the night. Darkness came quickly and stars shone like jewels in the sky.

Alice stared up at these stars. A warm feeling filled her, the kind people get when they return home after a long journey. She was where she belonged, no matter what sad or horrific events she experienced there. She was home.

Finally, Alice closed her eyes and drifted off to dreamless sleep.

*****

"*NO!*"

The Queen sat bolt upright. The yell escaped her lips before she could stop it. Soaking in cold sweat, her heart raced and chest heaved. Wild eyes searched the fading recesses of her dreams. Alice had penetrated her nightmares once again.

"Your Majesty!" A maid girl rushed into the room, candle in hand. "Are you alright, Your Highness?"

"*Stupid* girl! Can't you see? It was only a nightmare, nothing more," the Queen of Hearts spat.

"Yes, Your Majesty." She bowed her head. "I just…"

"You just *what*, girl? Did you expect to save me from some unknown terror? *Foolish* girl! Why, you would do no more assistance to me than a fly would to a spider. Now, leave me. And by the Old Mock Turtle, extinguish that light!" barked the Queen.

With a flick of her wrist, a bitter wind blew out the small flame and left nothing but a trickle of smoke rising from the candle wick. The maid was filled with terror.

"Yes, Your Highness." The maid gave a quick curtsy before hustling away.

Thoughts raced through the Queen of Heart's mind. *I have to send out more troops. I need to find Alice.*

Only then, would her mind be at peace.

*****

"What do you suppose they are?"

"Well, they are most definitely *not* flowers."

"I guess I've never seen any flowers like these. Could they be *weeds*?"

"Don't be silly, Daisy."

"Yes, who has ever seen a weed like *that?*"

The one called Daisy gasped. "You don't suppose they could be *humans*?"

"Honestly, Daisy. There are hardly any humans around these days."

"Have you ever *seen* a human, Iris?" Daisy asked.

"No, I have not, but I don't need to have seen a human to know there are hardly any humans that aren't in the Queen's dungeons," Iris said hotly.

"*Shhh*, flowers! That one's moving!"

"Rose, you don't think they could be *dangerous*, do you?" Daisy inquired.

"I really don't know," Rose whispered.

Daisy gasped, "I think that one is waking up! Oh, so is that one! And that one! My petals! They're all waking up!"

"Well, you can't expect them to sleep forever," Iris huffed.

Alice opened her eyes and stared up right into the face of a large, crimson rose. As she was focusing on the sight, remembering the events of the previous day, she heard a gasp—from who was a mystery. Wendy and Red sat bolt upright with wide eyes, reminding Alice that she was the only one familiar with such things. Jack stretched his long arms as he started to waken. He sat up with sleepy eyes and ended up face to face with a smiling daisy.

"Hello, there," she said cheerily.

"Whoa!" Jack started back, suddenly wide awake.

Daisy laughed, "Oh, this one is funny!"

"Humph," a giant iris puffed.

Surprise and wonder filled the faces of the other four, but Alice wasn't at all surprised by the oversized, talking flowers. It'd been a long time, but it seemed only yesterday when she had her first interaction with the special blossoms of Wonderland. Though then, she was with an entirely different group of friends. And she was an entirely different size.

The rose smiled warmly at Alice. "Hello, dear."

"Hello," Alice said like it was entirely normal to talk to a flower that could talk back.

"I'm Rose. And this is Daisy." She nodded her blossom toward the daisy still giggling over Jack. "And this is Iris." She pointed with one of her leaves over to the large iris examining Kai with a smug look of disapproval on her face.

"It's a pleasure to meet you. I'm Alice…"

"An Alice?" Daisy interrupted. "I've never heard of an Alice." She bent over Jack and said with a smile, "Hello, Alice."

Alice couldn't help but giggle at this misunderstanding. "No, *I'm* Alice. That's my name, you see. That's Jack, and this is Wendy, Red, and there's Kai."

"Oh." Daisy's petals turned slightly pink as she blushed.

"Yes, so now we know *who* you are," Iris huffed. "But we still don't know *what* you are. That makes all the difference, you see."

"We're humans."

"Ah ha!" Daisy exclaimed. "I knew it!"

"Yes, but just because you were right about these *humans*," Iris said the last word with a disgusted look on her petals, "doesn't mean that you were right about that *ghastly* old white rabbit."

Those words clicked in Alice's brain, sending a spark of excitement through every nerve.

"Oh, do excuse them," Rose apologized. "They're always like this."

"Hmm? Oh yes. That's alright. But, what was that about a white rabbit?"

"Oh, just some white rabbit in a waistcoat that came hopping into our garden…"

"More like stormed into our garden, I'd say," Iris interrupted. "He nearly squashed the baby pansies and sent Lily's petals flying everywhere! That poor, flower."

"… Yes, well he seemed very distracted and worried. He said he needed to find *her*, but we obviously didn't know who the *her* was. Then he ran into the woods," Rose concluded.

"Yes, he was quite rude and abrupt. Never once did he apologize for the trouble he caused," Iris huffed.

"Now really, Iris. That was weeks ago!" Rose exclaimed.

"It doesn't change a thing. Not a single speck of pollen!"

"He is a ticklish one, isn't he?" Daisy giggled.

Rolling on the ground, Jack howled with laughter. Daisy tickled him playfully with her leaves. When Kai tried to drag him away, Daisy started tickling him too. His composure broke like glass as he too fell laughing under the tickling leaves.

Alice turned back to Rose. "The woods, you say?"

"Oh, yes. He was in quite a hurry to get there."

Alice thought for a moment. *What would the White Rabbit be doing in the woods?* What's more, who was he looking for? At least he'd gotten away from the Queen of Hearts…

The stuck up voice of Iris interrupted her thoughts, "What peculiar petals."

Red snatched her auburn skirts away from Iris' leaf hands. "We told you! We're *not* flowers!"

Iris huffed.

"Stop! Stop it!" Jack exclaimed, laughing hard.

He tried in vain to push Daisy and her leaves away. Kai finally managed to break out of reach. He sat back, gasping for breath.

"Well, thank you," Alice said to Rose. "But we really must be going."

"So long, then, dear Alice." Rose smiled warmly.

"Goodbye!" Daisy called as the five walked away from their garden.

They were a good distance from earshot—or petal-shot—when the group felt comfortable talking again.

"Charming," Kai commented sarcastically.

"They weren't *that* bad," Wendy tried in vain to keep the humor from her tone.

"At least you weren't being tickled to death by Daisy." Jack made a face, still breathing heavily from the thrill of it.

Kai huffed, "Trust me, I was."

Red turned the topic, "So, where are we headed?"

"The Tulgey Wood," Alice answered. "We're off to find my old friend, the White Rabbit."

Chapter Seven

Rabbit Hunting

By midday, they reached the Tulgey Wood. Though slightly darker and less colorful there than in the meadow, there was no shortage of curiosities and oddities. Many times Alice was questioned on what this was or what that could be. She always answered casually. After all, it wasn't strange to her anymore.

Alice stopped Red once from almost stepping on a group of mome raths: sickly looking flightless birds only as tall as a hand with spindly legs, long beak, and tufts of colorful feathers on their heads. It was a good thing that she'd stopped her, for despite their innocent appearance, one should never judge a creature by its looks. This was especially in the case of a mome rath.

The trees grew dense as the five drew deeper into the Tulgey Wood. The sky was nearly blocked out due to the thick branches overhead. Streams of sunlight flooded through the gaps in the leaves, illuminating the unusual patterns in the tree trunks. It was quite enchanting, the Tulgey Wood, with leaves that dripped instead of fell, and grass that whistled in the breeze.

A strange plant grew amongst the enchantment, with tall leaves the shade of chartreuse and veins as silver as starlight. Wendy gazed at it, dreamy thoughts floating through her mind in wisps. The thought was there, but when she went to ponder it, the thought disappeared. Stomach tightening with wishful yearning, she drew closer. But the thoughts slipped through her fingers like sand.

A face formed before her eyes, distorted and unrecognizable. Yet there was something about it… Wendy longed to see this face. It'd been so long since she saw him. An aroma emerged from the fern, growing stronger as she drew closer. So strange at first… but it melted into a comforting scent that caused her dreamy longing to grow into a strong desire. Yet as the image in her mind was unrecognizable, the scent was indistinguishable.

Wendy approached the fern, could almost grasp the memory. She reached out, touched the fuzzy leaves; and the face and scent were immediately clear. Eyelids grew heavy. She collapsed to the floor.

"Wendy!" Red exclaimed as she made a move to pursue her. Something itched the back of her mind…

"No, don't," Alice said sharply, yanking her back.

Shaking the dizziness away, she turned to Alice, worry in her eyes. "What happened to her?"

There was a pause, as if to check that Red would stay put. Then Alice crept over to Wendy and answered, "She touched the doze-fern."

"Doze-fern?" Jack questioned. "What's that?"

"The plant," she explained. "The intoxicating aroma causes hallucinations and tempts the victim to touch its leaves. Touching a doze-fern makes you fall instantly to sleep."

Red, Jack, and Kai hastily stepped away from the poisonous plant. Alice carefully dragged the sleeping form of Wendy off as she avoided its premises.

"Doesn't the aroma affect you?" Kai asked, beginning to feel the effects from where he stood, though he wasn't permitting himself to give in to them.

"A friend made me an antidote, making me immune to the smell."

Once at a safe distance, Alice let Wendy rest in place. She looked so peaceful, and Alice knew why. She too once experienced the realistic, blissful dreams of the doze-fern.

"Can't we just wake her up?" Red cried in a panic. Strange how this set her off. Nothing seemed to make Red panic, not like this.

"It's not that simple," Alice tried to explain, looking around. "See, she doesn't *want* to wake up. No one does while they're in the trance."

"Well, how do you wake her?"

"I need sap... from *that* tree." Alice pointed. "Red, would you get it? The tumtum tree's bark is thick and only a pair of powerful claws could tear it away fast."

Red nodded and closed her eyes, trying to calm herself down. The feeling was between pleasure and pain as she transformed into the black furred Wolf. She stalked over to the twisted, whimsical tree and dug her claws into its swirly trunk. She scratched at the rough surface until she pried out a chunk of bark sticky with golden sap.

Jack grabbed it and handed it to Alice. Dabbing her fingers in the sticky substance, she rubbed some on Wendy's nose. Almost instantly, Wendy jerked awake, sitting up with a jolt.

"What happened?" she gasped. "I... I thought I saw... and the smell... It was like..."

Alice explained what happened with the doze-fern as Red, her old self again, helped Wendy to her feet. A look of relief crossed Red's face.

Wendy wiped the sticky sap off her nose with the back of her hand. "What is this stuff?"

"Tumtum tree sap," Alice said. "We're lucky there was one around."

Wendy smiled weakly, the effects of the doze fern still dwindling in her mind. She shook her head, reminding herself that it wasn't real. No matter how convincing it was or how it brought back so many happy memories, it wasn't real.

"I'm alright. Let's keep going," Wendy insisted. But that was a lie. She wasn't alright; not yet.

They continued walking through the wood, careful to avoid any more doze-ferns or mome raths for the rest of the afternoon.

Kai looked up at the sky though it was hard to see it through the tree branches. It appeared blue, but it wouldn't stay that way. From personal experience, he knew it was harder to travel at night as a group than to travel alone, especially in these strange lands and different worlds.

"Alice?" Kai spoke up. "How are we supposed to find one rabbit in this whole wood?"

A smile stretched across her face, the kind that made him wonder at her sanity. "Oh, trust me; I'm quite positive we won't have to find anything."

"I thought we were on a rabbit hunt," Jack stated. "How are we supposed to find the Rabbit if we're not hunting?"

"You must've misunderstood. What I meant was that I have no doubt it won't take long for *him* to find *us*."

"But how do you know?" Kai asked. "What makes you think he'll find us."

"Well," Alice's grin turned a bit sheepish, "it's just like Iris said. There aren't many humans left in Wonderland that haven't been imprisoned."

*****

The Queen of Hearts paced back and forth. They were supposed to have been here ages ago. *Where are they?* she thought. *Honestly, how hard is it to bring up one prisoner?*

She'd received the news this morning. Her soldiers had finally caught them, or at least one of them. Which one, she was yet to discover. Very few knew the difference between those two. But the Queen of Hearts could tell them apart. She would know who it was when they brought him to her.

The doors flew open with a heavy swish, drawing the Queen's immediate attention. In a great commotion and scuffle, a group of soldiers entered the room. Two guards had firm hands on their prisoner who was struggling with great effort. But it was no use; there were too many of them for him to escape.

The prisoner was covered in bruises and cuts from many a brutal beating. He had messy red hair and determined green eyes. Freckles dotted his nose, though they were swallowed up by the blood and bruises. The Queen of Hearts knew who he was immediately. This would be a challenge. Not that it wouldn't have been challenging if the soldiers caught the other instead. They were both equally stubborn.

The Queen smiled with taunting politeness. "I'm so pleased you could join us, Tweedle-Dee. I'm sorry it had to be under such circumstances, but you know how it is these days."

Dee scowled. "Down with the chivalry, *Queen*. We both know why I'm here."

"Then you know what I want," she leered.

He spat at her, saliva splattered against her rich skirts.

With a flick of her wrist, Dee was thrown back into a rickety chair by an unseen source. He grunted as invisible ropes tightened around his wrists and ankles, binding him in place. The soldiers breathed heavily, no longer having to control their relentless prisoner.

The Queen of Hearts stepped closer. "Where did you hide her?"

Dee glared at her, blood trickling down his temple. "I don't know what you're talking about."

Unseen bounds constricted suddenly, digging into his skin. Dee groaned in pain, jaw clenched.

"Perhaps I didn't make myself clear." The Queen of Hearts stepped a little closer. "Where is *Alice*?"

"I don't know," Dee sneered.

He cried out as the bounds tightened again, tearing through skin, bruising muscle. Blood dribbled down his fingers and soaked his feet. The Queen's face was cruelly calm as she watched her prisoner suffer.

"Please, stop!"

A deadly silence wafted through the room. The other cards stared in utter disbelief at the stupidly outspoken soldier. The bounds on Dee's wrists and ankles loosened a bit as the Queen of Hearts' shock set in. Green eyes looked up at the one who'd spoken up for him. The Queen's dark eyes averted from Dee to the soldier.

"What did you say to me?" she questioned.

"Your Majesty, you're going too far," he said softly, almost regretting his loose tongue.

The pause itself was poisonous. Heels clicked against the floor as the Queen of Hearts approached the soldier. He gulped. Loathing disbelief filled her gaze. But she didn't falter.

In one swift movement, she drew his sword from his sheath and with one swipe cut his head clean off his shoulders. The body fell in a crumpled heap. The only remaining sound was that of the helmeted head rolling across the floor until it stopped at Dee's feet to stare up at him with empty eyes.

Some cards quickly dragged away the body and head in familiar routine. The Queen of Hearts turned back to her prisoner.

"Now, where were we? Oh, yes," she set the bloody sword aside, "I wish to know where you are hiding Alice. If you cooperate, I would be willing to highly consider giving you a place in my armada. As you can see, I now have an available position."

Dee looked up from the pool of blood where the head had rested at his feet. His glare was of pure and utter hatred. To see him sent chills up the Queen's spine. It wasn't the glare itself that made him so fearsome, but the fact that that kind of loathing had never before been in those eyes. That in itself was what would've caused anyone to tremble in his gaze.

"*Never*," he hissed.

Bursting past the guilt, she rushed up so their faces were within a breath of each other. She stroked his face with the back of her fingers. What a mocking gesture.

"What a shame. Such bravery, such nobility," she brushed away the dirty hair that fell over his eyes, "such a *waste!*"

Fingernails dug into his skin and swiped across his face. Dee cried out painfully, the new cuts on his face stinging with vigor and bled freely.

The Queen of Hearts turned away. She wasn't entirely surprised at his constant refusal. The Brothers Tweedle were renowned for their fun, loyal, and brave personalities. Dangerous combination.

"You'll never win, Queen."

She wheeled around to face him. His eyes fixated on her and it took all of her strength not to tremble in their gaze. Few things scared her, and those hauntingly unnatural eyes were among them.

"You'll never find her," Dee continued, almost amused. "But as you continue to search and search, your loathing will grow stronger. You'll become desperate, frantic. You'll go *crazy* in your searching. You won't listen to reason, no matter how many times it screams in your face. You'll become restless. And in your restlessness you will become careless and clumsy. Soon, you'll have a rebellion under your very nose and when it rises you will have no power to stop it. There will be no peace for you, Queen." He smiled as blood dripped in his eyes. "You will never find her."

Anger bubbled up in the Queen's chest. "*I WILL FIND HER!*" she bellowed. She turned away from him. "Take him to the dungeons."

*****

"When's this rabbit going to find us?" Jack asked.

"He will soon. Don't worry," Alice responded.

"But how do we know he's even in this forest? He could've left for all we know."

"Rose said he came here to look for someone."

"Yes, but she also said that was weeks ago," Wendy acknowledged.

Alice didn't answer. She knew they had a point, but this was all she had to go on. The White Rabbit was the only one she knew had escaped from the Queen of Hearts. He was her only hope.

As her mind wandered, her guard slowly disappeared, and it wasn't until it was too late that she realized it.

There was a snap and a swish. With a yank, they were jerked up in the air. Squashed together, they found themselves trapped high in a large net, strung up like caught fish. Alice let out a pitiful scream, eyes instantly squeezed shut. Her body quivered slightly. She hated heights so much.

"Get your foot out of my face!"

"What happened?"

"Don't poke there! I'm ticklish."

It was unclear who said what.

A hearty laughing sounded from below, stilling their struggles. "That'll teach you not to come prowling into *these* woods! Now, let me see. You don't appear to be cards. Spies, perhaps? Coming to take me to the Queen, are you? Well, I'd think *not*!"

"We aren't spies!" Kai announced, his shout more of a growl under the circumstances.

"That's what they all say. Why should I believe *you*?"

Alice wrestled with herself, forcing her eyes to open and struggling to look down at their captor. It was difficult, but she finally was able to move into a position to see him clearly without having to see how far above the ground they were.

There he was: The White Rabbit. Larger than a normal sized rabbit, and he was whiter than one typically would be. He had long ears, wore a black waistcoat, and had an expression that seemed slightly pompous for a rabbit, but Alice knew he really wasn't.

"Why should I believe you?" the White Rabbit questioned again, twitching his nose as he smiled with the victory of his grand catch.

"Because we're telling the truth!" Wendy persisted.

"Not a very good excuse, is it? I'm sure that I've heard better farfetched lies than that," he said smugly.

"Now really, White," Alice cut in, though her very bones were trembling, "is this any way to treat an old friend?"

White's eyes grew even bigger than their usual large state. "Great Uncle Jackrabbit! Is that really you, Miss Alice?"

"It certainly appears so," Alice said, smiling through her fear. "Now, are you going to let my friends and I down or are we going to dangle from the treetops all day?"

"Oh, yes. Quite right." White hastened to untie a hidden rope on the ground. "So sorry. I'll have you down in a moment."

With a lurch, the net gave and the five were taken down with it, screaming and shouting in surprise. Alice happened to scream the loudest. They landed in a hard heap of arms and legs. Soon they untangled themselves and were back on their feet.

"Do forgive me. The Queen has spies and soldiers everywhere! Hardly know who you can trust anymore," the White Rabbit fumbled, ashamedly wringing his paws.

"It's good to see you, White." Alice stooped down and threw her arms around him in a tight hug.

He sighed, "And you, Miss Alice."

She pulled away and stood. Her legs were a bit shaky from the thrill of being up so high, but she was thankful to be on solid ground again.

Remembering the others, Alice introduced, "Oh, right. White, this is Red, Wendy, Jack, and Kai. Everyone, this is the White Rabbit."

"Hello," the four said in unison, still dusting off from their fall.

"The pleasure is mine, I'm sure," White exclaimed, giving an extravagant bow as he did so. "Now, it's getting late. You had all better come with me. You don't want to be out in the dark in these woods, unexperienced as you are. Not you, of course, Miss Alice. But you know how it is."

It wasn't too long before White stopped and announced, "We're here."

There wasn't anything particularly special about the area, except perhaps a patch of nasty looking snapdragons that nipped the air in trying to reach them.

Looking around, Jack voiced, "Where exactly is *here*?"

White grinned toothily and pushed aside a large bush, revealing a gaping rabbit hole.

"We're going down *there*?" Kai declared, being the broadest of the group.

"Quite right." White nodded affirmatively. "It might be a tight fit for some of you, but no matter. It's enchanted so that anyone I wish, no matter their size, will be able to fit. Now, go on!"

Jack looked down the dark hole and gulped. "Ladies first?"

"Since when have you been so noble?" Wendy smirked teasingly.

She jumped down the hole without hesitation. Screams echoed instantly, farther and farther down. Whether it was from excitement or fear, no one could really tell.

"Right, well go on. No need to dawdle," White persuaded.

The Rabbit gave Jack a little shove forward. Jack looked down the dark hole once again, swallowing a lump in his throat.

Turning to Red, he asked, "You're sure you don't want to go first?"

Red rolled her eyes and pushed him, causing him to pitch forward and fall down the hole with a drowning yell. Shaking her head with an amused smile, she saluted the White Rabbit before she too jumped down the hole with a whoop of delight.

"I like her." White grinned.

When it was Kai's turn, he simply stepped off the edge and disappeared down into the darkness. He gave one surprised exclamation, but other than that, no other sound was heard.

"After you, Miss Alice."

Alice walked to the edge and gazed down into the endless darkness. Her fear of heights tingled, but oddly enough, going down rabbit holes never entirely scared her. She jumped high and plunged down and around and around… She laughed and screamed with delight. The tunnel came to an end abruptly atop a pile of pillows.

The room was bright and roomy despite being underground. There was a short bed to one side, a few chairs, a small table, a little stove, and a few other furnishings. But there was ticking, ticking, ticking all around. Watches dangled from the ceiling like spiders on silk, clicking their repetitive song in chorus. The other four sat at the table, exhilaration from the slide still plastered on their faces.

Alice's inspection did a double take by the stove, breath compressing when she saw her. White blonde hair fell in silky waves down her back. Had her skin gotten paler since last they'd met?

"Celeste?" Alice asked.

The woman turned, silvery blue eyes widening, her smile broadening. "Alice!"

Skidding to her feet, Alice rushed to embrace her friend. She squeezed her eyes shut in happiness. They were like sisters to each other, not like the sisters they'd both in turn lost, but the sisters they both needed.

Alice finally pulled back, overcome with questions. "But, how…?"

"It wasn't easy," Celeste answered her friend's unspoken question, "but I escaped the battlegrounds unharmed. I've been in exile ever since."

"Exile?" Alice's voice expressed her concern.

Celeste laughed. "Not to worry, Alice. I've been wanted and exiled since long before you returned to Wonderland."

"Nearly all of our friends are wanted and exiled, otherwise in Helena's dungeons," added the White Rabbit, who just gracefully hopped out of the tunnel.

After sitting silent for some time, the other four were about comfortable enough to ask some questions of their own. Wendy stood first, quick to join in the conversation. "Pardon me," she interjected, "who's Helena?"

Alice wasn't sure how to specifically answer that question. People in Wonderland possessed far too many names.

"The Queen of Hearts," was White's immediate response.

Celeste added just as quickly, "My little sister."

"But, if you're her *older* sister," Red observed, "then why is she the one on the throne? Aren't you the White Queen?"

"By right, yes, the crown should be mine," Celeste agreed. "But I'm afraid Helena has far more powerful friends than I do. She overthrew me, has tried to kill me on multiple occasions. Luckily, she hasn't managed that yet. And yes, I am indeed the White Queen."

Recalling that Celeste had yet to be introduced to her friends, Alice hastily spoke up, "I'm sorry; I just realized I don't believe you've met…"

"Not formally, no," the White Queen interrupted. "But I know who they are, and I'm certain they know who I am by now. So, I don't believe we are in need of any introductions. For now, dinner is ready, so I insist we resume talking afterwards."

She clapped her hands twice and bowls of soup appeared on the table, followed by seven cups of tea. Alice and the White Rabbit joined the others.

Alice looked up several times to make sure that Celeste and the White Rabbit were really there and not just some realistic dream. To her delight, it wasn't one.

Chapter Eight

Catching Up

"So, tell me," Celeste inquired, "what happened to you after Remus broke you out of the dungeons?"

Alice explained the fateful events of the night she hadn't put to words since she told her father what seemed ages ago. She told of how the Brothers Tweedle pushed her through the mirror, how her father hadn't believed her when she returned to him, how he sent her to the Facility, how she met Wendy who then introduced her to the others. She told of the interrogation they experienced together and how the strange Anne Christiansen helped them escape. Alice recollected how the five fell down the rabbit hole and toppled into Wonderland, how they met the talking flowers, and finally how the White Rabbit found them and brought them there.

Alice hardly left anything out. She knew the importance of details, even if their meaning were not revealed until much later. All the while, Celeste and the White Rabbit sat listening intently. The others listened too, but as they were part of most of it, they didn't drink it in as White and Celeste did. They put in their own little comments when Alice fumbled or had trouble remembering, though.

"Do you know who could've helped us and why?" The question flew out of Alice's mouth before she could stop it.

Celeste shook her head. "No, I don't."

"Nor do I," White added.

Alice sighed. She thought that maybe one of them had sent the help; but who could have sent it? Who would have known? Who was Anne Christiansen really? Questions kept popping into Alice's head and zipping around her mind like a swarm of rocking-horseflies. But it wasn't the time to ask them all, so instead Alice caught one question and released it off her tongue into the surrounding air.

"What's happened since I left?"

Celeste sighed, her face falling with some remorse, but she explained anyway, "Some of us managed to escape the battlegrounds that night, me included. I believe the twins were able to escape, though I've heard tale that Dee was caught and imprisoned. Chess escaped, of course, as did most of the troops. White was captured with the March Hare. After that night I went back into hiding. I have an assortment of hiding places around Wonderland that I've used before. This is one of the few that hasn't been discovered by Helena. It wasn't but a few weeks ago when White found me."

"What of Remus?" Alice managed to say with all the courage she could muster.

The White Queen hesitated. She gave White a fleeting look, not wishing to share this part of the story. Though White didn't wish to share it either, he relented, clearing his throat before he began, "Well, he was imprisoned, heavily guarded. Not that they expect him to escape by any means, but they fear who should come to steal him away. The Queen of Hearts doesn't know that you ever left Wonderland, Alice. She's been looking for you everywhere. She expects you to come and try to save Remus. That is, if she doesn't catch you first."

"Then she presumes correctly," Alice blurted.

The White Rabbit appeared taken aback, obviously not expecting such an answer. His ears twitched. The shock left him speechless.

Celeste nodded, saying softly, "I knew you would say that."

"But you can't go back there!" White pronounced, finding his voice once more.

"And why not?" Alice demanded. "You can't expect me to just sit here and do nothing!"

"You won't do nothing."

The voice was soft, but it caused everyone to fall silent. Alice had nearly forgotten that Wendy was there, being caught up in the moment and all. Wendy looked up, a look of adventure dancing behind her eyes.

"You won't do nothing," she repeated, "because we'll help you."

White was appalled, nearly choking on his sputtering words. "What... What... You can't do this!"

"Why?" Jack spoke up.

"Well, because... because... Well, you're just children!"

Kai's face grew dark. "We're not children anymore. We've been through much more than most ever experience in a lifetime."

"I thought you would've learned that by now," Alice said softly. She swallowed the memories that proved her point, of a sister who abandoned her, of a drunken father who blamed her for her mother's death, of a night where she was yanked from Wonderland.

White looked quite torn, aware of most all of these hardships she'd faced. "But… of course I have, Miss Alice. I only meant… It's just that… It's too dangerous!"

"Dangerous? Ha!" Red huffed, rolling her eyes. "Do you honestly think we don't know what *dangerous* is?"

"No… No, of course not…"

"We've seen more danger than your furry little tail could hardly imagine," Jack pushed.

"I never said you didn't!" White huffed.

"But you were thinking it."

"I did no such thing!"

"Enough!" Celeste exclaimed, her tone of authority and finality: the tone of a queen.

Everyone snapped silent, most eyes turned to the White Queen. The White Rabbit and Jack still glared at each other, though.

"That is quite enough," Celeste scolded. "We still have important matters to discuss. If you would all please leave your argumentative behavior at rest until *after* we are done. Now, White, would you please?"

White tore his large, black eyes away from Jack's glaring ones. Sheepishly, he turned to Alice with a desperate look, whiskers twitching.

"They took my pocket watch, Alice," he explained pleadingly.

Alice's anger left her instantly, replaced with dread. She found it difficult to speak.

"Wait, they took your *pocket watch*?" Jack taunted. "So what? Was it an *unbirthday* gift?"

The White Rabbit looked utterly bewildered. "Of course not! Honestly! No one has celebrated an unbirthday since Remus…" but his voice trailed off, eyes falling to his paws.

Alice grimaced, realizing how important Remus was to preserving the mad joy Wonderland was renowned for. Even such simple things like unbirthdays…

Attempting to ignore the flood of emotions, she forced herself to say, "So, they took your pocket watch?"

White sighed, glad to return to the subject. "Yes. The soldiers searched me when they caught me. They took my pocket watch. I don't think they realized what it really was. They wanted to give it to the Queen of Hearts. I tried to find it and get it back when I escaped, but there was no time. They still have it, Alice! If the Queen of Hearts finds out…"

"Yes, I know," Alice whispered. "It wouldn't be good."

Wendy spoke up, "Alright, am I missing something? Or is that just me?"

"I'm lost, too," Red agreed. "What's this about some old pocket watch?"

"*Some old pocket watch?*" the White Rabbit put heavy emphasis on each word as he said them. "It is most definitely not *some old pocket watch*! Why, I've never heard such… such… *absurd* propositions! I can't even… How could… It's not…"

Alice cut in, "White's pocket watch isn't just any pocket watch."

"Um, Miss Alice," White whispered between his teeth, leaning close. "Are you sure they can be trusted? Because I'm not so sure about that wild haired one over there…"

Jack scowled at him.

"Yes, I'm sure even Jack can be trusted," Alice reassured with a smile before continuing. "The watch enables him to travel between worlds. It's been passed down in his family from generation to generation." Alice turned back to the White Rabbit. "Alright, so we'll add that to our mission. We go to the Queen's castle, find the watch, find Remus' heart, save him from the dungeons as well as anyone else down there, put the heart back inside him, and kill the Queen."

White blinked. "But, how can you... I mean, Remus... You can't... Impossible!"

"Well, there has to be a way, hasn't there?" Alice threw her hands in the air. "I mean, if she could take it out, who's to say I can't put it back in?"

White's mouth lolled open in disbelief, revealing long front teeth. "But I... Well..."

Annoyed with White's inability to complete his sentences, Alice whipped around with hands on her hips. "Celeste?"

Her silvery blue eyes rose to meet Alice's. "It is possible..."

"I knew it!"

"But," she continued, "it won't be easy. It might even be painful. And, you have to find the right heart! That is crucial. I don't believe Helena will have damaged Remus' heart. To possess the Mad Hatter's heart would be like owning an extravagant trophy to her. If you do this, you must be careful. It'll be dangerous, Alice, more dangerous than last time, for now Helena is determined to catch you."

Alice sighed, trying to find the right words to explain her determination. "The first time I came to Wonderland I was trying to find my sister. The second time, I tried to find myself. This time, I'm going to find Remus. I'm going to get my Hatter."

Later that night while everyone was falling asleep on top of blankets on the floor, Wendy whispered over to Alice, "You never told me you had a sister."

Alice swallowed the lump in her throat. "I never thought to mention it."

"What was her name?"

"Lorna."

"Do you mind telling me what happened to her?"

Alice was silent for a moment, staring at the ceiling. *What did become of her?* All she could say was, "I don't know. I'm not even sure if she's alive or dead, where she is, what she's up to. Lorna… ran away when I was ten."

"Oh, Alice, I'm sorry."

"Don't be." She shrugged. "She couldn't stand it, I suppose. The first time I came to Wonderland, I was trying to find her. And I guess I can't blame her for running away. I did the same thing, after all."

"But you went back."

"Only because I thought Lorna would come back, at least the first time," Alice admitted. "And I was afraid of leaving something important behind. But the last time, I had no intentions of going back. There was no reason to. Wonderland is my home now, not England, not my father, not even Lorna."

Wendy sighed, "I suppose I understand. But I do wish that you had a better family in England, Alice. It's always nice to know you have someone still waiting for you, who has loved you all your life."

"That does sound nice." Alice smiled at her. "But I think I'm pretty blessed to have my own growing family, one that I chose."

"I can't argue with that."

"Good night, Wendy."

Wendy smiled lightheartedly. "Good night, Alice."

Chapter Nine

A Rather Odd Cat

Slippers stuffed with pudgy feet squeaked across the floor, layers of silk mauve skirts sweeping around her legs. The Duchess' amethyst wisps of hair were piled up atop her head like candy floss. Yellowish eyes scrutinized the prisoners as she passed their cells, her crimson lips pursed with disgust. Though her face was powdered pallid, a single mole perched black beside her hooked nose. It was shocking that her ruffled collar didn't choke her due to her folds of chins. But the Duchess didn't show discomfort, only determination and revulsion.

There was one footman beside her, an overly large frog walking along on floppy feet. His bulbous eyes were dazed, looking up at the ceiling as if the mold there were interesting. It was as if he were sleepwalking. But at least he was conscious enough not to drop the tray of tarts he held with his webbed front flippers. The Duchess was almost scarier than the Queen of Hearts; and no one could afford to drop the Duchess' tarts.

Maniac babbling echoed down the passage from the heavily guarded cell in ceaseless garbling. It wasn't like the special guest wasn't normally chatty. But ever since he'd come into the Queen's custody, well, he wasn't often in the mood. When he did talk, however, it was a good idea to pay attention should he reveal something of value amongst his nonsense.

When the Duchess reached the cell, she snatched up a tart from her footman and shoved it in her mouth. "What has he been burbling this time?" she smacked, not bothering to swallow before speaking.

A soldier—a typical one in dark white armor adorned with a blood red heart on the helm and other major pieces— addressed her question, "He's on a rampage about some great epiphany of his. He's been talking faster than a rocking-horse fly about complete nonsense, but it's at least somewhat clear."

The prisoner jumped from the shadows and pressed himself against the prison bars, blue eyes flashing with dead madness. "What do you feel?" he hissed between a stretched smile.

The Duchess raised a thin eyebrow at his messy hair and stubbly jaw. She gave an equally maniac smile, revealing jumbled teeth and tart bits. "Is this another one of your riddles? Ravens and writing desks and all that?" She didn't wait for his response before she frowned and answered his question, "I am frustrated, *Hatter*. I feel *frustrated* with you."

The Mad Hatter shook his finger disapprovingly. "Nay, not what you think you feel, not what you want to feel, not what you think you want someone to think you think you feel. But what do you *feel*?"

She cocked her head slightly. "Bored."

"WRONG!" the Hatter bellowed, pushing himself away with such ferocious force that the door rattled.

The cards drew their swords instinctively, shocked by the flip in their prisoner's mood. The Hatter's face darkened as he paced back and forth, pulling at his filthy hair. All the while, the Duchess watched in scrutiny, mildly amused by such display of anger. She shoved another tart in her mouth.

The frog footman stared dreamily off at a shower of dust falling from the rafters.

"See, we all feel... Yes, we feel everything, *everything* all at once!" the Hatter rambled, somewhere between frustration and desperation as he paced. "But we only chose one emotion, one face, one *hat* to put on the outside so it only seems like we feel only one feeling. Yet imagine what it'd be like to show exactly what we're feeling the moment we feel it, like piling every hat on your head precisely when you have the urge to do so. Wouldn't then we all be considered mad? When in reality, everyone feels everything at any given moment, so wouldn't the ones who chose only one feeling to display be just as insane as the ones who express everything instantaneously? And just the same, all with every hat would be as sane as those with one hat so really feelings and expressiveness have nothing at all to do with madness or sanity. It's about... *humanity* and *tolerance.* Whether all those hats could topple over and hurt somebody else. So we go about wearing only one hat but feeling, *feeling, FEELING...* everything..."

The Hatter stopped pacing and looked around him, baffled. His hands rummaged around his pockets, patted his thighs and chest—definitely his chest—as if searching.

"Missing... Something's missing, and I can't..." He checked everywhere, grasping at the spot where his heart should've been. "... feel..."

The Duchess leaned forward and grasped the prison bars with her chubby hands. She smiled with wicked madness. "*What do you feel?*" she leered.

No one noticed the eyes that watched from the rafters except for the frog footman, who thought that it was merely dust particles glinting in the fire light. But that didn't explain the shadow of a gleaming smile poised just beneath those watchful eyes.

The Hatter looked up, dazed, mournful, broken. "… Nothing. I feel nothing."

*****

Thus far, the only plan was to stay in hiding with the White Rabbit and Celeste until there actually were any further plans. The group began taking turns everyday emerging from the hole to look for food or reset traps for intruders. They would go in pairs, just in case. But Celeste didn't join in such ventures, since she was the most recognizable and likely to be caught if discovered. White tried to point out that Alice was just as wanted as the White Queen, but both women were quick to acknowledge that she wasn't as recognizable. Besides, they would need more than just White who was familiar with the Wonderland landscape.

The only issue with the new routine occurred when Jack was paired with the White Rabbit during one shift. Jack ended up leading White into one of the traps for the intruders, leaving him hanging there in the large net. When Jack returned to the hideout later without White, he got criticized intensely by Red despite his protests that it was *innocent revenge*, and Kai was sent to release the Rabbit. After that, everyone deemed it wise that the White Rabbit and Jack shouldn't be left alone together.

The White Rabbit got his own revenge soon enough, though. He left a small flock of mome raths in Jack's sleeping mat one night. As he knew, it's not wise to disturb a mome rath, especially a flock of them, no matter the size. When Jack went to bed that night, he discovered why that was a wise virtue in Wonderland. It resulted in many bites and scratches from the typically docile creatures, complete with a mouthful of colorful feathers and a loud racket of mome rath warbles. Apparently, Jack was also extremely allergic to mome raths, sneezing for days. He developed a unique and unusual craving for cheesewood.

White had quite a laugh that night and several nights thereafter, but just as Jack had been yelled at by Red, so did the Rabbit by Alice. You could say they got similar consequences for their actions. That didn't necessarily make them even.

One day, Alice and Red emerged to scavenge for food. Already they'd collected some cheesewood—extra for Jack—and some ham-and-eggs flowers, which Alice insisted was delicious despite its peculiar appearance. Red soon encountered a large bush with numerous amounts of small yellow berries scattered about golden leaves.

"Alice?" Red beckoned. "What are these?"

Alice came over to investigate. "Those are giggle-berries."

"Giggle-berries?"

"Don't worry, they're not toxic…"—as if that was Red's concern— "…Unless you count uncontrollable laughter as toxic." Alice smiled, the kind that made you doubt her sanity. "Maybe Celeste could make a giggle-berry tart tonight."

Red eyed the bush warily. "It's a little big for a berry bush, don't you think?"

Alice looked at it sideways and shrugged. "What can I say? Laughter spreads."

Even as they picked, Red was still unsure of the berries. But after a taste, she had to agree with Alice. They were so sweet, making her happy for no reason in particular. She ended up laughing for three minutes straight, something she hadn't done in years. The berries seemed to remind her of happy, hilarious things. Red enjoyed it.

As she was picking, she ventured to the other side of the large bush to get more. Soon, she couldn't see Alice anymore, but she didn't notice much. Red was sure that Alice wasn't far. Her wolf senses told her so. But she didn't realize just how far away she really was. All she knew was that Alice wasn't kidding when she'd said that laughter spreads.

From somewhere above, or behind, or beside her, a singsong voice echoed through the air, "You know, it would be nice to say *hello*."

Red jumped, scattering giggle-berries as they flew out of her basket. She looked around warily. She wasn't scared, a little startled, perhaps…

"Who's there?" she called.

"Of course," the cheery voice went on, "hellos are getting so overrated these days. Sometimes I wonder where proper greetings and etiquette are going to."

Red spun in circles trying to find the source of the voice, but it seemed to come from everywhere at once. She tried to sniff the air, but there was nothing distinctive, different, or unusual about it.

"But then again," the voice said in its bouncy rhythm, "it might help some if every once in a while I revealed myself before I start to speak. I might try that next time I come across someone. But then again, maybe I won't. I'll just have to see."

And then she saw it. A wide smile hovered in a nearby tree. Just a smile, nothing attached. Of all the peculiar things Red had seen in this world alone, this was by far the strangest. Red didn't know what to make of it.

She replied rather unsure, "Hello?"

Two large multicolor eyes and a pink nose dropped down from nowhere and landed above the smile. "Hello! Oh, I knew it would work! But sometimes it's quite a bother being noticed. Everyone's eyes gaze at you all stunned when you appear out of thin air. At least, that's how it is for me. But since you have decided to say hello, I suppose I will bare it for the time being."

And so, a furry body appeared behind the obscure face and a fuzzy head fit around the eyes, nose, and seemingly out of place smile. Two pointy ears fell on top his head and a large, fluffy tail grew out of his body. His coat was hard to describe. It seemed to be one color in one moment, then as you began to process it, the shade seemed completely different the next. One instant it was every color imaginable, the next it seemed opaque and invisible. Red finally decided not to focus on it. Trying to comprehend it was giving her a headache. The cat's grin widened to touch each ear.

"And I quote the wise Blue Caterpillar, '*Whoooo arrrre yoooou?*'" the floating cat asked.

"R-Red," she said, though she didn't mean to stammer.

"Hmm… What an unusual name. I don't know many creatures named after colors. I do believe my mother's friend's father's pet's neighbor was named Turquoise. Or was it Evergreen? You know, though, I've never heard of it spelled with two *R*s before."

"No, there's only one," Red explained.

"That makes more sense. Though, it would be more interesting for it to have two *R*s. You should think about that."

Red didn't respond.

How many giggle-berries did I have? she wondered. But surely this couldn't be her imagination, no matter how many berries she had.

Where's Alice? Red thought next, thinking that she'd know what to do. After all, Alice was familiar with the oddities of Wonderland.

Finally, she spoke up, "Do you mind if I go fetch my friend? I'm sure she'd *love* to meet you."

The cat's face seemed to grow brighter. "You have a friend? Oh, that's nice. Is this friend a *true* friend?"

Red was taken aback by the new subject of conversation she just walked into. "Uh, I suppose."

The cat clapped his paws together. "Oh, that's *wonderful*! I was hoping that you would have one of the true kinds! Those are the rarest ones. Not many have those kinds, you know. I am *mad* that I'm so lucky to have managed to have so many. I am indeed a lucky cat. I would like to meet this rare kind of friend. It is exciting to meet such. And I suppose our conversation will be more interesting with three."

Then he laughed gleefully, chuckling, giggling, cackling, howling, roaring! It's hard to explain exactly what his laugh sounded like. One could only describe it as ecstatic, mad laughter.

Red laughed awkwardly. She still didn't know what to make of this cat, if it even was a cat. Leaving the cat and his madness behind her, she slipped away to find her friend. The thought crossed her mind not to even mention the cat to Alice and to just return to camp, but she shook it off.

Red quickened her steps, circling the giggle-berry bush until she came to the other side. It wasn't too long before she literally ran into Alice.

"Where have you been? I've been looking for you," Alice said after collecting herself.

"There was this cat," Red started to explain. "I said I'd introduce…" Her voice trailed off, unable to find the right words.

"What is it?" Alice asked, "What's up?"

"I am," the singsong voice mused.

The two girls looked up to see the multicolored, wide smiled cat perched atop the giggle-berry bush. He seemed quite amused with himself at his little joke.

"So this is your true friend!" His smile widened, though it didn't seem possible. "Hello, Alice."

"Chess!"

"You know him?"

"Of course!" Alice explained, "Red, this is the Cheshire Cat."

She looked sideways up at the cat again. "Oh. That explains a lot."

The Cheshire Cat swished his tail, passing it through the bush like smoke. "Yes, I've already had the pleasure of meeting Scarlet. She said hello."

"It's Red," she corrected.

"Oh, yes. I knew it was some kind of color."

Before Red could roll her eyes or say a word, a twig snapped. They whipped around, frozen in shock.

"Do excuse me, ladies," Chess pardoned himself, disappearing into thin air.

Red melted into the Wolf without a second thought. Bristling dangerously, she lowered herself to pounce if the need arose. Alice stayed put, narrowing her eyes at the spot where the intruder would emerge. She drew her sword and held it ready.

From out of the underbrush appeared Kai. Alice sighed in relief, sheathing her sword. Red transformed back to her normal self at the sight of their friend.

Kai raised his hand in greeting. "They wanted me to call you back for—"

A rock dropped on his head, knocking him out of consciousness. He fell heavily to the ground.

"Kai!" Red and Alice shouted, rushing over to his side.

Chess hovered above them. "Sorry, I was under the impression that he was a spy. I didn't realize he was a friend." He gasped, "Oh, Burgundy! Is this another true friend of yours?"

Red groaned. "Yes, I suppose."

She and Alice hoisted Kai up with some difficulty, though not much. The Cheshire Cat floated down and grabbed the collar of Kai's shirt, helping to pull him up. Putting one arm over Red's shoulder and the other over Alice's, together they started to drag Kai slowly to the hidden rabbit hole. Chess floated behind, holding the baskets of scavenged food.

"Crimson!" Chess called to Red. "That was a mad trick you did. Simply mad!"

"Was that a compliment?" Red asked Alice.

"In Wonderland, that's the highest you can get."

Chapter Ten

Painting Roses

Helena brushed the white petals tenderly with her paintbrush. Those roses were to be handled with care. The only person she trusted to paint them was herself. Not even the Duchess, especially not the Duchess, was allowed to handle them. Solemnly, she smeared more red paint on the flowers. Very few of those roses were completely red. Helena liked them partially red and partially white. It was special.

There were only two others who had ever painted those roses. One was her sister. The memory came blasting through her defenses before she could stop it.

She was only a small girl at the time, Celeste older but still a child. The gardeners were supposed to plant red rose bushes for the young queen, but their mistake was that instead of red, the roses turned out white. Sweet little Celeste didn't want her sister to be disappointed or angry with this simple mistake. So she began painting them. She was almost done, but Helena had gone to look for her dear sister and discovered what was happening.

Helena moved on to another rose as she recalled the incident. Her lips were almost smiling, her eyes almost happy.

The young White Queen tried to explain the mistake, but Helena wouldn't listen. She was so happy. She couldn't believe her sister would do something so kind, so sweet, so mad. By the end of the day, they had all of the roses painted: half red, half white.

That was one of the last times they were happy together. One of the last times that Helena could remember them being sisters. It all changed soon after that. It began before then. It just hadn't taken drastic turns until they were older, until Celeste betrayed her.

The Queen's twitch of a smile vanished almost instantly and the glint of happiness faded just as fast. Her calm state turned to anger and the painting she did for comfort seemed childish, a petty thing to do.

In her rage, she lashed out. With a slash of her arm, she struck a white rose with her brush. The blow jostled the flower and left behind a single red line across its petals. The paint dripped like blood down the purity of the white.

The Queen of Hearts gazed at this rose with a new interest, cocking her head. Her act had torn the rose slightly and the blood red paint seemed to emerge from it like a wound. It was as if the rose was bleeding, wounded by the Queen's hand.

Fingering the dripping petals, she came with a resolve to satisfy her cruel heart. This rose was like her sister, and the Queen would not rest until the results were the same, not until her sister's blood was spilled. Only then would her heart be satisfied. Only when she had Alice in her grasp and Celeste's bleeding heart in a box would she have peace. There was no other way to satisfy her longing, none that she could see, at least.

She gingerly put her hands around the bleeding rose. At her touch, the white petals browned. The rose withered away in the Queen's hands. A glint came to her eye and a smile upon her lips, but instead of happiness or goodness, the glint was evil and the smile was cruel.

Ruined, the rose died.

*****

"Here, put this on your head." Celeste handed over a bag of ice.

Kai winced as he placed it on the bump on his head. It hurt terribly, but he didn't express just how terribly.

"And drink this." She passed him a cup of a deep purple liquid.

He stared down at the drink with silent repulsion. "What is it?"

"It's a tonic for the pain." She winked.

He emptied the cup in one gulp. Instantly, with a slimy shudder, the pain disintegrated. With a grateful smile, he nodded toward her. "Thanks."

Celeste waved it off. "I usually have spare pain killing tonics around. They tend to come in handy." She placed the tonic bottle on the shelf alongside numerous other strangely shaped medicine and potion containers.

The Cheshire Cat sat on a chair's arm, seeming fairly tangible now, his multicolored eyes watching the sway of the ticking clocks hanging from the ceiling.

"Well, Great Uncle Jackrabbit! It's good to see you again, Chess," the White Rabbit exclaimed, slapping his paw on the cat's back. Of course, it didn't connect, only passed through like smoke.

Chess' smile stretched, tail swishing. "Yes, it's always good to see old friends, especially these days when they're all locked away. I remember popping in and seeing the March Hare a few days back, just in time for tea, too. Of course, there's never time for tea now."

"You've seen my cousin?" White asked excitedly.

"He *is* your cousin, isn't he? I had almost forgotten. Yes, I've seen him, as I believe I just mentioned."

"So, he's alright? He's escaped?"

"Who did?" The Cheshire Cat's eyes looked vaguely at White.

"Well, the March Hare. He's escaped the Queen's dungeons?"

Chess gasped. "He *did*? Oh, this is frabjous news!"

"No, no!" White shook his head. "You were just telling me if March escaped or not."

"Was I? I must've forgotten. How would I know if he escaped?"

"But, you said that you saw him the other day."

"Saw who?"

"The March Hare!"

"Oh, yes. I do like that rabbit. Nice fellow. He's your cousin isn't he? I saw him not too long ago, sometime in the brillig. I just popped into the dungeons and there he was! It was a brilliant surprise. Now, what were you saying, White?"

The White Rabbit sighed, "Nothing."

He cast exasperated black eyes on Alice. She laughed to herself, knowing how easily forgetful and distracted the Cheshire Cat could be. Most of the time, it was comical to listen to the conversations Chess had… unless you're the one that he was conversing with. In that case, it could be very exasperating and confusing, especially if you wished to get information out of him.

Then her face slacked. What was that the Cheshire Cat said before?

Chess slowly faded away, his smile the last to disappear.

Bewildered, Wendy asked, "Where did he go?"

"Oh, I'm not gone." The Cheshire Cat's voice came from everywhere at once. "I just appear to be so. Sometimes, it's so much better to be invisible. Nobody knows where you are and there are no eyes staring at you constantly."

"I never thought about it that way," Wendy admitted truthfully.

"Yes, most don't think of such things. It's also quite humorous to watch how everyone tries to find me when looking in the opposite direction." The cat slowly appeared right behind Jack's head. "Hello!"

Jack jumped in surprise, losing his footing and falling to the floor.

The Cheshire Cat rolled over and over in midair, chuckling with maddening laughter. Red helped Jack to his feet.

Composing himself instantaneously, Chess said, "I apologize for the scare, Quack."

"I wasn't scared, just surprised," Jack huffed. "And it's Jack."

"That's right! I suppose I was close, though. I'm not too good at names. It takes me a while to get them down. Let's see, so you're Jack." He turned to point at Wendy. "And you're Breezy."

"Uh, actually, it's Wendy."

"I knew it was something along those lines." He turned to the wounded Kai. "And you must be Kuvasz."

"Kai," he grunted.

"Oh, yes. They're both dogs, aren't they? And then, of course, Ginger!"

111

Red sighed, "We've been through this before. My name is *Red*."

"Well, I got the same color," Chess chuckled, "just different shades. Isn't that right, Alice?"

Alice didn't hear him. Her mind was elsewhere. Her heartbeat sped behind her ribcage, but she had to know.

She formed her thoughts into words. "Did you see Remus?"

Giant eyes the size of pocket watches turned to Alice. "The Mad Hatter? Works with the March Hare? And isn't he the White and Red Queen's…"

"Not now Chess!" she burst. "I need to know, and I don't have the time or patience to put up with your madness! Now tell me, *did you see Remus?*"

A sickening feeling entered Alice's gut as the Cheshire Cat's smile faded to near disappearance. She had never seen him without his smile. It was a strange sight, almost incomprehensible. But his grin returned quickly, though not as wide.

"Yes, I did happen to see the Hatter."

"How is he? What did he say?"

"Like I said, I happened to *see* him. What is it with humans and not taking anything literally?"

"Chess, focus!" Alice cut in. But a second voice had said the same thing at the same time: Celeste.

"I didn't talk to him; he didn't see me. The Duchess was seeing him, and he was talking more nonsense than I do! After that, though, by what I saw, he's not good. Dirty, unkempt, solemn, heavily guarded… And his hat was smashed on the floor. But what could one expect from

112

someone without a heart? The sight nearly wiped the smile right off my face!"

Alice's heart sank. *He ruined his hat?* It was unthinkable. The Remus she knew would never smash his hat. It was the one he wore at all times, the first one he ever made. It held his most precious childhood possessions: his mother's aquamarine scarf, his father's pocket watch, the pincushion Celeste gave him when she first taught him how to sew, and the scarlet feather quill he'd stolen from Helena's office. They were his treasures, his memories. That hat was Remus. Now it was smashed, broken, and destroyed… just like Remus.

A small tear slid down Alice's cheek. It was unbearable. She couldn't leave her Hatter like that. She couldn't stay in that rabbit hole, safe, while Remus sat in that cell, lifeless. It was too much.

She made her decision right then and there.

It was another beginning that started it all.

Standing with a start, she grabbed the closest sack she could find and began to pack it with provisions.

The White Rabbit hopped to his feet. "What in Wonderland are you doing, Miss Alice?"

Without looking up, she answered, "I'm going to get him."

"Who?"

"Remus," she replied, not faltering in her packing. "I'm going to find his heart, find a way to put it back in him, and then rescue him. And while I'm at it, I'll find the pocket watch and save the others trapped in the dungeons."

"But… but…"

Shouldering her full sack, Alice sighed, "We've been through this! I'm going, and nothing you say can stop me."

"But, the Queen! She's looking for you everywhere! She has spies and… and soldiers… and… and…"

"Well, I'm going no matter the cost."

Alice looked out over the others in the room, at the shocked, expectant eyes staring at her. Over half of them had followed her into this place, trusted her to show them the way. The others she'd known since she was a child, when she was half mad with depression from her sister's disappearance, when all she wanted was to go home. They'd helped her not only get home then, but find a true home later in Wonderland. Alice couldn't be more grateful to any of them. They were more of a family to her than any biological ties she had in England, even the other Facility escapees she'd only known for a few months.

She sighed. "Look, I can't ask anyone to risk their lives to come with me. But, if any want to join me, I would be very appreciative." Alice looked at the White Rabbit. She'd been running after him since she was ten years old. "Feel free to stay here if you wish."

The pause that followed set a weight to the heavy silence in the air as her words sank in. Alice knew it was a hard choice to make between risky adventure and safe comfort. Honestly, she wouldn't blame any of them if they decided to stay.

Wendy didn't have any difficulty with her answer and announced without hesitation, "Well, I'm coming."

"As am I," Red added.

"Count me in," Jack declared.

"Let's get this Hatter." Kai's voice rumbled low with his thick accent.

"You can't expect me not to join you, Alice," Celeste said gently, matter-of-factly. "As you might recall, I love Remus, too."

"Well, I suppose I'll tag along," the Cheshire Cat sang absentmindedly, gaze following the swinging watches again.

Alice smiled as she let out the breath she didn't know she'd been holding. But still, there was one more who had yet to answer. Maybe it was the little girl in her, but for some reason Alice felt his response was the most important.

She looked down her friend. "And you? What will you do?"

The White Rabbit looked up at Alice. There was fear and apprehension in his black eyes, but such decisiveness that she knew his answer before he spoke it. "No matter where you go, Miss Alice, I will follow."

Chapter Eleven

Frumious Bandersnatch

"How much longer?" Jack whined.

"We've only been walking for an hour," Wendy laughed. "Quit your whining!"

Jack grinned playfully. Out of the corner of his eye, he caught Red's smile and felt a warm glow in his cheeks. He liked when he made her laugh or smile. It was difficult sometimes, so it was like a small victory every time he managed it. Jack looked away quickly as her green eyes glanced over at him.

Thanks to Celeste, everyone was fitted with the new traveling clothes. She even managed to make a new waistcoat for the White Rabbit. All garments were made of leathery fabric procured from the lady's-slipper plant—excellent for shoes, hats, or clothes—and adorned with threadlike fibers from the Queen-Anne's-lace flower. How the White Queen had been able to finish them all, or know they'd be needed, was a mystery. Even so, she'd even managed to prepare several necessary potions and ingredients by the time Alice proposed their immediate expedition.

Alice had a sneaking suspicion Celeste knew all along when they were going to leave.

The Cheshire Cat hummed a cheery tune as they walked through the Tulgey Wood. Mostly he kept invisible. Every so often, though, he appeared floating in midair with that oversized smile on his face. Either that or just parts of him were revealed, especially his smile, sometimes only his eyes.

He seemed to finally get some headway on the Facility escapees' names. For one, after plenty of Eyes, Kevins, and Kyles, Chess at last got used to calling him Kai. Wendy's name was almost down—he was stuck on Wanda at the moment—and Jack's was nearly there. But Red's name kept as nearly unpredictable as ever, all different shades of the color.

Alice hung back, allowing the others to move ahead of her. Soon, she fell in step with the White Queen so she could talk to her privately.

"I know what you wish to ask me," Celeste said before Alice could open her mouth.

"You do?"

"Honestly, Alice, after all this time, seeing incredulous things, finding the unbelievable true, you still use the tone of surprise."

Alice laughed at her own mistake, but her smile soon faded into seriousness. "Well?"

Celeste sighed. "The method of putting a heart back into its owner is a process that's been nearly forgotten for ages."

"*Nearly* forgotten? So, there are those who know how?"

"Very few, but yes, there are those who do."

"And are you one of them? Do you know how to put back one's heart?"

"I had to." The White Queen lowered her eyes. "Living with a sister who was learning the arts of dark magic every day in secret, I had to learn the ways of undoing such horrors. And though I loathe it and never use it, I had to know how to create them. I had to train myself in both arts of

117

magic, the good and bad. So I found someone who knew both but had the same priorities as I do."

"So, how do you do it?"

She pursed her lips together, narrowing her eyes as if revealing such a thing was strenuous. "First you must find the heart. And it *must* be the right heart; otherwise if you put the wrong heart in then you and Remus would die an excruciatingly painful death. Once you have the right heart, you need to be completely calm. One wrong move, one small fear in mind, and all is lost. You must plunge your hand—holding the heart—into the owner's chest, release the heart, and pull your hand out again. But it will be painful, for both you and Remus."

"But how would I get my hand through his chest?"

"The same way Helena took the heart out: *magic*. See, the heart wants to return to its owner. It'll be able to get through and enable your hand to pass through as well. It's different to take a heart *out*. You must have powerful magic in order to do that. But taking out a heart automatically casts a sort of spell that enables it to be able to return. All it needs is someone to put it back in."

Alice thought a moment. "That doesn't sound too bad. Not as hard as I thought, at least."

"It gets worse. Returning the heart comes with a price; magic typically does. As soon as someone puts the heart in, they will feel every pain the owner feels forever more."

"So, if I put his heart back, I will share in all of Remus' pain?"

"And he will share in yours."

Alice nodded resolutely. "Then it's a price I'm willing to pay. Remus will have to be, too."

Red awoke with a start. *Something's wrong.* She could feel it, instincts shaking all over. It was almost like… No. She shook her head, stopped herself from thinking that way.

Fang isn't here; he can't be, she kept telling herself. *He could never find out where I am. He's not in Wonderland.*

Besides, now that she thought about it, this wasn't like that. This was different. It was new.

She looked around the camp. The coals in the fire pit glowed faintly, illuminating the sleeping forms of the others. The Tulgey Wood was quiet… much too quiet. There was definitely something wrong, but it wasn't familiar. There was something out there she didn't recognize.

Red got up gently without making a noise, one of the many talents she adapted before she'd been hunted by Fang. Moving slowly away from the campsite, she sniffed the air. She needed to know what this new potential threat was. She smelled the wind once again. There was something very strange, something dangerous out there. Hardly making a sound, Red slinked deeper into the woods.

There was more than one creature, Red sensed, like a pack. But they weren't wolves. The smell of man also perked her nose. But this wasn't the same scent as someone like her, where she could smell both man and beast in one. The men had to be among these strange creatures. Curious and cautious, she continued following the invisible trail.

It took a while, her senses tingling vigorously as she drew closer, but soon she found it: an abandoned campsite. Her gaze darted every which way. A fire pit was smoking in the center of a ring of tents. Red knew this place was far from abandoned. Still, she warily drew closer, the hair on the back of her neck prickling.

Nearing the fire pit, she saw the traces of footprints in the ash. The flames had been recently stamped out. Wooden stakes partially encircled the pit, heavy chains attached to each. Empty now, it was obvious that whatever they used to hold was big and strong.

Something was dreadfully wrong.

The wind shifted.

Red whipped around just as teems of armored soldiers surrounded her on all sides. She cursed under her breath. How did she not see it sooner?! These were definitely the Queen of Hearts' soldiers—*What did Alice call them? Cards?* —judging by the crimson hearts on their tassets, spaulders, gauntlets, and helms. Every one of them had a blade raised in her direction.

Then Red saw them, the creatures that cast that peculiar scent. Massive and hairy, they appeared to be a blend between wolf and hyena. Dark grey fur covered their muscular bodies, thick shabby black hair sprouting on their necks and the ends of their tails. Long claws shot out of great paws, and numerous yellow teeth gleamed in the moonlight. Deep empty pits for eyes glared at her. She noted especially their long snouts and powerful jaws. Muscles flexed and ready to spring, their lips pulled back in a ferocious snarl. They lurked just behind the soldiers like waiting nightmares.

"Put your hands up!" ordered one soldier. His armor was rusty, battle worn. Red respected that. She'd kill him last.

She slowly raised her arms.

"What're you doing in these woods?" he barked.

Red shrugged. "What can I say? I like nature."

"Don't use that tone with me!"

Red smirked, rethinking her previous considerations of a quick death for this one.

"Who's with you, girl?"

"No one."

"Don't lie to me! Who's with you?"

"You mean *besides* you?"

"Don't smart mouth me!"

"Well, then I'm all by myself."

Red felt a glimmer of déjà vu, reminding her of the Facility. This guard reminded her strongly of Mrs. Bones. Or maybe Mrs. Prig? She couldn't decide which, but the thought made her want to laugh.

Another soldier said to the first, "I don't think she's going to break."

Red smirked. *The Facility couldn't break me either.*

"Fine!" spat the first soldier. "We'll take her to the Queen, then."

She raised her finger to stop them. "Now *there* we might find a problem."

"And what might that be?" he mocked.

"I have no intentions of going with you, and I certainly have no desire to see the Queen."

"You don't have a say in the matter. You're surrounded, unarmed, defenseless…"

"Now, you really shouldn't judge a girl by her appearance," Red put, savoring the drama of the situation.

"I've had enough of this nonsense!" He nodded to another soldier.

Red shrugged. "I tried to warn you."

Instinct took over, a tingling sensation between pain and pleasure coursing through her inside and out, and she transformed into the Wolf. The soldiers shuffled back in surprise, leaving them unprepared for the blow. Red rammed her body into the closest soldiers, knocking them off their feet. Her magnified strength was enough to knock several unconscious.

"Give the bandersnatch the signal!" someone roared.

A soldier banged his sword against his shield thrice. The beasts immediately sprang to attack.

In the back of her mind Red evaluated that though they were much bigger than her, she was far more limber, and she was faster. She dodged attacks, using her sharp teeth to draw blood. Her claws, though not as long as her attackers', managed to tear through the bandersnatch's thick hide.

Stinging pain racked through her body as she herself was dealt many wounds. Her black fur was stained with blood, both hers and her victims'. As far as she could tell, she had no serious injuries.

Bandersnatch bodies lay dead around her. But still many more were all too much alive. The soldiers hung back, occasionally making an attempt to strike the Wolf. She bit one soldier's forearm off after he tried to stab her.

Despite her victories, Red knew that she wouldn't be able to get them all, not by herself. There were too many of them.

Feigning the opposite direction, she managed to clamber out of the pile of attacking beasts and ran around the campsite. Both bandersnatch and soldier followed in hot pursuit. Before they could reach her, she stopped, threw her head back, and howled as loud as she could. Then a bandersnatch sank its teeth into her foreleg.

With a jolt, Jack abruptly woke at the sound of the Wolf's howl. It had pierced through his dreams, sent a shiver up his spine. But the howl seemed so out of place in those woods, no matter how dark and mysterious it was. Something about it made Jack uneasy.

He looked around camp. The fire was out but for a small trickle of smoke. The Rabbit was twitching his leg irritatingly, as if trying to kick something—or *someone*—away. Jack smirked, wondering what awful things he was doing in the White Rabbit's dreams.

Of course the Cheshire Cat was nowhere in sight, not surprisingly.

Kai lay in a position that made him appear awake. But Jack knew he was asleep. This was the way he'd slept at the Facility, and—as Jack learned—how he slept every night. Kai slept in such a way that he was ready for action as soon as it arrived. He slept in a way that would make him prepared to attack and protect. He slept like a soldier.

Celeste slept like a queen, though her bed was certainly far from regal. Wendy was curled up in a ball, looking very sweet and innocent as she slumbered; almost childlike. Alice slept as if she were trapped in a nightmare and couldn't wake herself up. Jack knew what that was like.

He almost relaxed, almost believed there was nothing to worry about. Perhaps the howl was only in his dream. Then he noticed it: everyone was there, except…

"Red," he whispered.

It all clicked. Anxiously, he scrambled to his feet and shook the others awake.

"Red's gone!" he exclaimed.

"What?" Kai sat up instantly as Jack knew he would. "What is it?"

"Red's gone," Jack repeated.

Wendy stretched her arms over her head, yawning. "She probably went on walk or something."

"No, but I heard her—"

A skin crawling howl pierced through the sky like a dagger, cutting him off midsentence. The sound made everyone freeze. Then all was eerie silence.

Alice gulped. "White, remind me again: are there any wolves in Wonderland?"

The White Rabbit's eyes were wide. "No."

All went into a complete frenzy, or as much of a frenzy as a bunch of half-asleep people could be. Still, there wasn't a wisp of sleep left in their minds.

"Where is she?"

"How do we find her?"

"Where could she have gone?"

"*Calm down!*" White proclaimed.

Everyone fell silent, even Jack.

"Good," the White Rabbit went on, exasperated. "Now, before we lose our heads, let's just think this through—"

"Kai?" Wendy interrupted, noticing her friend's absence first.

Kai looked up from the edge of camp where he'd been silently inspecting the area. As they were discussing all the possibilities, Kai wasn't paying attention. He pointed to a trail hidden to the untrained eye that led deeper into the woods and on.

"She went this way," he announced without explanation. "Follow me."

It took a moment for his words to compute, but when they did, no one questioned him. Kai was the kind of person you never defied, the kind of person you follow no matter what. That's just how it was. So they followed Kai without complaint or question, confident that he knew what he was doing.

The Tulgey Woods was dense and dark, the shadows themselves seeming to hold a murky depth to them, but Kai still managed to find Red's trail, traveling quickly yet cautiously.

"I didn't know you could track," Jack stated, impressed by another thing his brotherly figure could do.

"One learns a lot of things when hunting the Snow Queen."

Celeste suddenly tensed and she stopped abruptly, eyes glazing over. No one noticed the slight reaction but for Alice.

"Are you alright?" she asked.

"Yes, I'm fine," Celeste answered, brushing off the bottom of her foot absently. "I stepped on a thorn."

Alice frowned, sure that there was more than Celeste was letting on. She knew that look. But she could tell that Celeste didn't want to talk about it.

"Where's the Cheshire Cat?" Wendy asked, looking around for the cat. He was nowhere in sight.

"Oh, he'll turn up," White assured. "He always does."

A mournful howl filled the air again, this time much louder than before.

"This way," Kai whispered grimly.

It didn't take them long after to discover the campsite. In a split second, they took in the horrible sight. Corpses littered the ground, some human, others a strange canine beast. Soldiers clad in dark white armor surrounded an exceedingly angered green eyed Wolf, weapons drawn. The large canines circled the Wolf, drool dripping off their chins.

Red's teeth were bared in a vicious snarl. Claws protruded from her paws like nasty daggers. Blood stained her matted fur, and the hair on the back of her neck bristled terribly. She was a horrific sight. They'd never seen Red this way, and it scared most of them.

"Oh great," Alice sighed. "Bandersnatch."

"Gesundheit," Jack whispered.

"No," Alice tried to explain. "*Bandersnatch*. They're those big, wolfish creatures over there."

"Lovely," Wendy huffed.

"What's the plan?" the cheery voice of the Cheshire Cat hummed as he formed above their heads.

"We attack!" Jack responded instantly. "We have to help her."

"Yes, but how?" inquired the White Rabbit.

"Now really, White." Alice questioned, raising an eyebrow, "Where's your imagination?"

Red knew she was done for. She was surrounded on all sides, and her foreleg screamed in pain. *Where are they?* Deciding it only made her vulnerable, she chose not to howl again and hoped that somehow the others had heard her already.

One bandersnatch snapped at her, but Red was too quick. She dodged the sharp teeth and struck its shoulder. Her foreleg exploded in protest. But the bandersnatch jumped back, continuing to circle her behind the others with a bad limp.

The noise of hungry growls diminished. A humming tune echoed from overhead, so mad and out of place that all were distracted. Red only processed it for a second before knowing help had arrived.

Everything happened in a moment.

The Cheshire Cat appeared with Celeste directly beside the Wolf. Instantly, Celeste sprayed liquid in Red's eyes, the potion stinging, before raising her hands.

A soldier only had time to say, "What in Wonderland?"

Beams of light streamed out from the White Queen's hands, engulfing the whole campsite in a dome. Red blinked, surprised she could still see easily. But the soldiers were blinded, and the bandersnatch reared in anxiousness with their loss of sight. The liquid in her eyes must've enabled her to see.

"Go!" Celeste proclaimed.

The others entered the white light, eyes also protected by Celeste's concoction. They took the swords from the soldiers' hands and bashed the back of the men's heads to knock them unconscious. The soldiers couldn't stop them. They never saw it coming.

Shaking her head to snap out of her shock, Red caught on quickly. She sprang on the staggering bandersnatch, ripping their hide with her claws and teeth.

The beasts were still dangerous, even without their sight, but at least she now had the advantage.

Soldiers swung their swords frantically or poised for the unknown. Some hit each other with fatal blows in thinking them the enemy. Bandersnatch turned on bandersnatch in maddening blood thirst, thinking the other as the Wolf. Soon, all bandersnatch lay dead and the remaining conscious soldiers held their arms up in surrender.

Breathing hard in exhaustion, Celeste dropped her hands and the light disappeared. The spray substance in their eyes slid off like tears. The soldiers blinked rapidly, probably unable to see properly anymore.

"May I do the honors?" the Cheshire Cat asked cheerily.

Celeste nodded in response, regaining her composer.

Chess smiled wider as he disappeared and reappeared above the heads of the soldiers. His paws hugged glass flowers that had been growing nearby. In rhythm, he dropped each one on the soldiers' heads. Petals shattered. Each soldier in turn fell unconscious on their faces.

"Oops." Chess shrugged with mock regret.

Red morphed back into her normal self, hugging her wounded arm close. She was completely bloody and beaten, but alive.

"Red!" It was said all at once.

Jack ran up to her first, almost going for a hug, but Red stepped back defensively. "Jack; bleeding."

"Oh, right." His face turned scarlet. He felt like an idiot, but grinned anyway when Red smiled a little at him.

Celeste approached, informing, "We should return to camp and get you fixed up. Someone can stay and look around, though. There may be some supplies we can collect."

Wordlessly, Alice decided to stay. Wendy, Jack, and White returned to camp with Celeste and Red, but Kai and the Cheshire Cat joined her in investigating. Curiously, the three approached the tents.

The first was full of sleeping mats and other personal belongings: watches, journals, letters, maps, and clothes. The next three were the same, though a few weapons were scattered about. Kai helped himself to a couple daggers. The fifth tent was filled with boxes of food and barrels of water, which was odd for a campsite, but helpful for the scavengers. The floor of the sixth tent was littered with bones and tufts of fur, heavy chains striping the ground. It must've been a place for some of the bandersnatch to stay. Kai and Alice worked together to put the unconscious soldiers inside, only after tying them up did they realize that Chess had disappeared.

Recovering from the exertion, Alice led Kai to the last tent. A scuffling pricked her ears. Kai stopped her. Alice held her breath. Something was inside. Whether it was bandersnatch or soldier or even mome rath, she couldn't tell.

Kai put a finger to his lips. She nodded, stooping to pick up stones and held them at the ready. Silently, he braced himself and counted off his fingers.

One.

Two.

Three!

He whipped back the tent flap as Alice raised her stone.

Both froze in shock.

A tall young man stood in the center of the empty tent, strapped tightly to the supporting pole. His flaming red hair was soiled, but his viridescent eyes still glittered with inextinguishable spirit. Freckles sprayed out over his nose and under his eyes. His neck and arms were black and blue from bruises, his face and hands splotched with blood.

The man looked up, his gaze falling on Kai. He didn't flinch, though no recognition came over him. Then his eyes found Alice. A smile stretched across his face so wide that his lips began to bleed.

"Alice!"

Chapter Twelve

Drowning Time

"Dum!" Alice rushed forward to untie her friend.

"You know him?" Kai asked, though he wasn't sure why he was surprised. "Is there anyone you *don't* know here?"

Alice made a face at him as she loosened Dum's bounds.

"Honestly, mate," Dum spoke up good-naturedly, "she probably knows more than I do."

"Kai, this insufferable nuisance is Tweedle-Dum." Alice gave Dum a poke in the ribs. He smiled at the compliment.

Once released, Dum hugged her close despite his obvious injuries. "It's good to see you, Alice."

She returned his embrace. "It's good to see you too."

He pulled back to hold her at arm's length, exclaiming incredulously, "By the old Mock Turtle! How did you get back?"

Alice glanced back at Kai. "It's a long story."

With a sigh, she scrutinized Tweedle-Dum. Bruises inked down his arms, no doubt his legs as well. Scratches where his skin ripped proved evidence of countless beatings, his face being especially bloody. His right eye was ghastly yellow and his lips were cracked and swollen. An ugly gash above his left knee oozed blood, though not too much, and a long vibrant line across his throat moved strangely when he swallowed. Still, despite all of it, his eyes gleamed mischievously and his playful smile struck a mad appearance.

Alice thought briefly of how similar he looked like his brother underneath his deformed features. Of course, the Brothers Tweedle were completely identical. Few could tell the difference between them, especially with their personalities being so close, but Alice knew the difference. This was Tweedle-Dum. But then where was Tweedle-Dee?

Shaking her head, Alice exclaimed, "You look terrible!"

"Thank you." He grinned cockily. "I've been working on it."

"Wait until Celeste sees you like this. There's no telling how she'll react." Alice sighed. "We'd better get you to camp. She's sure to have something to fix you up."

"Seeing the White Queen again will be healing enough."

Alice and Kai helped the unbalanced Dum outside the musty tent and into the woods. With Kai able to find the hidden trail back, the two of them were able to lead the limping Tweedle to their camp boarders.

At first, they couldn't see it. There were only dark trees, gleaming glass flowers, shifting shadows.

"Mome rath," Alice groaned.

The air in front of them shimmered like a curtain, the password making Celeste's concealing enchantments briefly visible. The three hobbled through the enchantment and entered the campsite. Red was being tended to by Celeste, who was preparing a potion for her. Wendy sat between Jack and the White Rabbit, who must have gotten in another fight for they were either ignoring or glaring at the other. The

Cheshire Cat sat right beside the fire, staring oddly into the flames. No one looked up.

"Guess what we found!" Alice announced as they staggered toward the newly aroused fire.

"Food, I hope," Jack mumbled without turning around.

"Well, yes, but that wasn't the answer I was looking for."

They all looked up at once, taking in the sight. Each reacted differently. Jack fell off his stump in surprise. Wendy ran over to help. Red looked confused. Chess' smile stretched even farther, eyes reflecting the fire's glow. Celeste gasped and nearly dropped her potion bottle as her hands flew to her mouth.

"Great Uncle Jackrabbit!" the White Rabbit exclaimed.

"Sweet peppermint tea!" Celeste snapped out of her shock. "Dum, are you alright? What happened?"

"We'll all tell our grand stories later," Dum insisted as he was helped to a sitting position beside the White Queen. "But for now, I personally would enjoy a bit of that healing tonic you're making. It appears that this one over here needs some too." He nodded to Red.

As soon as the tonic was ready, Celeste gave Wendy some to apply to Red's wounds while she herself took care of Dum. He observed her with great interest as she doctored him, not bothering to hide it even when a deep blush rose up Celeste's neck. As soon as the pasty tonic was applied to the wounds, they began to mend and heal.

Looking around at the group, Dum proclaimed humorously, "Are we all just going to sit here and stare at one another or are we going to actually introduce ourselves? By the old Mock Turtle, I don't care if it's cheesy! Honestly, I only know half of you." He laughed. "I'll start. My name is Tweedle-Dum, but just call me Dum." He dramatically gestured to Red who sat beside him. "Now it's your turn."

She raised her eyebrows, but didn't protest. "I'm Red."

"That's a nice name. May I ask, is it a nickname or are your parents merely creative in their choices of names?"

"No, it's a nickname. My real name is Rubina Ellen Daim. My initials are R. E. D. Thus, Red."

"I like it. It's… original."

"Thanks."

Dum turned to Kai. "I didn't catch your name earlier."

"Kai," he said simply.

"And I'm Jack," Jack spoke up.

Dum pointed to each in turn. "So it's Kai and Jack. Alright, so who are you?"

"Wendy."

"Is that right? I don't think I've heard that name before. It's nice and… breezy." He smiled at his own joke.

The Cheshire Cat cackled much harder than the joke was worth, nearly disappearing.

Wendy shrugged. "My Uncle Jim invented it."

"Really, I didn't know that," Alice spoke.

"Many people don't know that, actually."

Then Dum noticed the White Rabbit. "White! I thought you were still in the dungeons. You escaped then, eh?"

"Yes, I very much did. Probably got that manxome Knave into trouble while I was at it, too. But enough about me, what about you? What happened?"

He grinned in amusement. Dum held out his hands mysteriously, ready to spin his tale. "Well, Dee and I just escaped from the battlegrounds and were running from the Queen of Hearts' cards. We kept on the move, never staying in one place for more than a few days. Now don't doubt that we kept an eye out for them, but we never saw any friends. We invaded a couple of the cards' campsites and stopped a few troops out hunting for Alice and the White Queen. We even managed to get some on our side, and now they're spying on Helena for us. Anyway, it was our mother's birthday, so we decided to visit her grave to, you know, say hello—"

"Oh, that's nice," the Cheshire Cat interrupted. "I do enjoy it when someone tells me hello."

"—But Helena must have known we would do that because a surprise party was there waiting for us, as we expected of course. If there wasn't one, then we certainly would've been deeply disgraced! Where would our reputation have gone if there wasn't? But at least she thought us important enough to send a *surprise* party. It was a messy business; I got a cut on my forehead that left a scar—if you can tell—and a nasty bump on the head."

"You really should be more careful," Celeste mumbled.

"We got away from it alive," Dum reassured her before returning to his tale, "not together, mind you. Somehow we got separated. Next thing I know, I hear Dee's been captured and sent to the dungeons! I was actually trying to find you, Celeste, when I heard this. Of course, I was determined to get Dee out of there and was making plans to do so when these old brutes got in the way and caught me! They beat me, of course, threatening that they'd take me to the Queen of Hearts. One frumious card gave me that nasty gash on my knee just for spite! And then, before the week is over, I hear a great commotion outside my tent. There were several crazy noises, some I knew as bandersnatch and others men's voices. But there was another noise I'd never heard before that left me in uffish thought; kind of like a wail, but deeper, like someone was crying out in pain, but eerier. Anyway, later came an almost blinding light—that was probably you, Celeste. Good thing I was inside my tent, otherwise *I'd* be blind! Then Alice and Kai found me and took me here." Dum gestured around him in conclusion.

Alice sat ponderously. *So we have to save Tweedle-Dee too.*

But Red laughed, bringing her from her thoughts. "Yeah, that *howl* was me."

"Really?" Dum asked. "I didn't think it sounded human."

"Well, you're not wrong."

He raised an eyebrow and grinned. "Now I am very much interested in hearing your story. How'd you get back to Wonderland, Alice? How'd you find me? Tell me everything."

So they told him, everyone helping to fill in the blanks. They told him about the Facility and the mysterious Anne Christiansen. They told him how the White Rabbit had found them and how Red found the Cheshire Cat—though Chess insisted it was he who found her. They explained their mission to find Remus' heart, rescue everyone in the dungeons, and get White's pocket watch back. Red also told her story of finding the soldiers' campsite, which everyone else was very much interested in hearing her side of it. And finally, they told him about their ingenious rescue plan to help Red and how they found Tweedle-Dum.

"Whoa!" Dum puffed out his cheeks. "So much to say. First of all, brilliant rescue, absolutely mad! Second, what is a *wolf* exactly? It sounds strange."

Wendy nudged Red as if to say, *Show him.*

Red smirked. Closing her eyes, she let the sensation wash over her. The pain she used to feel during this change, like she was being turned inside out, was not so painful anymore. She felt herself melt into the Wolf.

Dum started back. "Cabbages and kings!"

Red changed back to herself quickly, blushing slightly and lowering her eyes.

"Thank you for that explanation." Dum regained his composer in amusement. "Thirdly, who helped you escape the… whatever you called it?"

"Facility?" Wendy suggested.

"Yes, that! It sounds like a horrible place. Boring and painful, a terrible combination."

"Yes, it was. But we don't know who Anne Christiansen is," Alice responded, though the predicament was beginning to bother her now that she thought about it.

"Lastly, can I join in on your expedition?"

"Yes!"

All eyes turned to the White Rabbit, astonished.

White smiled sheepishly, wringing his paws. "What? Don't look at me like that. After all, we need all the help we can get."

*****

She dreaded coming down there, but ever since the Duchess' report from her previous visit, Helena had an itching to go down and see for herself. There was always a tinge of guilt whenever she thought of what she'd done to the Mad Hatter. She'd never intended it to go so far. Her revenge wasn't supposed to include Remus. But he'd taken the side of the White Queen. Besides, the Duchess was right. Other than the White Queen and Alice, the Mad Hatter was the biggest threat to her reign. Still, that didn't make it any easier when she stepped into the dungeons to find Remus sitting on the floor in his cell. He was humming, swaying back and forth, more mad in that moment than she'd ever seen him. Did that happen? Did taking out a madman's heart make him even more of a madman? A worse one?

When Helena approached, the soldiers bowed to her and moved out of the room. She stopped just a pace away from the iron bars that separated them. Instantly, Remus' eyes snapped open, a dull and empty blue. His humming stopped. Helena had to remind herself to breathe.

He spoke first, cocking his head, "Why are you here?"

Helena swallowed, trying not to betray her reason. "I don't know," she lied.

"Yes you do," Remus said steadily. "You can't lie to me. I know when you lie."

Taking a deep breath, she stated, "I've come to see if you have anything of importance to say this time."

"Time." The word echoed in the room. Remus' eyes flicked around as if to follow it. "Time is all messed up," he said calmly, his train of thought flowing from his mouth. "Forevers are seconds. Words come too soon or too late. Some stories last forever, others seem to come only yesterday... or tomorrow. Strange, isn't it? Time has gone mad."

"Why are you saying this?" she muttered.

He grinned madly. "Blood, sweat, and tea, sister! That's what it takes to achieve all great and terrible things."

"No, not that." Helena shook her head. "About time. Are you saying that time is running out? For what? For who?"

Remus shook his head and scowled, clenching his fists to his knees. "Not running, no, no. Where's it got to run off to? It's not wasting, either... Drowning." He relaxed, eyes looking up at the ceiling as if reading words etched in its surface. "Time is drowning, drowning, drowning away in stale tea and desperate *madness*... Tick tock, tick tock... Time is drowning."

He began humming again. The sound sent a shiver down Helena's spine. Then Remus began to sing softly to the eerie tune:

"Time is drowning,
Hearts are burning,
Heads are rolling,
Nothing can save you now,
Tick tock, tick tock;
"Creatures talking,
Weak are rising,
White Queen's nearing,

139

Nothing can save you now,
Tick tock, tick tock;
"Cards are bleeding,
Crowns are sweating,
Tea is spilling,
Nothing can save you now,
Tick tock, tick tock;
"Red Queen, here's your warning,
Wonderland's raging,
Alice is coming,
Highness, time is drowning,
And nothing can save you now,
Tick tock, tick tock, tick tock…"

Breathing hard, Helena turned on her heel and left, trying to hide the tears in her eyes. Remus stayed, though, swaying to his music and murmuring over and over, "Tick tock, tick tock, tick tock…"

*****

"Wait!" Tweedle-Dum exclaimed that next day as the group continued to travel through the Tulgey Wood. "So you really saw and *fought* with actual giants?"

Jack nodded. "Yep."

"Cabbages and kings! There aren't any giants in Wonderland, both fortunately and disappointingly." Dum paused to think about that. "Well, there are giant flowers, giant birds, giant dogs… but no actual *giants*."

"What are you two talking about?" The White Rabbit hopped up to them, his ears having pricked at the word *giants*.

"Jack was just telling me about how he's had encounters with giants," Dum explained when Jack didn't.

White stared incredulously at Jack. "You've been to Giant Country?"

Lowering his eyes, he shrugged. "What of it?"

"He didn't tell you about the giants?" Dum asked just as incredulously.

White waved this off, absentmindedly. "Jack and I haven't been on the *best* of terms." Face scrunched in thought, he asked Jack. "How did you get there?"

"Beanstalk."

"How'd you get the beans?"

"The *what?*"

"Beans! The magic beans to grow the beanstalk."

Jack shrugged sheepishly. "Oh. Well, I didn't get any beans. I found the beanstalk."

"*Found* the beanstalk?!" The White Rabbit's jaw dropped.

Suddenly defensive, Jack snapped, "Why? What if I *found* the beanstalk? Why all this fuss that I entered Giant Country?"

By this time, everyone stopped walking, intrigued by the conversation.

"Because Giant Country is a very difficult world to get into!"

"What do you mean?" Alice spoke up.

"Well, see, my pocket watch is the most predictable way to travel between worlds. It's a specially made portal creator—such things are very rare to come by. There are other ways to travel, of course. Portals, for instance, are some but they are very difficult to make and harder to find, yet it's more common to stumble into them. Some are random and unrecognizable. But most worlds have their own special way

141

to get there. Some rabbit holes, for example, lead to Wonderland. Neverland takes the Second Star to the Right as its means of transport. One just needs to fly to it, not actually making it to the star, but intentionally fly to it and one will eventually break into Neverland. Mirrors make excellent portals, but they're also unpredictable. I believe one world is very random in their portals; going anywhere from wardrobes to paintings to trains—"

"Alright, this is all very interesting stuff, but I don't see how this has anything to do with the subject," Jack grumbled.

"I'm getting to that!" White exclaimed. "Giant Country's unique route of travel is through magic beans and giant beanstalks! There are very few magic beans and hardly any have been planted to grow into giant beanstalks. It is also one of the most difficult of portals to create! That's why it's very hard to get into Giant Country without a specially made portal creator, like my pocket watch. And that's why I find it most peculiar that you just so happened to have *found* a giant beanstalk just abandoned like that!"

Silence grew heavy around them. No one moved as they absorbed what the White Rabbit was saying. Even the Cheshire Cat was quiet. You could almost see the thoughts buzzing around their heads. Dread filled Alice's gut like a growing fungus.

Finally, Celeste spoke up in a far off voice, "You're saying that someone intended for Jack to find the beanstalk."

It wasn't a question, but she got an answer anyway.

White sighed. "Yes, that is *exactly* what I'm saying."

Chapter Thirteen

Questions and Discoveries

Helena tried to get her mind off of the Hatter's words by keeping busy. There were many things she could've done, but presently she figured it was time to write a progress report. That was definitely a good way to keep her mind occupied.

But why would a queen, much less the Queen of Hearts, need to compose a progress report? After all, she was at such a rank that she should've been the one receiving such reports. In fact, there was a small stack of them on her desk beside her.

Some were from her searching parties. All said the same thing, not surprisingly. They still hadn't found Alice or Celeste. There were more prisoners on the way, and a few were on some suspects' tails. The only peculiar occurrences were the reported disappearances. Perhaps the subjects of Wonderland were going into hiding, probably trying to find refuge in the Diamond Mountains or even the remnants of Underland. Whatever the case, it was an issue the Queen needed to look into another time.

Some reports were from her spies, saying pretty much the same thing except that they've heard wind of a rebellion. But this was no news to Helena. After all, rebellious camps had been in Wonderland since she'd come to power. None lasted long. The Queen of Hearts was able to stomp them out quickly, almost effortlessly.

Others came from the cards guarding the castle. These were short and few. There were no invaders but for those crazed ones who tried to singlehandedly breach the castle. They were taken down with little second thought.

There were some from the training cards, the soldiers ready to fight. Many were ready enough. The majority just practiced for fun. Most of the warriors in the Queen's army were former residents of Underland, longtime enemies of Wonderland's former king but gladly served the Queen of Hearts who helped them obtain their revenge. As much as Helena valued them for their ferocity and brutality, she was glad they kept busy training. Anything to satisfy their thirst for violence.

There were others from the caretakers of her *pets*. The bandersnatch were multiplying steadily, though slow. Those that were old enough were being trained to fight and track, hunt and kill. The jubjub birds were doing fine. Many were already grown and trained. The eggs should hatch any day, which was at least progress. And Helena's *special* pet was doing excellently. It was just as dangerous as ever; maybe even worse.

As for the cards holding the prisoners, those were the shortest of all. The prisoners didn't do all that much except for composing an endless array of chatter. It was amazing how the mad people of Wonderland could entertain themselves so easily. Tweedle-Dee and that March Hare were ones for picking fun at the cards, which made the guards agitated, which made the prisoners delighted. But the Mad Hatter…

Helena shook her head, trying to get rid of the awful memory, the terribly haunting song, and the pitiful *madness*. Calming herself, she proceeded to write her own progress report in ink red as blood.

When the Queen of Hearts signed her name at the bottom of the parchment, the doors burst open.

"Your Highness!" the soldier rushed in.

Annoyance quickly inflamed to fury inside her. The doors banged shut and the soldier was slammed against them by an unseen force. The light flickered and dimmed despite the brightness outside.

The soldier was lifted off his feet and his throat tightened. Groping at the invisible hands squeezing his neck, he gasped out for breath that wasn't there. His eyes bulged, his tongue wagged, and his legs danced crazily in midair.

The Queen's face darkened. "You dare enter my presence without permission?"

The soldier shook his head frantically. His lips formed the word *please* several times.

"And what would cause such arrogance to your Queen's rank?" She stepped closer. "*Speak!*"

He clawed at the tightening forces holding his throat, his face a bright scarlet. "Message," he croaked out with difficulty.

"What message?" she barked.

With a trembling hand, the soldier produced a crinkled letter from his pocket. The Queen snatched it. The parchment was creased from the stiffness of the soldier's grip. She read the sentence quickly.

The magic vanished and the soldier dropped to the ground. He wheezed as he took in great breaths, back pressed against the wall. But the Queen of Hearts didn't pay him attention. She smiled, rereading the sentence.

The soldier gulped. "What are you going to do to me?"

Dark eyes turned on him, but she still smiled. "I suddenly have no desire to kill you. I hope you've learned your lesson. You're free to go, before I change my mind."

He scurried out of there before she could have second thoughts.

The Queen of Hearts took the note and walked back over to her desk. With a flick of her wrist, the progress report she'd finished burst into flames and was incinerated in seconds. Gingerly, she placed the parchment on her desk. Taking up a quill, she wrote a new progress report that included the new bit of news she just received.

She wrote her signature at the bottom of the page and folded this letter into an envelope, her royal insignia on the edge to keep the letter sealed. There was no need to write an address.

Opening her drawer, she took out a small crystal letter opener. She closed her eyes, focused, and sliced through the air. A fissure ripped open the air before her just large enough for a letter to pass through. The Queen stuck her progress report in the slot before it closed.

She placed the crystal letter opener back in her drawer and locked it with a faint twitch of her finger. Helena looked once more at the parchment, reading those four words:

We have seen Alice.

*****

The idea that Jack was *intended* to enter Giant Country hung over the travelers for the rest of the day. Questions built up, thoughts were stored away for later pondering, until there was no choice but to breach the subject again. Of course, it couldn't possibly be a matter to discuss at the moment. So the subject merely loomed over them, unspoken, until night fell and they set up camp. Being the most rationally thoughtful in the party, the White Rabbit took control of interrogating the facility escapees to further conduct his theories.

Red was the first to be deliberated on.

"So, someone was *hunting* you?" White inquired ponderously after hearing the basics of her story, as well as the others'.

Red twisted the end of her braid between her fingers. "Yes, I was hunted by a wolf who was hired by somebody else. Who hired Fang, I couldn't tell you."

"You're sure it had nothing to do with your past?"

She froze, eyes flicking up to glare at the Rabbit. "What do you know about my past?" she questioned dangerously.

White winced, her sudden change of mood scaring him. He was suddenly afraid the Wolf would take over and, well, deal with him the same way most canines dealt with rabbits. "Nothing! I was just being thorough, that's all."

"No, it has nothing to do with my past," Red retorted dryly. "Leave it at that."

Dum took that moment to question, "So is Fang a wolf or a man?"

"Both," she explained, relaxing slightly. "He can change between wolf and man."

"So like you? Except, you know... *woman*."

Red hesitated. "I suppose."

"Can we please get back on topic?" The White Rabbit exclaimed exasperatedly.

"Yeah; sorry, mate," Dum apologized.

White sighed, passing a paw over his face, and turned back to Red. "Do you know *where* you went?"

She shrugged. "I don't know what the world was called."

"Can you describe it?"

"Mostly forested, lots of different kingdoms, plenty of magical creatures. There was magic everywhere, kind of like here except... more; much more. It was like it was—"

"Enchanted?" White put in.

She nodded.

"Hmm..." He paced back and forth, whiskers twitching in thought.

Red looked nervously at Jack, but he'd just realized that the plant behind him was eyeing him, literally. Curly stems branched off the other and at the end of each stem grew a glass eyeball. The doll's-eye vine twisted to stare at him with dozens of eyes. Jack shifted over, suddenly uncomfortable. Red tried unsuccessfully to hold back a smile as he scrutinized the plant, clearly uneasy.

"Do you know where she went?" Wendy asked, bringing them back on topic.

"Yes." The White Rabbit looked up from his thoughts to Red. "You traveled to the Enchanted Forest."

Kai huffed and muttered sarcastically, "Well, that makes sense."

White continued, the gears in his head turning, "I assume you were hiding in a hollow tree when you entered that world."

Red furrowed her brow, but nodded.

"Most hollow trees are the Enchanted Forest's primary route of transportation," he explained mostly to himself. Apparently that was his way of ending the conversation. He clearly had a habit of going down rabbit trails.

Without warning, he veered the focus on Kai. "So, you entered the Realm of the Snow Queen?"

Kai shifted a bit, but answered, "Yes."

"And how did you enter it?"

"When the Snow Queen captured Gerda, she opened a portal. Before it closed, I was able to get through."

White grunted, "Makes sense, seeing as the Realm is nearly impossible to get into since the Snow Queen closed most of the portals. But you didn't arrive at the same spot as the Snow Queen?"

"I did," Kai corrected, "but she was gone before I entered."

"Yes, yes, the time difference can be delayed somewhat if the portal is beginning to close. At least you were close enough to the Realm for it to push you out that way instead of the way you came," he muttered to himself. "Do you know why the Snow Queen wanted Miss Gerda?"

"No. Believe me, I've asked myself the same thing for far too long."

White started pacing again in his concentrated thoughts. His nose wrinkled, eyebrows scrunched together, and his ears were twitching now: a sure sign of his deepest thinking.

Kai rubbed the scar on his chin agitatedly. He didn't like recollecting his failure. The only thing that kept him from breaking down was his resolve to rescue Gerda somehow.

"What are you thinking, mate," Tweedle-Dum asked the White Rabbit.

"What would the Snow Queen want with an innocent young woman?" White thought aloud. "Unless she was in something far darker than we know of…"

"No!" Kai protested, standing abruptly. "No, Gerda would not get into anything like that, not willingly, not without telling me."

"Then that could mean," he concluded without even faltering, "she may not have been the intended victim. Perhaps she was simply used to lure the *actual* victim."

"What are you saying? That Gerda was the bait so that I would go after her?"

"Precisely," White stated. "It's only logical. You'd obviously be of more use to the Snow Queen than this girl you've been describing, at least from what I can figure."

Wendy beckoned Kai to sit, trying to calm him down. He was breathing heavily with agitation, but he relented in placing himself beside Wendy. Though Kai didn't think the conversation over, the White Rabbit moved on to Wendy without disruption or hesitation.

"Tell me about this Shadow."

Wendy did her best to explain the concept of the Shadow being both part of Peter Pan and part of Neverland, thus its own creature at the same time. She didn't make it sound any less confusing than when she'd explained it to Alice, but the White Rabbit didn't seem to have trouble understanding.

"So, it was the Shadow that led Pan to your room?" he inquired.

"Yes, it was hiding there for Peter to find."

"Curious," White muttered, his ears twitching frantically.

Alice caught Celeste staring into space rigidly, a usually bad sign. But she quickly blinked and returned to normal. In fact, she soon began collecting some of the doll eyes for ingredients from the doll's-eye vine that was freaking Jack out. Confused, Alice tried to focus back on the conversation.

"What is it, Cotton Tail?" Jack asked.

The White Rabbit didn't even acknowledge the insulting name calling. "Isn't it a bit peculiar that the Shadow just so happened to pick Miss Wendy's bedroom as a hiding place when there were plenty of other nooks and crannies for a shadow to hide in? Why *her* room? It could've chosen anybody's room… And why not a lamppost's shadow or behind a building? But no. It decided to hide in Miss Wendy's room."

"You can't honestly believe that Peter's Shadow intentionally chose to lead Peter to me *knowing* that he would take me to Neverland," Wendy guffawed.

"Not intentionally, no," White agreed. "A shadow wouldn't do such things without its master's consent. But somehow, I believe the Shadow was *drawn* to your window. What attracted the Shadow, I don't know. Perhaps it was a kind of spell, though a spell of that magnitude requires years of practice and considerable amount of talent to lure a specific shadow to a certain spot. Even to control someone else's shadow is next to impossible. But *something* must have caused the Shadow to enter your room."

Eyebrows knit together, Wendy couldn't respond. What exactly was he suggesting?

The others sat in interested and suspenseful silence.

Finally, it was Alice's turn in the White Rabbit's mind.

"But I've already told you how I came to Wonderland," Alice implied.

"Yes, I know that you fell down a rabbit hole and ended up here, but the question I want answered is *why* you fell down that rabbit hole? I'm pretty sure you wouldn't just hop into any rabbit hole you came across. After all, I'm aware of your acrophobia. Surely there was a reason you chose to do so?"

Confused, Alice cocked her head. "But, it was because I saw *you*."

The White Rabbit was quite taken aback. "*Me?*"

"Yes, you! I saw a white rabbit in a waist coat and I followed it because… because I had this feeling. I thought you'd take me to Lorna, or you'd lead me to a world of my own." Alice lowered her eyes as if she'd revealed a childhood secret. She recovered quickly. "And you seem to be the only white rabbit who wears a waist coat. *You* led me to the rabbit hole and I followed *you* into Wonderland."

"But, Miss Alice, I didn't lead you anywhere!"

She felt perplexed at this point. "But… I saw…"

"I don't know who or what you saw, Miss Alice, but it wasn't me."

152

She closed her eyes tight, rubbing her throbbing temples. Confusion sent waves through her that gave her headaches. Wendy placed a comforting hand on her shoulder.

When Celeste spoke, her voice sounded vague and far off. "Someone wanted all of you to travel to each world," she breathed. "Someone was looking for you, hunting you. They probably still are."

And for some reason, Alice couldn't help but think of Anne Christiansen.

Chapter Fourteen

Just Play Along

The past night's discussion still lay thick in the air the next day, especially on Alice, Wendy, Red, Jack, and Kai. Questions raced through their heads, questions that forced them to look at their experiences in a new light. Unfortunately, it was not a pleasant light to be looking at.

Was someone else manipulating their time in the different realms this whole time? Was that same someone to blame for all of their hardships and miseries, maybe even their joys? Was any of this tied to the mysterious Anne Christiansen? Arguments with opposing possibilities played out in each mind. It was maddening.

The Tulgey Wood was quiet, except for the scampering of mome raths and a following sneeze from Jack, not to mention the humming of the invisible Cheshire Cat. There was also the tinkling of bells-of-Wonderland—darling little colorful flowers that rang like bells—or the occasional blast of trumpet flowers would sound every now and then. On second thought, perhaps it wasn't so quiet after all. But no one felt the need to talk, and that in itself made the nonexistent silence weigh heavy around them.

No one particularly noticed how the woods thinned or how the sun and sky expanded in visibility overhead. None acknowledged the lacking of exotic wildlife such as doze-ferns and mome raths as they walked on. And so, because of this unawareness, it was a great shock when they broke out of the Tulgey Wood and found themselves in the middle of a colorfully paved path.

The White Rabbit stumbled back. "Great Uncle Jackrabbit!"

The Cheshire Cat appeared overhead, shrouded in his own mist. "Are we supposed to be out in the open?"

"Of course we aren't! We'd better get off the road before someone sees us."

"It's too late," Celeste murmured.

She nodded left down the winding road where ten armed soldiers rode toward them.

"Cabbages and kings!" Dum muttered, raking his fingers irritatingly through his flaming hair. "Alright, everyone, just play along."

Because no one else had any better ideas, and no one else seemed nearly as calm with the present situation, they decided to follow Dum's improvisation. Except for Chess, who disappeared immediately. Alice and Celeste, being the most wanted, hung in the back of the group, keeping their heads down. White was prompted to take off his waistcoat just in case, but he wouldn't hear of it.

The soldiers, clad in dirty white armor embellished with bloody hearts, were upon them quickly. They rode what appeared to be horses without mane or tail, but with a coat that looked as if a sheet of water was draped over them to make their somewhat reflective skin. The cards pulled their steeds to a halt.

"State your business," the head card ordered.

Dum answered boldly, casually, "Queen's work. Honestly, mate! What'd you expect?"

"Queen's work, eh? What's your assignment?"

He shrugged. "Find the Alice girl."

"And your rank?"

"Head of my team!" Dum waved his arm at the rest of the group. "We work undercover to retrieve information about the Alice girl for the Queen."

A different soldier smirked under his helm. "What's with the bunny?"

The White Rabbit looked appalled. "*Bunny*? You, sir, need to learn to keep such rash opinions to yourself! I most certainly *am not* a…"

"That's Fluffy," Dum cut in. "He relates more to the animals, able to retrieve information better from them."

White sputtered, clearly disapproving of this new fake name, but he wisely stopped complaining. Jack smirked.

The head card grunted, "And who are you?"

Dum continued to lie easily, "Thrush. That over there's Si." He gestured to Kai, who didn't entirely approve of the fake name, either. Dum turned to Jack. "And this is…"

"Harry," Jack interrupted, not wanting to be called something that could be used to make fun of him later. But he stood stiff, shocked. He hadn't expected the name of his best friend to pop out of his mouth. It made long buried feelings rise up.

"I'm Moira," Wendy said with a sweet smile.

"Ellen," Red said bluntly, also using her middle name.

"Pleasance," Alice muttered.

Celeste opened her mouth to say the name on her tongue, but she stopped before saying the first one that came to mind. Somehow, using her sister's name didn't seem like such a good idea. That left her off guard and her mind went blank.

The card nodded to her. "What's wrong with that one in the back."

Dum was quick to answer, "She's mute. But you should see her with potions. Incredible!"

"Her name?"

"Lily," he replied smoothly.

Celeste looked up in surprise. She'd always loved that name; she'd even wanted to name her future daughter that. She recalled telling such to Tweedle-Dum once long ago, but she didn't think he would've remembered. Yet, this was the name he chose as her alias.

Dum gave the soldiers a look as if daring them to keep questioning. One of the watery horses shivered, causing its coat the ripple immensely. The beasts were becoming restless, ready to move on.

The head card grunted, "Carry on."

The hairless equine carrying the Queen's cards rode off down the road. Everyone seemed to exhale at once.

"Really? *Fluffy?!*" White fumed. "That was the best you could come up with?"

"I think it suits you," Jack jeered.

White glared at him.

Jack moved on to his friend, slapping Kai's back good naturedly. "Well, hello, Si!"

Kai huffed, "Could've been worse. I could've been the one called Fluffy."

Jack laughed, glancing at the White Rabbit out of the corner of his eye. "Right you are, Si. Right you are."

Red commented on Dum's performance, "Smooth."

"I never thought I'd say this," Alice added, "but nice lying, Dum."

Dum pulled a corky smile. "Thank you. I will take that as a compliment."

Maddening laughter sounded as the Cheshire Cat reappeared floating in the air. He rolled over and looked down at the others with crazy multicolored eyes. Inhaling dramatically, he exclaimed, "Oh! That was fun! Let's do it again!"

"NO!"

"Alright then," Chess said in his usual singsong voice. "If that's the way you feel about it."

An obscure silence rang in their ears. Alice cracked a smile. Then, as if they all had an overdose of giggle-berries, everyone started laughing hysterically! Nothing could stop it. It wasn't your typical laughing fit. It was the type of laughter you get after experiencing something so odd with your friends all that was left to do was laugh.

Each laughed differently, which made it all even funnier. The White Rabbit laughed heartily and slapped his thighs. Chess laughed maddeningly, spinning through the air. Kai laughed as if he hadn't laughed in a long time, but it was smiles and bellyaches all the same. Jack rolled on the ground. Dum snorted. Red clutched her stomach. Wendy's was high and bouncy like hiccups, a highly contagious laugh. Celeste's was like chiming bells, her face in her hands to hide the amused tears rolling down her cheeks. Alice's was real, breathtaking laughter.

Heaving and trying to catch his breath, White gasped out, "Alright, we'd better get going before those soldiers find out that there is no Thrush, head of an unusual team of spies."

They heaved their last breaths of laughter and recovered from the insanity quickly. Jack shuffled to his feet and helped Wendy up as she wiped her watering eyes.

"Alright," the Rabbit announced. "Follow me."

He turned left and started to hop down the rainbow stone road. The others began to follow. But Alice stopped after taking one step. The smile vanished from her face. A tremor went up her spine.

This isn't… right, she thought. She wasn't supposed to go that way, she could feel it. Her heart tugged at her.

Alice. It was a voice; she wasn't so sure it was her own.

She turned and looked down the road leading right. *What's down there?* Something was down there. She needed to know what it was. There was a feeling, a calling. She couldn't ignore it. It was like when she couldn't ignore the rabbit in a waistcoat seven years ago, or the way the looking glass seemed to call to her last year.

"Are you coming, Alice?" Wendy asked.

Alice tore her eyes away from the path to look back at her friends. "I think we should go this way," she called.

The White Rabbit shook his head, slightly astounded. "But, the Queen of Hearts' palace is this way."

"I know," she admitted. "But, I have this feeling…"

Celeste stepped toward her. "What kind of feeling, Alice?"

"It's just… It's like I *need* to go this way. Like it's calling me."

Celeste didn't reprimand her. Instead, she closed her eyes and stood very still, very calm. It wasn't like when she usually received insights. What she saw behind those lids, no one knew except her.

She slowly nodded. "Alright."

Opening her eyes, she followed Alice. Wendy was right at her heals, and soon everyone was following her away from their initial destination.

"But, Miss Alice, are you sure?" the White Rabbit asked as they walked down the path together.

"No, I'm not sure," she admitted. "This is probably one of the most unsure things I've ever done. But I'm doing it anyway."

*****

The Duchess was convinced that someone had stolen her tarts.

"It was him!" she accused, pointing a fat finger in the Knave's face.

The Knave of Hearts rolled his scarlet eyes, scratching his ginger whiskers. "Again? Really?"

"Yes, *really!*" she scowled, her yellow eyes flashing. "This time, you're busted! Caught! Bamboozled!"

"Running out of synonyms?" he groaned. "Anyway, why would I want your filthy tarts? Your sneezing chef puts far too much pepper in them!"

"Pepper is beside the point!"

"What about your footman? Aren't they always trying to have a go for your treats?"

The frog footman gulped, eyes bulged.

"I know it was you!" the Duchess insisted. "Your breath smells like putrid slithy toves and *my* TARTS!"

"ENOUGH!"

Both of them nearly jumped out of their skins, especially the frog footman who seemed jostled awake at last. The Queen of Hearts had her fingertips pressed against her brow, trying to still a growing headache.

"Your… Your Highness," the Duchess stuttered.

"I said *enough!*"

The Duchess clamped her mouth shut, which better improved her appearance. It didn't do much, but still.

"I am so sick," the Queen huffed, "of your constant bickering over the same. Bloody. NONSENSE!"

"But he… he stole my tarts," the Duchess said weakly.

"I don't care if he stole your bloody tarts! He's from Underland; of course he's stolen them at one point or another!"

The Knave spoke up, "If I may—"

"You may not." She looked up at last, resting her elbow on the arm of her throne. Her dark eyes were bloodshot and thick circles hung under her eyes. Her complexion was even paling. The Queen of Hearts had never looked more fearsome. "If I hear one more word about any of this blasted tart business, I will personally have both of your heads. Don't think either one of you is so important to avoid my punishments. You only serve a purpose here because I have allowed you to; don't think for a second it's because I *value* you. Duchesses and knaves can be replaced. It doesn't matter what you may have done for me in the past, if you annoy me again, you will be on the wrong side of my wrath."

The Duchess trembled so much her amethyst locks fell out of their bounds. The Knave of Hearts shifted uncomfortably, tugging his ruffled sleeves over his hands. As for the frog footman, he was long gone.

The Queen sighed and closed her eyes, sitting back in her throne as if to melt into it. Calmer now, she stated, "Now, if you don't mind, there is one small thing you can do for me."

"Anything, highness!" the Duchess exclaimed enthusiastically.

"Name it and it's yours," cried the Knave, desperate for orders to keep him occupied.

Her eyes snapped open. Leaning forward, she roared, "BRING ME ALICE!"

Chapter Fifteen

Eat Me

"What were those creatures the soldiers were riding?" Kai asked.

"Aquistrals," Dum answered simply.

Jack snorted, "Funny, I'd think they were water horses."

The White Rabbit was quick to insert an explanation, "An aquistral is a truly marvelous creature. It's the result of when a quistral touches water. The quistral then gains a watery coat, becoming an aquistral. An iquistral is the result of when a quistral touches fire. They then gain a fiery coat, though."

"So, if an iquistral looks fiery and an aquistral looks watery, what does a regular quistral look like?" Kai questioned.

"Regular quistrals have thin, mousy colored skin," White went on. "They're quite skeletal in appearance. Regular quistrals are a lot less common than aquistrals or iquistrals. Most quistrals are the young ones and babies."

Alice wondered why Kai was so curious about the horse-like creatures. He didn't normally seem to strike up conversation or ask questions unless there was a specific purpose in it. Maybe he was just trying to get a better feel of Wonderland's oddities. She shook her head, thinking to herself that he'd probably never get used to such strangeness. Wonderland was simply too unpredictable.

Thankfully, there were no more soldiers to encounter on the road. But the lack of excitement seemed to set everyone on edge. Surely something was going to happen, especially when they least suspected it, and even more so now that they were out in the open. Nothing happened, though. It only pushed the question: was something wrong? And if so, when would they find out?

Jack sighed, beginning to miss the absurd humming that had kept him blissfully agitated and distracted. The Cheshire Cat had long disappeared. The sun beat down on him with such dreary heat, it made him both drowsy and sweaty. His only source of entertainment was watching the White Rabbit, thinking of glorious tricks to pull on him. Of course, he wasn't actually going to do any of them; not unless the Rabbit called for it anyway. That overdressed bunny had a habit of getting on Jack's nerves.

The sun glinted off something gold hanging out of the White Rabbit's knapsack. Jack scowled slightly. He hated gold. Still, he watched the object as it slowly emerged from the knapsack each time the Rabbit hopped. It looked like a box of some sort. Of course, Jack didn't mention anything about the runaway box.

Jack stared at it as it fell with the smallest *clink* onto the rainbow stone road. No one noticed, just him. Without a word, he picked up the small box to inspect it. Despite his loathing for gold, he still had a strange attraction to it.

What was inside? Why would the White Rabbit have some tiny little chest? Looking closer, Jack noted the words *Open Me* engraved on the lid.

I've never taken orders from a box before, Jack thought to himself. *But if it really wants me to…*

He obeyed the box.

His stomach growled.

Inside lay small heavily iced cakes with *Eat Me* written on each in delicate icing. They smelled heavenly, like sugar and tulips. His stomach rumbled again, his mouth watering. They looked so good… But Jack hesitated. He examined the box closer to see if there was anything wrong with the cakes. All he found were the words: *Open Me*.

He was still apprehensive, but the thought that the Rabbit had been hiding cakes this whole time made him want to eat them even more. Jack shrugged. It couldn't hurt to take one cake from the White Rabbit's secret stash.

A cake made it to his mouth quickly. His tongue exploded with the scrumptious sweetness of the pastry. Perhaps just one more…?

He'd taken up another cake when Alice noticed.

"Don't—"

She was too late. Jack swallowed it before she got the words out.

"—eat that," she groaned.

"What?" Jack shrugged, shutting the glittery box. "Fluffy here's the one who's been hiding food."

"I'll tell you *what!*" Alice barked, marching over and snatching the box away. "Because you ate *this*, you'll start shrinking any minute!"

Jack furrowed his brow. "Shrinking?"

Right as he said it, he shrank so fast he hardly had time to scream until he was only fifteen centimeters tall. Miniature Jack shouted in outrage. The White Rabbit laughed tremendously.

"I knew you would go for it!" he exclaimed. "I've been preparing those for days. I knew you'd take the bait!"

"You get your fuzzy little rear over here so I can give you a piece of my mind!" Jack yelled, stomping his feet.

"Oh, I'm so scared!" White mocked. "The tiny little boy is going to hurt me. Whatever shall I do?"

Jack punched his tiny fists in the air in frustration. "Just wait until I'm normal sized! I'll tear that fuzzy tail out and tie your ears together! I'll kick you so hard you'll end up in another realm and won't be able to sit for weeks! I'll rip every tooth out of that mocking smile!"

The White Rabbit clucked his tongue. "Naughty, naughty, naughty! You shouldn't be so frumious while you're whiffling about down there in your tiny little tantrum."

"I don't know what you're saying, but I'm going to make you regret those words!"

Alice rolled her eyes, looking disapprovingly at the White Rabbit. "Really? Was this necessary?"

"My apologies, Miss Alice." He stifled back a snicker. "I just couldn't resist!"

"I'll use you as a punching bag!" Jack ranted, "After I'm done with you, that little rabbit's foot of yours isn't going to be so lucky! I'll cut your ears off and hit your head with your own foot!"

Red stooped down and picked him up. "Jack, that's enough."

Dropping his fists, he clamped his mouth shut.

"Good. If you behave yourself, I'll let you ride on my shoulder until we find a way to get you back to normal," she bribed.

Jack nodded solemnly, still upset he'd gone from being over being so small. Red carefully placed him on her shoulder. He had to push aside her black hair like a curtain in order to see clearer. Holding tight to her jacket to, Jack dangled his legs over her shoulder. To keep her hair out of Jack's way, Red quickly pulled it back into one long plait.

"Don't worry, mate," Dum assured Jack. "I'm positive that the *very* talented White Queen will be able to whip up an antidote faster than a rocking-horsefly!"

Celeste blushed and lowered her eyes.

"Can you?" Jack asked hopefully.

"Well," Celeste began, trying to find a way to explain. "Yes, I'm able to prepare an antidote. But this particular antidote will need… *time* to prepare."

"How much time?" Red questioned.

Instantly, Jack's hands flew to his ears, her voice nearly exploding his eardrums.

"Sorry," she apologized softly.

He waved it off like it was no big deal; his ears still rang.

"So, how much time does it need?" she asked again, gentler.

Celeste looked sheepishly at Jack. "At least twenty-four hours."

"Twenty-four hours!" he cried.

"At least."

Jack groaned in annoyance, vengeful thoughts flying through his head once again. This new fact made the White Rabbit howl even louder. Boy, did he hate that rabbit!

"I should probably get started now," Celeste went on. "It will only take me a few minutes."

Alice agreed with a nod.

The White Queen set to work, removing her bag and kneeling by the side of the road. Fumbling through the satchel, she drew out a pinch of orange power and threw it on the rainbow stone in front of her. It burst into flame, small but hot. Withdrawing her arm from the bag again, Celeste produced a small cauldron and placed it on the fire.

Wendy's eyes widened. "How can you fit a *cauldron* in your bag?"

"It's a special bag," Celeste explained without looking up from her preparations, "with the ability to hold whatever I want it to."

Impressed, Wendy commented, "Well, that's a useful thing to have."

Celeste smiled, reaching back in the bag to dig around for something. Hissing in pain, her hand jerked back with bleeding fingers.

"*Borogove!*" she cursed, sucking her wounded fingertips. "That *manxome* snapdragon!"

Dum looked dumbfounded, a smile tugging at his face. "Did you just say what I think you just said?"

Her face turned scarlet, but she smiled sheepishly.

"What?" Jack asked. "What's wrong with what she said?"

"Nothing is wrong with what I said," Celeste said softly. "It's just how I said it."

"Said what?" Red questioned.

"Borogove," Alice responded.

"Which means?"

Dum grinned mischievously. "It means that our dear White Queen just *cursed*."

168

Celeste turned even redder. She turned back to her work quickly, trying not to look into Dum's eyes. He stared at her as if he couldn't believe it, but he was obviously impressed. It wasn't everyday his sweet Queen used a curse word.

For those who weren't familiar with Wonderland lingo, they had to take a moment to process the reactions. So *borogove* was a curse word, and, as Alice later told them, also a badger-like creature with a long corkscrew snout and orange spots down its back.

Celeste busied herself by pulling ingredients out of her bag's endless array of contents. She recited the amount and type as she plopped them in the cauldron, "Three quistral tears, eight crushed bread-and-butterfly wings, four drops of blood from the bleeding-heart flower, one tablespoon of tumtum tree sap." Finally, poring a jar of liquid in, she murmured, "And a half-gallon of tea."

"What kind of tea?" Dum inquired.

"Chamomile."

Jack rolled his eyes and muttered, "Of course it's chamomile. What else would it be?"

Only Red heard him. She stifled back a laugh, but her shoulders betrayed her, so Jack knew.

The boiling liquid was a shiny brown color when Celeste was through. As she poured it into a container, she said something about how it had to sit for at least twenty-four hours until the liquid became transparent. Quickly gathering her things and returning them into her bottomless bag, she threw a pinch of blue powder on the fire, causing it to go out in a flash; not even leaving a charred mark on the rainbow stone.

Once Celeste was ready and the White Rabbit had regained his composure, though his shoulders still shook with silent laughter, the group continued their journey down the road.

*****

"*What?!*" the Queen of Hearts bellowed.

Knees shaking, the man was more frightened than the servant girl quivering in the corner. He dared not look his Queen in the eye. He was at least smart enough to know better than to respond. He'd heard of what happened to those who upset the Queen of Hearts. Unfortunately, he had a feeling that his name would be added to the long list of her victims.

"What do you mean you made a *mistake*?" she shouted.

He opened his mouth but nothing except for frightened noises came out.

"Quit your burbling, fool! Speak!"

He spoke without exactly meaning to, something seeming to loosen his tongue. He didn't know it was the Queen's doing. "We m-made a m-mistake. The g-girl wasn't Alice as w-we thought."

"*How* could you make such a stupid misjudgment?!" she screamed.

The servant girl cringed and squeaked in fright at the tone in her mistress' voice. She tried to focus on her mending, but she kept poking her fingers for lack of concentration.

The man shook tremendously in fear. "She... She fit the d-description. H-had blonde hair and b-blue eyes."

"*Do you realize what will happen to me if this is found out?!*" the Queen raged.

The man fell back on the floor in fear. The servant girl was practically in tears, flinching terribly as she stitched her seams with trembling hands.

The Queen of Hearts thundered, "*IF THIS IS FOUND OUT, I'M GOING TO BE…*"

Red sparks and black lightning bolts flew across her fingers as she raised her hand high overhead. Before she could fry the card, the doors flew open and in came the Knave of Hearts. She looked at him with a wrath so dark; but fear hid behind such darkness. It was a fear like none she'd ever felt, but no one saw it. They saw only the anger.

"Your Majesty!" the Knave exclaimed, masking his own nervousness with anticipation.

"What is it?" she snapped coldly.

"Sorry to interrupt." He glanced at the soldier trembling on the floor with no pity. "But, we've found her."

"Who?" The Queen lowered her hand doubtfully, the sparks minimizing.

"Alice," he responded. "And Celeste…"

"*Do not speak her name!*"

"My apologies, Your Majesty." The Knave inclined his head. "But, they have been spotted together."

Rage still pulsed in her veins, but it was calm and cool. She wasn't losing her head. "How? When?"

"A group of cards just arrived," he explained. "They say they were attacked by Alice and company, as well as others traveling with them. They say they're the only survivors. If you ask me, they were let off easy. Nearly the whole team returned."

171

Relief flooded through her. Everything was back on track.

The soldier, having listened the whole time, hoped this might mean mercy. As soon as he began to relax, a shower of red and black lightning bolts came down on him. His body jolted and seized. The servant girl squealed.

Allowing the electricity to shut off, the Queen looked at the charred body with a satisfied gleam in her eye. "Lana," she ordered the servant girl, "remove this one from my presence."

Trembling and ashen, Lana took the body by the arms and dragged him away. Helena turned to stare out her window. The relief had washed over her face and she didn't wish the Knave to see her thus.

"What do you wish me to do with the survivors?" the Knave of Hearts asked casually.

"We only need one mouth to talk," she responded without turning. "Thus, we need only one to explain what happened. Show the rest what happens to those who fail me."

"As you wish, Your Majesty." He bowed deeply, probably glad to be back in the Queen's favor after the tart incident, before he let the doors shut behind him.

Helena looked over Wonderland. She looked over the Tulgey Wood and the Mimsy Meadows. She looked beyond that, all out over her kingdom. It was *her* kingdom, no one else's. It was *her* Wonderland. She'd taken it; she wasn't about to give it up. Soon, she wouldn't need to worry about any revolt or sister or Alice to take it away from her.

Those words Tweedle-Dee told her had haunted her but a little while. Helena knew they were meaningless words told by a scared story-teller. He had no idea what she had up her sleeve. He had no idea what was coming. Once it came, she would no longer need to inflict fear to control her people. Fear was but her temporary companion until the ultimate, all powering companion came.

As for Remus' song… No, she needn't dwell on the song of a madman.

She gingerly touched the window glass. "I am coming for you; both of you. You'll be gone before long, Alice. And soon, my dear sister, you'll be mine."

*****

The road turned the wrong way. So Alice didn't follow it anymore. She led the others onward through the shrubbery and overgrowth, finding themselves back in the Tulgey Wood. Many felt far more comfortable now that they were no longer in the open, even if they were following an invisible path and led by a girl with voices in her head. Or was it a feeling in her heart? Did it even matter?

The Cheshire Cat had yet to make a reappearance since the encounter with the soldiers on the road. At least the silence was no longer complete now that they were in the woods. Mome raths warbled, mumblebees murmured, and trumpet flowers blasted. Still, where did Chess go?

Tweedle-Dum ventured ahead of Alice, always one to dive headlong into adventure. He enjoyed the thrill that surged through him when he looked around corners or through bushes, expecting the unexpected. Most of the time, however, the unexpected ended up being nothing but a stray mome rath or a colony of active fire ants. These, of course, he stamped out immediately before they caused a wildfire. The thrill subsided for lack of unpredictable surprise. Still, hope proceeded with every turn.

As he peaked through an overgrown hedge, surprise waited there for him. Dum jumped back from the shock of it. He took another look to make sure he wasn't seeing things. He jumped back again with realization that his eyes weren't playing tricks on him. Frantically, he beckoned the others to hurry up, which they did when they saw the wild look in his eyes.

"What is it?" Alice questioned.

Dum motioned for them to follow suit. "You need to see this!"

"What's going on?" Jack asked Red from her shoulder.

"Dum saw something," she responded softly.

"Well, what did he see?"

"We're about to find out."

Dum pushed aside the leafy hedge as they all crowded around to see what lay behind. A shack stood in the middle of the clearing, protected by a horror of a creature. An enormous bird lay there asleep, white, red and black sprayed across its feathers, some blue hints in the wings, tail, and crown. Long, thin legs stuck out of its body and elongated, razor sharp talons protruded from each toe. It had a long pointed bill slightly open to reveal numerous sharp teeth and an indigo tongue.

"What *is* that thing?" Wendy asked.

Celeste answered, "*That* would be a jubjub bird."

Dum nodded. "Right you are, Celeste. Right you are."

Chapter Sixteen

Beware the Jubjub Bird

"You're sure we need to go in there?" Kai asked, not unsurely, just to be certain.

Alice nodded. "Positive. I just don't know why." Well, that wasn't exactly true. She had some idea, but it was more of a feeling, not a resolute thought. Besides, the voice in her head was silent of a sudden. Not much help to prove her reasoning.

"Well, what do we do?" Jack shouted so everyone could hear him. "There's a giant tub-tub bird in the way!"

"Jubjub," Dum corrected.

"That's what I said."

Red stifled back a laugh.

"Look, whatever we're going to do, we'd better do it quickly," Wendy spoke up, trying to play rational. Maybe all those years with the Lost Boys had given her some motherly instincts which were beginning to show now that she wasn't cooped up in the Facility anymore. "That jubjub bird isn't going to sleep forever! I personally want to figure out our plans and priorities before that thing wakes up."

"Wendy's right," Celeste agreed immediately. "Whatever we're going to do, we need to do it soon."

"Well, we can't just run in there," the White Rabbit pointed out. "It could be a trap!"

"Of course it's a trap!" Dum exclaimed, throwing his arms in the air. "But it's not like we haven't walked into traps before, mate."

"Well, yes. I'm just trying to be realistic."

"We don't have a choice," Alice put. "I mean, we haven't got anything else to go on. If we don't go in, where else are we going to go? The Red Queen's palace? I don't think so; not yet at least. We don't have enough people here to storm the castle. I doubt we'll even get Remus out in the state he's in. Our only option is to see what lies in that shack. There has to be a reason why that jubjub bird is guarding it. It's not like you see one every day!"

White sighed. "I see your point, Miss Alice. But we can't just go in there based on a gut feeling. There has to be some logic to this situation."

"We're in Wonderland, mate," Dum pointed out. "Since when has anything been logical?"

"True, but I still don't want to have the lot of us go gyre and gimble into the jaws of that jubjub bird!" the White Rabbit rambled.

"That's odd."

Alice turned back to Red, who'd spoken so softly she hardly heard her at all. Eyebrows furrowed, Red's nose was scrunched up like something was off. On her shoulder, Jack looked concerned too, based on her reaction.

"What is it, Red?" Alice questioned.

"I smell something."

Having grabbed his attention, Dum was quick to point out, "Well, a giant man-eating bird is right over there."

"No, not the bird." She turned her head around, muttering, "A cat."

"A cat?" Jack questioned sarcastically.

"Or a mouse…"

Jack held on tight as Red started towards a nearby bush. Crouching down, she moved aside the leaves to peak through. Jack clutched onto the folds of fabric as she did so. A sword shot out of the bush just a hair's width away from Red's face.

"Make one false move and you'll feel the wrath of me!" proclaimed the sword's wielder.

The sword was the size of a needle.

Its wielder was a mouse.

She was large for a mouse, with tan fur and pink ears. Black boots covered her back feet, and she wore a purple leather jacket. The mouse had her sword pointed directly at Red's nose.

"Put that thing away before you take someone's eye out," Jack snorted, still clinging onto Red's shoulder. He tried to ignore the fact that the mouse was bigger than him.

"Don't you use that tone with me!" the mouse threatened, switching her sword between Jack and Red.

He raised his hands up in defense, probably supposing he should've kept his mouth shut since he was unarmed. Red just stared at the sharp point of the tiny blade, her eyes crossed.

The mouse eyed Jack with a frown. "What happened to you, Tiny? Eat a shrinking pastry?"

"As a matter of fact," the White Rabbit hopped up casually, "he did."

She only glanced at him a moment with a raised eyebrow. "These two with you, White?"

"Well, actually," Alice stepped up, "they're with me."

She felt like blushing when the mouse looked up at her in awe and admiration, dropping her sword at her side. "Alice?"

"Yes, that'd be me," Alice responded with a sigh. "Old Mock Turtle, why must all of our meetings with old friends be so violent?"

"Oh." The mouse looked at her sword sheepishly before sheathing it. "Sorry about that."

Red stood, thankful the sword was out of her face. Jack was relieved, too, though he'd probably never admit it.

The mouse looked over her shoulder and shouted, "Dinah! It's perfectly mimsy. Come on out; it's Alice!"

An orange cat with the look of a kitten emerged from the underbrush. Dinah wasn't oversized; she couldn't talk either. However, she was nothing close to an average cat. Alice couldn't help but feel a flood of emotions on seeing her old pet. Dinah must have thought the same thing as she patted up to Alice and rubbed against her legs.

Alice stooped to stroke the cat, whispering, "Pleasure to see you, too, old friend."

Dinah purred in response.

Celeste approached. "Is that the Dormouse?"

Dinah meowed as if offended of being forgotten. Celeste knelt to scratch the cat behind the ears and all was forgiven.

The Dormouse waved, kicking her feet. "Hey, Celeste!"

"Greetings, dear Dormouse."

Jack mumbled, "You have the most creative names here in Wonderland."

The Dormouse eyed him. "Got a problem, Tiny?"

"I've got a name, you know," he retorted.

"Don't care." She twitched her whiskers. "*I'm* calling you Tiny."

Before Jack could say something he'd most likely regret, Alice interfered by asking, "What're you doing here, Doe?"

Big, brown eyes turned up to her. "We were trying to break into the Queen's heart vault."

Her stomach flopped. "Heart vault?"

"You know, where the Queen keeps all her stolen hearts," Doe explained, kicking gravel absentmindedly. "Dinah and I've been trying to get in for days! But *Mister Evil Bird* is kind of hard to get past."

"You sure like giving names, don't you?" Jack inquired.

Red shushed him. "Must you always pick a fight with *everyone* we meet?"

Mind racing, Alice continued, "You mean that shack the jubjub bird is guarding is the Queen's heart vault?"

"Uh, *yeah*! That's what I just said, wasn't it?" Doe twirled her tail around. "We were going to get the Hatter's heart back before we storm the castle."

"*Storm the castle?!*" Celeste exclaimed in extreme concern. "Just you two?"

Spitting in hilarity, Doe was thrown into hysterics. Dinah made a chuffing in the back of her throat like she was giggling. Unable to talk through her uncontrollable squeaking, Doe tried unsuccessfully to calm down.

Talking between gasps of breathless laughter, Doe managed, "Oh, no! I was talking about the army!"

"*Army?!*" everyone stated unanimously.

"Well, yeah. Everyone against the Queen of Hearts formed an army. We've been getting ready to storm the castle for quite some time. Just wait 'til you all come back to camp. They're sure to be mimsy! They'll make Alice leader! The White Queen will return to the throne again!" Doe squealed, "Oh, frabjous day!"

"Whoa, whoa, whoa! Slow down," Alice insisted, her head spinning. "Before any storming the castle or taking over the kingdom happens; we've got to get Remus' heart back."

Doe waved it off casually. "Ah, that should be *easy*! With all of us against one *slightly* oversized bird, we'll be in there in no time!"

"I'm with Doe!" Dum pronounced, raising his hand in agreement.

"It's not as easy as you think," the White Rabbit spoke up.

"*White!*" Doe whined, pouting. "It's not like we're going up against a jabberwock!"

"No, it's not," White agreed. "But a jubjub bird is still very dangerous, even for a group of armed people. We'll need to be careful."

"Question," Wendy spoke up. "What's a jabberwock?"

"It's like, um, what you'd call a dragon," White explained.

"I have a question," Dum inquired. "What's a dragon?"

"It's like a jabberwock."

"Oh…" Dum nodded, pointing at the Rabbit cleverly. "That makes sense."

Celeste sighed, "Well, if we're going to take on a jubjub bird, we'll need a plan."

"And weapons," Kai added, rubbing the scar on his jaw.

The White Queen smiled, patting her satchel. "Do you honestly think I'd go on an adventure like this and *not* bring weapons?"

*****

Helena looked grimly over her map of Wonderland. Tracing the shoreline of the Sea of Tears, her touch never disturbed the waves' movements on the enchanted map. Her stroke veered over to the domain of Underland. Though no longer belonging to the cruel reign of the King of Diamonds' enemies, the land still kept its title. The territory now belonged to Wonderland. But the Underlanders, the ones loyal to their murdered king and prince, still lived devoted to the Queen of Hearts for slaying the King of Diamonds. They served her, forming most of her army. The Knave of Hearts himself was once of Underland, having committing himself to her as his people did. The Underlanders were a bloodthirsty lot, eager for battle and owning steadfast loyalty. Their loyalty belonged wholly to the Queen, for she had avenged them.

The tiniest of tears fell from her eyelashes. It splashed on the Ruins of Underland, washing over the stone remnants of what used to be a great castle. It trickled down over the Mimsy Meadows and slid across the Tulgey Woods. The tear grazed past the Sugar Desert and only briefly touched the Diamond Mountains. Finally, it fell over the side of the map and burst into a trickle of vapor as soon as it hit the floor.

Helena willed herself not to let another tear fall. Tears showed sadness. Tears showed fear. Tears showed weakness. She couldn't afford to show any of those. Not even today. Especially not today.

"Your Majesty," a sweet little voice spoke up.

Helena turned her gaze to the young servant girl standing at the base of the platform.

The girl cocked her head. "Why do you hate your sister so?"

She had a round face and curious hazel eyes. Her hair was fair and freckles splayed over her rosy cheeks. She looked up at the Queen with no fear or hatred. There was none of that in those youthful eyes, only curiosity.

"I am so sorry, Your Highness." Lana scooped the girl up in her arms, her eyes full of fear. "My daughter doesn't understand such matters of authority. She's but young and stupid. She didn't mean what she said. Please, don't be angry."

Helena looked from Lana's face to the young girl's. She still didn't look afraid, even in her mother's quivering arms. All she wished was an answer. It was an innocent request from an innocent girl. For a moment, Helena saw herself in those big eyes.

"No need to be frightened, Lana," Helena insisted softly. "I'll do your daughter no harm."

Lana was hesitant. Helena didn't blame her. Lana set her young daughter down, though Helena knew that she still didn't fully trust her Queen.

"Why do you hate your sister, Your Majesty?" the girl asked again.

Memories flashed through her mind, but she shoved it aside. Helena stepped down from her pedestal and sat in her throne. The girl looked at her, waiting for her response. Lana stood back, frantic eyes glancing at her daughter, then the Queen of Hearts, then her daughter again.

"What is your name, child?" Helena said at last.

"Mary Anne."

The edge of her mouth twitched in a tempting smile. "Well, Mary Anne; that is not a question to be asked lightly."

"But I asked my momma and she says she doesn't know," Mary Anne spoke innocently. "And I don't see how anyone could hate their sister like you do. I would love my sister if I had one."

How could she respond to such a question? Rage didn't come as expected, only calm sorrow. Helena swallowed the lump in her throat. "My sister did something... horrible to me."

"Can't you just forgive her?"

She laughed humorlessly, sadly. "It's not something so easy to forgive. What she did, it was unforgivable."

"What did she do?"

Helena bit her lip, forcing a smile. "She took away someone I loved. That is all you need know."

"Can't you just find someone else to love?"

Her smile wavered but remained; one couldn't help it when talking to children such as Mary Anne. "That is not so simple either, Mary Anne."

Mary Anne looked down at her feet for a moment before looking back up at the Queen to say in all truthfulness, "I hope someday you'll forgive her and not hate her anymore."

At this, Helena was speechless. It had been so long since anyone talked to her like that. No one wished her anything as innocent as the hope of this child. For once since her childhood, Helena's heart melted. To think a child could do something no one else was able to do was astonishing.

183

As Mary Anne skipped away with Lana holding her hand, Helena wished she could stay. And that, too, was astonishing.

If things were different, would she have been happy? Would she have found love again, had a daughter like Mary Anne after… if only…

Helena hugged her stomach and wept.

*****

Alice didn't particularly like jubjub birds. One tried to eat her once, and when something has tried to eat you, it's kind of hard to forgive and forget. It had nearly succeeded, too, if it wasn't for Remus. He chopped off its head before it could swallow her. She still remembered how the vicious bird got her legs trapped in its beak, the relief when Remus killed it and its bite slackened. One of her legs had broken and both were soaked in blood. At least Celeste was there to fix her up.

Alice shoved the memory out of her mind. *Focus, Alice. Stay focused.*

Assuming the others were in place—*depending* on them to be in place—Alice tightened her grip on her sword and slowly emerged from her hiding place. Silently, she crept up to the heart vault and the sleeping jubjub bird.

Holding the hilt with both hands, she slowly raised the sword. She hoped everyone was ready. If she failed, she'd need all hands on deck.

Since when do I use pirate sayings? she thought amusingly.

Loosening and tightening her grip to unstiffen her cramping hands, she prepared to strike. The jubjub bird was just a few paces away. Just a little closer…

A crack echoed in the silence.

Alice felt her heart drop. She glanced down at her feet where the small bones of the jubjub bird's last meal lay. How could she be so careless?

The jubjub bird stirred, ruffling its feathers and stretching its legs. Its eyes snapped opened, revealing lime green irises as it awakened. Alice froze, busted. The jubjub bird leapt to its feet in a flash.

Frozen in fear, Alice found herself face to beak with the monstrous creature. Feathers fanning around its head, the jubjub bird opened its maw and screeched so loud her teeth rattled. Alice made a face at the foul stench of its breath. She stared down its throat, its sharp teeth, its long blue tongue…

Finally coming to her senses, Alice swung her sword. Blood sprayed. Its indigo tongue landed with a thud on the ground, sliced clean off.

The jubjub bird faltered, gargling in pain, giving Alice the perfect opportunity. She turned and ran. It screamed again, sounding hollow for lack of tongue. Alice glanced back.

Where did it go?

She spun in circles, confused and frightened.

"Alice, look out!" Wendy screamed.

She just had time to look up and see the jubjub bird's underside before razor talons closed in her shoulders. Alice screamed. Her sword dropped. The ground fell beneath her feet. She tried to struggle, but it only tore up her shoulders.

Her head swam as she looked down, the ground getting farther away. She wanted to squeeze her eyes shut, but she was petrified. *The ground can't possibly be that far away*, she tried to rationalize. But her fear of heights continued to obscure her vision.

She saw them run to help, watched as Wendy took aim and threw her knife. The jubjub bird lurched, gargling a scream. Pain shot through her shoulders as talons ripped her muscles. Alice's cry mixed with the bird's mangled shriek.

Through tears, she saw Red leap and transform in midair. Claws extended and teeth bared, she soared overhead and landed on the jubjub bird's back. Alice heard, as if from far away, screeching and snarls. She felt the talons slacken and she fell. Snapping out of her stupor, she screamed as her limbs flailed in the air and she landed heavily on the ground.

Blood flowed freely from her shoulders. To Alice, everything was a hazy blur. She heard her name many times. Her chest felt heavy, the breath knocked out of her. She tried not to think of how high she'd been. It made her head hurt. Then she heard the scream, the yell, and the yelp all in unison.

Rising, she took in the scene quickly. Red—still a wolf—was up with teeth bared viciously, but her hind leg seemed to hesitate off the ground. Kai was splashed with blood, sword raised to strike. Dum lay unconscious on the ground, hair matted with sticky crimson, and Wendy was by his side trying to wake him. Dinah, Doe, and little Jack were on top of the jubjub bird; clawing, plucking, and stabbing with mini swords. The White Rabbit was pinned under the jubjub bird's claws, struggling to be free, and Celeste threw balls of white hot light at the giant bird to distract it.

Alice felt her body rise of its own accord. Finding her fallen sword, she took it up in her hands. It felt heavy all of a sudden, but Alice still managed to lift it.

The giant bird snapped at Red and Kai, but didn't strike yet for sword and claws. The two could only keep the bird back while the White Queen burnt its wings. Alice ran. She raised her sword above her head, gave a great yell as pain exploded through her wounds, and plunged the blade straight through the jubjub bird's heart. It gave a crazed scream before it fell over dead.

Everything grew hazy. White wiggled out from under the bird's giant body. Red transformed back to herself and ran with Kai towards Alice. They didn't reach her in time to catch her. Staring down at the bird's corpse, Alice collapsed.

Chapter Seventeen

Of Hearts and Deception

Alice snapped awake, fully healed and mildly exhausted. She checked her shoulders immediately, just to be sure, but her torn wounds were gone. Celeste must've taken care of her while she was out.

Celeste! She pushed aside all remaining exhaustion. *What happened to the others?*

Looking around, she took in her surroundings. Relief flooded through her. Tweedle-Dum was awake, Kai clean of blood, Red's leg appeared well, and the others seemed just as they always did. Well, all except Jack, who was still only fifteen centimeters tall.

The jubjub bird's corpse lay where Alice had slain it, sword still sticking out of its chest. Dark blood continued to flow and form a puddle on the ground where it lay. Not much time had passed since it was killed.

"Alice!"

She turned just as Celeste pulled her into an embrace.

"Thanks for fixing me up," Alice murmured.

"Of course! What was I going to do, let you bleed to death?"

Alice shook her head and stood, drawing the attention of her friends.

The Dormouse scurried up, squeaking excitedly. "You're awake! Can we go now?"

"Go where?"

"Inside the Red Queen's heart vault!"

Her breath caught in her throat. Alice had nearly forgotten about the heart vault. Well, she supposed she'd been a little busy trying to keep everyone alive. The urge to reclaim Remus' heart came crashing back with a flood of emotion.

"I suppose we should after all the trouble it's caused us," she admitted, managing a tight smile.

The shack looked much worse from up close, old and weather beaten, barely managing to hold itself up. Celeste was quick to open the door, anxious. Hinges creaked eerily. Alice's heart plummeted.

There was nothing bust dust and cobwebs.

Chest compressing, Alice watched as Celeste walked in cautiously with hands running across the rickety walls. Dust clung to the White Queen's fingers as she felt in the corners, her fists thumping against the splintered wood. Finally, after walking around the perimeter, she turned back to her companions. Her gleaming eyes and solemn face said it all. She couldn't find any enchantments.

"We went through all that, for *this*?" Kai's voice held a tinge of disappointment.

Dum grumbled, "Cabbages and kings."

"No, no, no, no, no!" Doe squealed, pulling her ears in frustration. "This can't be! After all our research, Dinah; after all our hard work… I was so sure. This *has* to be it!"

"But why was a jubjub bird guarding this shack?" the White Rabbit questioned to himself, trying to make sense of this. "You don't just happen upon a jubjub bird like that. There must be an explanation!"

Alice and Celeste stood in mirrored silence. Looking at her friend, Alice saw the same shock, the same disappointment, the same loss. Perhaps they could've consoled each other, but it seemed impossible in the state they were in.

Dinah mewed.

Red rubbed her temples irritatingly, her face screwed up in silent discomfort.

"Are you alright?" Jack asked in concern while trying not to fall.

"Throbbing," she said between her teeth.

"Your head?"

"It's causing my head to hurt."

Dinah mewed again, scratching the floor.

"Agh!" she groaned loud enough to grab the others' attention. "What's thumping? It hurts by head."

Something pawed at Alice's leg. She looked down to find an anxious Dinah, meowing. Stooping down, Alice questioned, "What is it?"

The cat promptly strutted over to the room's center and began scratching the floor with her white paws. Alice's brow furrowed. *What's wrong with what I'm seeing?* The shack, the jubjub bird, Red's headache, Dinah's unspoken message, the floor… The floor?

Dinah's scratching fell rhythmically, hollowly on her ears. *Wait a moment…*

Alice turned on her heal and stepped outside. She stamped the ground as hard as she could, trying to engrave the feel and sound in her mind. She then entered the shack, squeezing past her friends. There was a week spot in the floor where Dinah stood digging. Alice went to it, making sure the cat moved aside, then stomped.

That's not right.

"Alice…?" Kai started, but broke off when Alice's foot smashed through the floor.

She looked up at them with a smile, her foot still in the hole in the ground. "I think I know where the vault is!"

"Under us," Celeste whispered, her silver blue eyes scanning the floor with the same mad hope.

"Under us?" Doe squeaked.

Pulling her foot out, Alice saw the empty space below the floorboards, the flickering light just beyond. She stepped back, stooping down to feel for some hidden notch that would indicate… She felt the click and tugged up the trapdoor to reveal a dark staircase leading down to the Queen of Hearts' vault.

"Yep." Alice beamed. "We go down."

Shelves lined the walls, filled to the brim with square boxes. Open cabinets filed down the center for more storage for more containers full of more hearts. Each box had a label. Most simply said: *Unknown*.

Three pedestals stood in the very front of the room. Black and scarlet metal vines intertwined to form the daises. An intricate box sat on each pedestal, far more elegant than the others in the room. The ones on the left and center lay closed; the one to the right, however, was open and empty.

Alice walked up to the pedestals, examining the center box made of pure diamond. It radiated with a rainbow aura. Even in the dim light it cast rays in every direction. She read the label embedded in its side.

"*My dearest father, the King of Diamonds*," Alice read aloud.

Curious, she slowly opened the lid. Her heart leapt. She gasped, jumping back in horror.

"My father's," Celeste said calmly behind her.

Mutely, Alice could do nothing but stand and watch while she waited for her heart to slow. Celeste walked up to see for herself, eyes shining with tears.

"Helena ripped it out of him. She went even as far as to stab it, willing to kill…" but she couldn't finish. Tears dripped off her chin. Celeste closed the lid on the pierced, silent heart. Swallowing hard, she continued, "My father was a good man, the best king Wonderland has ever known. Yet she puts his heart on display like a trophy proudly announcing how she killed her own father to avenge the Underlanders."

Alice clenched her jaw in silent loathing. How could anyone do such a thing to their own father? No, she didn't have the best when it came to fathers, but that certainly didn't mean she would ever consider going to such lengths. It was sickening what vengeance could do to a person.

She watched Kai approach the empty box of white stone. Light blue cracks webbed through it, hauntingly beautiful.

"*My big sister, Celeste,*" Kai read the label aloud, "*the White Queen.*"

"No doubt Helena's been saving that ever since she took over. Maybe even longer," Celeste spoke with a humorless huff. "She wishes to tear out my heart and put it on display, just like our father's."

"This is it, Miss Alice!" the White Rabbit interrupted excitedly. "This is what we've been looking for."

He stood by the third pedestal, unable to reach the box. The Dormouse quickly scampered up it and perched at the top. The small chest was wooden, detailed with a golden whimsical design. Something was beating inside.

Doe read the label, "*My little brother, Remus, the Mad Hatter.*"

"*Brother?!*" Wendy questioned in surprise. Alice turned to look at her just as she added, "Remus is her *brother?*"

"*Our* brother, actually," Celeste corrected.

"The oldest is Celeste, then the Queen of Hearts, and last is Remus," Alice explained as if from a distance, lost in memories. "He didn't want the crown, didn't want to be treated as royalty. Remus wanted to be loved for *who* he is, not *what* he is."

"And that's exactly what he got," the White Rabbit murmured in his own solemnity.

Her eyes moved between Wendy, Red, Jack, and Kai. "I'm sorry, I thought I told you."

Wendy shook her head assuredly. "It's fine."

"Just a bit surprising," Jack added, shouting for his small voice.

Alice nodded, not entirely aware, too lost in her own head. Slowly approaching the box containing Remus' heart, she heard it thumping inside that wooden cage. As if her body moved of its own accord, she opened the lid slowly. Her breath caught in her throat. Remus' heart pulsed against the wooded walls that held it. Still fleshy and healthy, it differed greatly from the King of Diamond's grey and rotting heart.

"Well, go on," Doe encouraged. "Take it, Alice."

Alice was solemn, frozen in place. She didn't cry, for her eyes were dry from past weeping. She didn't break down; everyone could admire her for that kind of strength. But inside where they couldn't see, her heart was aching. Inside, she was screaming somewhere in the back of her mind. Her stomach knotted, her throat tightened, but still no tears arose.

She lifted a heavy hand, her fingers close enough to sense the heat from the pulsing heart.

*****

He'd been screaming for the past ten minutes.

She heard it as soon as she flew into the dungeons where the prisoners were thrown into a maddening uproar. But they couldn't drown out the screaming.

"ALICE!"

The bloodcurdling shout caused Helena's insides to chill.

"What caused this?" she questioned the card who could barely keep up with her pace.

"Nothing we know of, Your Highness," he said helplessly. "He was fine, and then suddenly—"

"ALICE!"

"—that happened."

Helena burst into the room, biting back a gasp at the sight. Remus was in a frenzy, zipping about his cage like a mad man—or rather a *madder* man. He rattled the bars, he kicked up the food tray; he sent the remnants of his hat flying across the room. All the while, he shouted at nothing, "ALICE!"

She could hardly move, so filled with shocked horror. *What's happened to him?*

194

"DON'T DO IT, ALICE!" Remus screamed to the sky, throttling the iron bars that kept him from the outside. "ALICE! DON'T DO IT!"

"What's he doing?" the Duchess' obnoxious voice sounded as she joined the Queen. "It's not like she can hear him!"

"ALICE, DON'T TOUCH IT!"

It hit her like a blow to the stomach. Helena's heart dropped. Fury replaced sorrow in an instant. *Of course*, she thought furiously. *I should've known he had some inkling of magic.*

"Your Highness?" the Duchess questioned.

Her face turned scarlet. "FIND HER!" she ordered with a volume that rivaled the Hatter's. Turning in a flurry, she stormed out of the room and barked, "Ready my carriage! She's found the heart."

*****

"Alice."

It was a whisper so soft, a voice in the very back of her mind, yet it didn't sound like it came from her head.

"Don't do it, Alice. Alice, don't." The voice was urgent, like a cry from far away.

Alice withdrew her hand as if she'd been shocked, clutching her fist to her chest. Her ears strained to hear that voice again.

"What are you doing, Miss Alice?" the White Rabbit questioned.

"We've found the heart," Tweedle-Dum added, "now let's go."

Alice didn't respond. She just backed away from the pedestal, the box, the heart. Her head shook slowly like she was waking from a dream.

"It isn't right," Alice whispered to herself. "Something's wrong."

"Alice."

Alice turned toward the voice. It was so familiar.

"Alice, look…" Dum began, starting toward Alice, but Celeste stopped him.

"Wait," she said softly, her tone firm.

He did, certain that he could never intentionally or unintentionally disobey such a queen as she.

"Alice," it said again.

She followed it down the endless shelves, never altering her stride, never changing her steps.

"What are you doing, Alice?" Doe exclaimed after her.

She didn't seem to hear. *Where is it?* She thought, *Where is it?*

"Alice," the voice kept calling her name.

The voice seemed to be getting louder. She walked faster, faster, faster...

"Alice."

She stopped abruptly. Eyes venturing over a stack of crowded boxes on a low shelf, she ignored the calls of reason behind her, listening only for that haunting voice.

"Alice."

She crouched down, shoving aside beating and silent boxes, each labeled *Unknown*.

"Alice."

There was a hollow *thunk* and then the voice stopped. Alice ruffled through the very back of the pile. Her hand felt the wall behind the shelving, but there was something else. Another box hid in a dark shadow behind the shelves.

She pulled it out.

Old and soiled, the label had long since smudged away. It seemed so fragile, so insignificant. But there was something about it…

Alice put it in her lap, her own heart beating wildly. Placing her hands on the dusty top, she opened it.

A white flash blinded her vision.

In a blink, she found herself in the Queen of Hearts' dungeons. The large cell was dingy and dark, and many cards guarded the barred walls. She heard exhausted breathing behind her and knew instantly that she wasn't alone.

A man knelt on the floor, shoulders slumped, head hanging. Dark brown hair was tousled, matted, and slightly overgrown. The clothes he wore seemed to swallow him in a worn, wrinkled drapery of cloth. Holes gaped open on the soles of his boots. His hands lay limply in his lap: strong hands with dirt and blood under his fingernails. Blue eyes stared down at something on the floor.

Before him lay a smashed hat, collecting dust. Shards of broken glass clung to the fabric beside a crushed watch. The feather wilted in a rusty red. Cobwebs were strung between the needles in the pin cousin, and the sash was fraying.

Alice had tears in her eyes as she reached for him. "Remus."

His blue eyes snapped up to meet hers. She had the slight sense of nostalgia, remembering the Hatter when his eyes used to shine with joy—eyes the same as Celeste's. He had Helena's dark brown hair; the perfect mix of both sisters. His wide smile, however, had been his own.

But Remus wasn't smiling now. Wistfully, hoarsely, he whispered, "Alice."

The vision vanished in an instant.

Alice sat staring down at Remus' real heart. A pang stung her chest.

That's the thing about visions. They're so cruel. They show pictures and snips of a message. You only have a split second to make sense of it all, never shown the whole thing, before your yanked so harshly back to reality at the exact moment you wish to see more. It's pure cruelty.

Alice couldn't possibly imagine what it was like for the White Queen, who received more visions than anyone she knew.

Swallowing the lump in her throat, she closed the lid and called back, "I found it." She scrambled to her feet and returned to the others, the dirty box in her hands.

"Found what?" Red asked.

"Remus' heart; I found it. Now, let's get out of here."

"Hang on, Miss Alice," the White Rabbit interrupted, placing a paw on Alice's elbow. "How do you know?"

Alice bit her lip. "Because he told me so."

Chapter Eighteen

Oh Frabjous Day

"Just wait 'til we get back to camp!" the Dormouse went on excitedly. "Everyone will all be mimsy! Old Mock Turtle, they're going to be absolutely outgrabe! What luck we have, huh, Dinah? I mean, we're returning with the White Queen, a Tweedle, the White Rabbit, Alice, and four new recruits! Besides, Operation Hatter's Heart is accomplished and now we can finally move to the next step."

"And what would that be, Mousy?" Jack asked from his perch.

"Storm the castle, of course! Take back the kingdom! Put the White Queen on the throne where she belongs! Kill the Red Queen!" Doe exclaimed.

Celeste's face paled. No one except Tweedle-Dum and Alice noticed, he being the only one to take action. Dum snatched Celeste's hand in his, gave her a reassuring, sympathetic smile, and then simply walked casually with her, hand in hand. Neither let go.

"*Red* Queen?" Kai inquired suspiciously. "I thought it was the Queen of Hearts."

"The Red Queen is Helena's original title, the one she was born with," Celeste explained. "She changed it to the Queen of Hearts when she took over, a symbol of her reign. She's better known by it."

They walked ever deeper into the Tulgey Wood where even the slithy toves—green deer-like creatures with branched antlers and slimy fur—revealed themselves. The Dormouse rode on Dinah's back, leading the way to their destination. They were the only ones who knew where they were going, after all. Dinah would've been glad to give Jack a ride as well, but he was quite content on Red's shoulder.

Alice held the chest that contained Remus' heart close, feeling the rhythmic thumping against her torso. They'd put the heart in a different box since the old one was so shabby it didn't look like it'd last much longer. Alice left that box where she found it. Celeste had offered to put it in her bag, but Alice preferred to carry it herself. It felt right keeping Remus' heart close to hers.

"What's that?" Red's voice pulled her out of her thoughts.

Alice turned toward the sight, a shiver running down her spine. They were ruins, of sorts, long abandoned, claimed by the Wood. The gnarled table, the mismatched chairs, the evidence of teapots and knickknacks under a blanket of vines and dirt.

"A Mad Tea Party," Alice answered solemnly. *A dead Mad Tea Party*, she thought.

"They used to be so alive, randomly placed throughout the Tulgey Wood," Tweedle-Dum lamented in remembrance. He sighed, as if seeing the sight as it used to be. "Yes, there used to be lovely parties to join, superb places to tell stories, drink tea…"

"And plan a revolt in plain sight," the White Rabbit added. "Which is why the Red Queen had them all… cleaned out."

Dum dusted off a teapot, pouring out its muddy contents. He frowned, sighing again. "Come on. No point in sticking around." But he kept the pot.

Alice's gaze lingered on the sight, memories flicking through her mind, memories of a Hatter and a Hare and a Dormouse singing songs and celebrating unbirthdays during a lively Mad Tea Party. She hugged the box tighter. *How much has changed since those days?* A pit formed in her stomach. *Too much.*

"How long until we get there, Miss Dormouse," the White Rabbit asked.

"Please don't start calling me *Miss* again! I've told you to just call me Doe a thousand times. You sound like my father calling me *Miss Dormouse*." Doe shoved the White Rabbit playfully. "Anyway, it shouldn't take much longer. We should be there in a few minutes or so."

Alice caught Wendy doing a quick head count, making sure everyone was still there. It must've been one of the many motherly habits she picked up in Neverland. She remembered when Wendy had told her of her time in Neverland, sullenly supposing that perhaps when the Lost Boys returned from an exploit, not all of them would come back. Alice didn't even want to think of what that would be like.

"You know," Wendy pondered aloud, "it's been a while since the Cheshire Cat left. Do you suppose he'll come back?"

"He comes and goes as he pleases," Tweedle-Dum responded. "But he always turns up eventually."

Probably thinking this a reasonable enough answer, Wendy didn't pursue the subject of the Cheshire Cat, but the Dormouse wasn't so easily contented.

"Wait, Chess was with you?" she squeaked.

"Yes, quite a lot actually," Red responded.

"I was wondering where he'd gone!"

"What do you mean?" Alice asked.

"Surely he would've told you! Then again, he does fail to mention most important subjects," she went on. "Anyway, he's part of the rebellion, been a member for quite some time."

"Now, why would he fail to mention that?" Jack asked suspiciously. "Even the Cheshire Cat can't forget to mention something *that* big!"

"Then you clearly don't know the Cheshire Cat very much," White snorted.

Jack scowled at him.

"Oh! I smell a rivalry!" Doe cried teasingly. "How long has this been going on? When did this loathing start?"

"Since the first time they laid eyes on each other," Kai mumbled with a smile.

Doe bounced up and down with excited interest. "I can't believe I hadn't smelled it sooner! Were you the one who gave Tiny the shrinking pastry, White?"

His nose twitched in a proud grin. "Yes, indeed."

The Dormouse cackled crazily, clutching her stomach and legs kicking in the air. She laughed so hard that she fell off Dinah's back.

"Yeah, yeah, yeah," Jack scowled. "Laugh all you want, Mousy."

"Hey, it's not my fault you're so tiny, Tiny," Doe chuckled as she climbed back on the cat.

"Please don't encourage them," Red sighed.

Instantly, Dinah stopped and meowed loudly.

"I suppose you're right, Dinah," Doe consented. "We're probably already there. Now, what was that password?"

"Password?" Wendy asked.

"Yeah, the one to get past the concealment enchantments," she explained, brushing her whiskers.

Dinah meowed again.

"I know, I know! I'm thinking." Doe tugged at her big ears with concentration. "What is that password?"

The others suggested things like *White Queen*, *Jabberwock*, and *Bandersnatch*. Jack even proclaimed an, "Off with his head!"

"No, no, no, no, that's not it!" Doe squealed, pulling her ears over her eyes, tail twitching.

Celeste suggested *the King of Diamonds*, while Alice offered *the Mad Hatter*. But those weren't it either.

"The Walrus and the Carpenter hunting for dancing oysters in the Sea of Tears!" Dum proclaimed thoughtfully.

All heads turned to him, still comprehending this mad comment.

Dum shrugged. "What?"

"Not the Walrus and the Carpenter… That's it!" Doe exclaimed before whispering, "The Lion and the Unicorn."

The air before them shimmered. With the Dormouse and Dinah leading the way, they all stepped through the invisible barrier.

"Welcome to the rebellion!" Doe announced.

Alice's heart skipped a beat. The camp stretched on as far as she could see and beyond. All sorts of animals wandered about; most all of them could talk. Quistrals of each kind were tied to posts or being tended to. Borogoves scampered about for potential scraps. There were many men, fewer women, and even less children. But no matter the strangeness, it was no less of an army.

And in the middle of it all floated the smiling Cheshire Cat.

"There you are, mate," Dum stated, though Chess didn't seem to notice the gesture or their presence.

"EVERYONE!" Doe proclaimed to the rebellion, but no one heard her. "HELLO! I'VE COME BACK WITH… ugh. Dinah, would you please?"

Dinah bobbed her head, turning her nose to the sky and crying the most attention grabbing yowl ever heard. It could've easily rivaled Red's wolf howl. It worked like a charm. The Dormouse had everyone's undivided attention.

"Thank you," Doe sighed. "Now, I have some very exciting news for all of you. Firstly, we have some new recruits! This is Red, Wendy, Kai, and Tiny—I mean, Jack."

There were a few murmured whispers rippling over the crowd at this. Most humans were in the Red Queen's dungeons, after all.

Doe waved everyone to silence, clearly taking advantage of the attention. "Settle down. Right. Now, secondly, we've brought back with us our very own Tweedle-Dum and the White Rabbit."

This brought on more of an applause in excitement. Dum waved to some old friends of his. Or maybe he'd never seen them before in his life. Tweedle-Dum was like that.

"And thirdly, I'd like to announce that as of today, we have achieved in bringing back the Mad Hatter's heart! Soon, we'll put the *White Queen* back on the throne with our very own *Alice* to lead us into battle!"

With this, there was a racket of joyous triumph. The crowd surged forward around the group. Alice laughed as Kai helped Dum hoist Celeste up on their shoulders above the crowd where she'd be seen by all. Whoops of "Callooh, Callay!" and "Oh, frabjous day!" sounded through the air.

Alice found herself being lifted up beside Celeste above the crowd, biting back a cry of protest. She held the chest tightly against her. Despite her fear of heights, she couldn't help but smile. Happiness is contagious, and she was getting an overdose of it.

Celebration rang through the air and the festivities brought merriment to all. Soon, as the sky dimmed, everyone was laughing and dancing and having a grand time.

Red was pulled into the dancefloor by a kindly young gentleman while Wendy was asked to dance by a seven-year-old boy. Of course she accepted, the boy reminding her of the Lost Boys. All the while Jack watched from a leafy log, disgruntled and undersized.

"Whoooo arrrre yooooou?" a deep, drawling voice questioned behind him.

He turned sharply around. Sitting atop a small mushroom behind him was a blue caterpillar, old with a wizened face and half-moon spectacles perched on his large nose. He was smoking a hookah pipe, blowing colorful smoke rings out of his mouth. Jack blinked, having thought he was alone.

"I repeat," the Blue Caterpillar said, rolling his *R*s. "Whoooo arrrre yooooou?"

"I'm, uh, Jack," he fumbled before adding, "Jack Caldwell."

"Well, *Jack Caldwell*," he drawled as gold coins made of smoke fell from his mouth. "Do you care to explain why you are sitting here so distraught?"

"Well, I can't exactly join the party."

"Why?" A large yellow *Y* floated through the air.

"It's kind of hard to dance and join the fun when you're only fifteen centimeters tall," Jack tried to explain.

"I am *exactically* fifteen centimeters tall and I find no problem."

"But you're used to it, aren't you?"

"Aren't I?" He took a long drawl from the hookah pipe before continuing, "I most *certaintally* am not unused to it."

"So, you are used to it?"

"Definitally," the Blue Caterpillar answered, "but the question remains." He blew out a blue question mark.

"What question?" Jack was becoming very confused by this caterpillar's way of speaking.

"The one that remains," he said, rolling his *R*s again. "You have not answered *correctically* why you are so distraught."

Jack furrowed his eyebrows. He'd never been so confused, even in Wonderland. He handled the Cheshire Cat's madness, which until then had been the craziest creature he'd ever met. Now, this Blue Caterpillar seemed to bring on a whole new perspective of madness.

The Blue Caterpillar took another drawl from his pipe. "Explain to me exactically why you continue to stare at that *girl* with such melancholy."

"What girl?" Jack asked sheepishly. He knew exactly what girl.

"The one you were watching, of course." He puffed out a series of smoke rings that formed the silhouette of a dancing girl.

Jack watched as the smoke girl twirled round and round, her feet moving to the rhythm. The smoke evaporated quickly, but it stayed long enough for Jack to get the message.

The Blue Caterpillar stared at Jack with electric blue eyes. "I know where your heart lies, Jack Caldwell. I can see it in your *eyes*."

Jack swallowed nervously, instinctively looking away from the Caterpillar. This madness strangely hinted wisdom beyond his grasp. It scared him. The Blue Caterpillar scared him.

The Caterpillar grunted, "Hmm… Well, I suppose I should ask how exactically you are planning to fix your problem."

"Well, Celeste is working on an antidote, but it won't be ready until tomorrow."

The Blue Caterpillar puffed his hookah pipe rapidly, saying between puffs, "I presumably presume that the White Queen is preparing the growing drink to make you taller." A blue bottle with a tag reading *Drink Me* formed in the air before he continued puffing his pipe.

Jack kicked at a small pebble at his feet. "I suppose."

The Blue Caterpillar grunted again. Taking another drawl from his pipe, his eyes crossed slightly. The wrinkles on his face were deep.

"Fine." He looked up with dreary electric blue eyes, rolling the pipe through his fingers. "I have made the decision to help you." A pink *U* skipped from his mouth.

Jack waited for him to continue while the Blue Caterpillar kept puffing his hookah pipe. A cloud of colorful smoke hung in the air above their heads.

After a while, he mustered up the courage to ask, "Well?"

The Blue Caterpillar looked at him curiously. "Hmm? Oh, apologies." He held out his pipe. "Did you want a puff?"

"Uh, no, I'm good."

He shrugged, continuing to smoke hookah.

Jack stood in silence before trying again, "So, how are you going to help me?"

The Caterpillar looked up at him again. "Oh, yes. I do suppose I said I would provide my assistance. Very well."

The Blue Caterpillar looked down at his six feet, bent down, and grabbed a piece of the mushroom he was standing on with one of his six hands. He stared critically at the purple chunk before offering it to Jack.

"There."

Jack took the mushroom piece, confused. Before he could ask anything, the Caterpillar was talking again.

"Put that in the growing drink and it will speed up the process," the Blue Caterpillar said absentmindedly. "I have provided my assistance."

"Uh, thanks," Jack said, unsure of what exactly to say.

"Do not mention it!" He waved him off. "Now go, Jack Caldwell."

Jack hesitated a little before turning to go. When he looked back from a little way off, he saw the Blue Caterpillar still sitting on his purple mushroom, smoking from his hookah pipe and reciting, "How doth the little crocodile…"

Jack smiled to himself before going on his way again.

"Celeste!" Jack shouted. "Hey, Celeste!"

Celeste turned away from talking with some old friends to see Jack scrambling her way. He was still small, so it took him a while to reach her. She greeted him with a smile.

"Hey, Tiny!" Doe spoke up. "What's up?"

Catching his breath as discreetly as possible, Jack gasped out, "Celeste, could you get that growing potion thing out?"

"I've already told you, Jack. It won't be ready until tomorrow."

"I know, but just... just trust me."

Celeste felt sympathetic and brought forth the potion from her bag. It was a milky color, definitely not ready yet.

"Would you open it?" Jack asked, fumbling in his pockets for the mushroom chunk.

She did, placing it so its opening was directly in front of Jack. Once he had the mushroom in hand—secretly praying that it'd work and the Blue Caterpillar wasn't just messing with him—he dropped it. Almost immediately the liquid became transparent.

Celeste gaped at it, astonished. "But... how?"

"Here, you can use my mug," Doe offered.

"Thanks." Jack scooped up the potion into the perfect sized mug.

"Now, make sure to only take six sips," Celeste cautioned. "We don't need a giant Jack."

Jack nodded gravely, having dealt with enough giants. Gulping down six sips, an airy taste filled his mouth.

209

A tingling sensation ran through his body and before he knew it, he was back to his old self. He felt his face, the top of his head, as if he could feel the difference. He might've been a bit taller than he originally was, though.

"Wow," Doe gasped, looking up at him. "I guess the name doesn't fit anymore, but you'll always be Tiny to me."

Jack smiled, handing her back the small mug. After thanking the White Queen about a dozen times, he snuck out to the dancefloor.

The sky was getting darker, but still not late enough for anyone to get to bed. Jack, Red, Wendy, Alice, and Kai took turns dancing together, linking arms, clapping, and spinning round and round. Some animals led by an exuberant dodo bird were playing instruments to a merry, frivolous tune. The dancefloor was an uproar of excitement.

Dum began leading a group in a giddy, jolly song.

Hoisting his silver teapot in the air, Dum proclaimed, *"Twas brillig, and the slithy toves did gyre and gimble in the wabe!"*

"All mimsy were the borogoves!" Doe exclaimed.

"And the mome raths outgrabe," Chess sang merrily.

"Beware the jabberwock, my son!" Dum said mysteriously, bouncing from place to place. *"The jaws that bite, the claws that catch!"*

The young children squealed as Dum snatched his hands at them like claws trying to grab them. They gazed on him in great earnest, marveling at this story in a song. All the children in Wonderland loved the Brothers Tweedle for their fantastic stories.

Doe threw her fist in the air. "*Beware the jubjub bird!*"

"*And shun the frumious bandersnatch,*" the White Rabbit shouted, chuckling.

Dum stomped up on a long table, taking a quick swig of tea from his teapot before raising it in the air. "*He took his vorpal sword in hand, long time the manxome foe he sought!*"

"*So rested he by the tumtum tree, and stood awhile in thought,*" the crowd cried.

Dum crouched down and spread his arms out mystifyingly, causing the children's eyes to widen, as he recited, "*And as in uffish thought he stood, the jabberwock with eyes of flame came whiffling through the Tulgey Wood, and burbled as it came!*"

"*One, two! One, two! And through and through!*" the crowd chanted.

"*The vorpal blade went snicker-snack!*" Doe squealed, leaping with excitement.

Dum waved his arms dramatically. "*He left it dead, and with its head he went galumphing back!*"

The children squealed with delight.

Celeste walked up to the table, looking up at Dum affectionately. "*And hast thou slain the jabberwock?*"

Smiling, Dum took her hand and pulled her up beside him. "*Come to my arms, my beamish boy* – Or lass, I should say," he added with a grin.

"*Oh, frabjous day! Callooh! Callay!*" everyone praised.

"*He chortled in his joy,*" Celeste recited.

"*Twas brillig and the slithy toves,*" Doe chanted.

"*Did gyre and gimble in the wabe*," Chess caroled.

"*All mimsy were the borogoves*," Celeste sang, looking at Dum.

"*And the mome raths outgrabe!*" Dum proclaimed, kicking his leg in the air and ending the song with a bang.

Cheers erupted through the night sky.

Dum looked back at Celeste and kissed her full on the mouth. She kissed him back, holding him close. Dum dropped his teapot and responded enthusiastically, nearly hoisting her off her feet. This action, of course, brought on whistles and cheers from the crowd and squeals and giggles from the children even after the two broke away with bright smiles.

"Well, it's about time," the Cheshire Cat said cheerily, grinning wide and acting like this kind of thing happened every day.

It was getting late and the really old and some of the very young had gone to bed. Most of the children had received permission from parents to stay up for the stories. Many gathered about the campfire to listen to the most talented storytellers and the best stories, riddles, and poems.

Of course, Dum was pressed to tell most of the stories, and no one was disappointed. But every good storyteller loves to listen to stories as much as they love to tell them. Tweedle-Dum was no different.

"Why doesn't someone else have a turn?" he offered, looking over his friends. "What about you, Wendy? You look like the makings of a storyteller to me."

Wendy blushed. "I'm afraid I haven't told an actual story since I left Neverland."

Red elbowed her. "Come on, Wendy. I know that's not true! What about that one you told me back at the Facility when the boys were sick and it was just you and me? You know, the one about Hook."

"That's more of a riddle or poem than a story," she insisted.

The boy sitting in her lap looked up at her with interest. "Will you tell it to us?"

"Yeah, won't you tell us?" Dum encouraged, downing the last of the tea in his teapot.

"I'm sure it'll be brilliant," Celeste added, smiling warmly.

The Cheshire Cat appeared behind Jack. "Is Willa telling a story?"

Jack jumped in surprise, falling off the log. A burst of laughter rang out from the children and others tried their best to stifle their giggles. Jack's face was scarlet as he shuffled back up next to Red.

Grinning broadly now, Wendy relented, "Well, I suppose if you insist."

"Oh, yes please!" the little boy said excitedly, bouncing up and down on her lap.

"Alright, this is a poetic description of Peter Pan's sworn enemy, Captain James Hook." Clearing her throat, Wendy began her riddle-like poem:

"My song may seem jolly, but my words are not so;
My smile brings fear, and my name ever more.
I'm the hero, I'm the villain, I fight and I steal;
Distrust me, but trust that my anger is real;
Though you may not think I'm such a villainous crook;
You'll soon fear the name of Captain James Hook."

Stunned silence followed Wendy's haunting words. In but a few lines, Wendy was able to send fear into the bones of her listeners. Who would've thought such an innocent girl in appearance would have this rare ability to take a few words and make them have the same impact as if actually meeting this Captain Hook. It was a rare gift.

Alice wondered what would happen if Wendy told them what she considered an *actual* story.

The boy on Wendy's lap began to clap. Only slightly awkward at first, but then the others around the campfire began to applaud too. Wendy blushed as the children around her joined in.

The little boy whispered in her ear, "I hope I never meet Captain Hook. He sounds scary."

"I hope you never meet him either," Wendy whispered back.

"That was brilliant!" Dum praised enthusiastically. "I knew I saw a storyteller in you."

Some of the adults came over to gather the children for bed. Though there were plenty of protests and complaints, soon just the eleven travelers remained. The fire crackled and sputtered in the darkness. No one spoke for quite some time. Only a few others were awake, but they were off to the side, drinking tea and mumbling to themselves.

Celeste was the first to break the silence. "I wish... I could see Helena, talk to her."

"Why?" Jack asked. "Why would you want to talk to her?

"Don't you hate her for the evil she's done?" Kai added, "For the people she's hurt?"

Celeste looked between the two solemnly. "No. I could never hate my sister, no matter what she's done."

"But, she betrayed you," Jack insisted. Kai looked like he thought the same thing.

She kept her sad eyes on them. "Someday, you'll know how it feels to have the one you love most turn out to be someone you hardly know anymore. You'll know how hard it is to hate her, and you'll understand how hard it is to lose hope that she can change. You'll know how hard it is to believe the one you love has turned cruel and hard hearted. To accept this will be a difficult thing for you to do and to act on it will be the most difficult. Someday, you'll know how I feel."

Jack shifted uncomfortably. Kai lowered his eyes. They caught each other's eye, though. The message came across plainly. *Who could betray them?*

"What happened between you and the Queen of Hearts, anyway?" Red spoke up.

Celeste folded her hands in her lap. "I betrayed her."

"No, you did no such thing," Dum protested. "You did what was right."

Celeste looked at him pleadingly. "Did I? Did I do what's right? And if it was right, was it worth losing my sister for?"

At this, Dum had no answer. No one had an answer. None of them knew what to say. None of them felt they could relate to this kind of pain.

Celeste sighed. "It was my fault. Of course, we'd grown apart after our mother died. But that was my fault, too. I should've realized how lonely Helena was. I should've made more time for her. But I was too young and stupid to

215

recognize this and so I spent most of my time with Remus, helping my father raise him. I should've stayed closer with Helena."

Alice grabbed her hand. "You don't have to tell us if it's too painful or you don't want to."

"No, I have to," she insisted. "You all deserve to know what happened. After all, now you're all involved."

Celeste brought her hands to her mouth, uttering the few words of a spell she learned long ago. Blowing softly into her cupped hands, a mist came out of her mouth. Once a small cloud had formed in her hands, she released it so it hovered over the campfire. The flames grew fainter, as if knowing what was happening above.

Pictures formed in the cloud, showing them a scene of the castle. They saw a younger Celeste, though not much younger, and a young girl with long brown hair and mysterious dark eyes. Helena. They both appeared to be in their late teens. They were in the midst of an argument.

"I told you, he's not like that!" Helena exclaimed.

"Yes, he is, Helena," Celeste tried to reason. "They're all like that. He's a spy, just like any other from Underland."

"Nix is not a spy!"

"Think about it, Helena," she said as calmly as possible. "Has he tried to get information from you? Has he tried even the slightest to get to our father?"

Helena was silent.

"I've seen how he tries to manipulate you, sister. He's trying to get close to you to learn your secrets. He wants to use you to betray our father."

"No! Nix isn't like that! He told me he doesn't want to be that kind of person anymore. He said that he got out of that life for a reason."

"It's harder to leave that kind of life than you think," Celeste said. "To be the Prince of Underland, to be the son of our enemy; it's too unrealistic to be true. He couldn't have just walked out of that. It's just not possible."

"What happened to Anything is possible? What happened to We must give everyone a second chance?" Helena shot. "I know he's telling the truth. I know he's not a spy. Sissy, I love him."

"And maybe he's trying to use that to his advantage," she tried. "Maybe he's using you to take over Wonderland."

"What do you know?" she spat. "You know nothing of love! The only love you have is for Father, or Remus, or the people! You know nothing of true love! You don't care about me and my happiness!"

"Now, you know that's not true, sister. I do love and care for you." Celeste reached for her sister's trembling hands.

Helena pulled away. "No, you don't. Not anymore. Nix was right."

"What? What lies did he tell you?"

"He told me no lies!" The young Red Queen backed away.

"But don't you see, sister? He's trying to tear us apart. He teaches you dark magic and puts these rebellious thoughts in your head," Celeste persisted.

"He teaches me magic because I asked him to," she snapped. "And he does nothing but point out what I couldn't see."

"We have to turn him in."

"No!" Helena looked on her sister with hatred. "I will not turn him in. If you truly loved me, you will tell of this to no one."

"Helena…" Celeste looked pleadingly at her. But Helena turned and ran off, her eyes full of angry tears.

The picture in the cloud changed, showing Celeste in the gardens reading a potions book. This scene occurred maybe a month after the last. Helena stormed up into the gardens, quickly approaching Celeste. Tears streaked her cheeks, still flowing, and her face was puffy and red from distress and anger.

"HOW COULD YOU?!" she screamed at her sister.

Celeste dropped the book, standing to meet her.

"How could you?!" Helena screamed again. "You vile, insolent, evil…"

"What is it, sister?" Celeste asked, her voice quavering slightly.

"Like you don't know!" She scowled. "Our cruel father has just sent word of the news."

"What news?" The White Queen was confused.

"What news*!" Helena clenched her fists, laughing in cruel anger. "Why, the news of the Underland Prince's execution, of course."*

"What?"

"Yes, Sissy, our dear *father has sent my beloved's head rolling across the chopping block," she sneered. "Apparently one of the King of Diamonds' accomplices told him of her suspicions that Nix was an Underland spy; how she suspected that Nix was planning to kill our wicked king. That's right, Sissy. She!"*

218

"But, you don't understand. I had to tell Father. I saw Nix preparing a potion to kill him," Celeste pleaded. "I promise; I wouldn't have told if it hadn't been exceedingly necessary! I wouldn't betray your trust otherwise."

"And how would you know what a deadly potion looked like?" she questioned.

Helena eyed the book on the bench. The title was more than visible, revealing its subject. Her face filled with amazement and anger. Celeste blushed.

Looking back at her sister, the Red Queen blustered, "You? The anti-magic, perfectly pure queen is learning potions?"

Celeste's blush deepened.

"And you still betrayed me." She blinked. "How dare you."

"I honestly didn't know Father was going to execute him," Celeste pleaded.

"What did you think would happen?" Loathing bubbled up in her again. "Did you think he would give Nix a warning, a pat on the back, and let him go? Did you think he would knight him? Give him an award?"

"No, I didn't..."

"NIX IS DEAD!" she screamed. "It might as well have been your hand that killed him!"

Red and black sparks flew from her fingers. Celeste noticed, fearing what was coming. Helena, however, didn't seem to pay mind to the electricity flying from her fingertips.

"Sister..."

"Don't you dare call me that! You have lost the right to call me that!" Helena was seething with anger. "I HATE YOU!"

She raised her hand, releasing the red and black lightning to strike. Celeste was just as fast. She raised her hand; a stream of white light met the electricity with a shower of sparks. The light and the lightning disappeared instantly.

Helena looked at her sister in shock. No doubt the surprise of knowing her sister could do magic as well was probably enough to knock her off her feet, but as they both stared at each other, breathing heavily, you could see the change come over Helena. Those watching the scene in the clouds knew they were witnessing the birth of the Queen of Hearts.

Helena turned and ran.

The picture faded away as the cloud evaporated into the air, the fire ablaze once again. Everyone sat in awe. Celeste, however, was staring at her hands. She knew the scene by heart. This memory had gone through her mind countless times over the years since.

"Not long after Nix died, my father conquered Underland," Celeste murmured. "Helena disappeared for nearly two years before returning… She's never been the same since. She *hates* me."

Without another word, Celeste stood and walked off to her tent. No one tried to stop her. They'd just seen her saddest moment of her life thus far. They'd witnessed when two sisters were torn apart. Whether he'd meant to or not, Nix apparently succeeded in separating them forever. That moment had changed both Queens of Wonderland.

Chapter Nineteen

Spoiled Plans

The carriage was traveling fast, but not fast enough for the Queen of Hearts' liking.

"Move faster!" she bellowed to the driver.

He whipped the already bleeding quistrals. He didn't wish to disappoint the Queen. Nor did he want to make her angry. Making the Queen of Hearts angry meant *off with your head*.

The quistrals were already pushing themselves to the limit, but it still wasn't enough. Their mousy coats were soaked with sweat, backs lashed with the whip. Their breath heavy, wet, and cold, never had they run so hard or so fast.

More soldiers on their own quistrals followed the speedy carriage, or tried to follow at least. One card tried to drink from his canteen, but it was more difficult than he anticipated. Water sloshed out and landed on the quistral's back. As soon as the drops hit its skin, the effects spread quickly. The watery appearance spread over the mousy coat instantly, creating an aquistral.

The card was so surprised by this sudden transformation that he wasn't prepared for the next bump in the road. He flew out of the saddle and landed hard on the ground. Some of the soldiers faltered in their riding as if preparing to help the fallen card.

"Leave him!" the Red Queen barked.

Obeying immediately, they left the card behind and kept after the carriage. The new aquistral happily pranced off into the Tulgey Wood.

The Red Queen straightened her bejeweled crown perched at the base of her fancy, pinned up brown hair. Though she was in a hurry, she intended to make an impression no matter where she was. She placed her hands in her lap, the red silk enveloping her hands in a silky embrace. Her face was powdered white to conceal the dark circles under her eyes and the hollowness of her cheeks

Noticing the rapidly approaching turn ahead, she called out, "Don't turn. Keep straight ahead!"

The carriage flew off the road and burst into the Tulgey Wood. Swampy slithy toves darted out of the way on nimble legs. Mome raths scrambled aside, though some burst in explosions of feathers when trampled underfoot. Helena's heart beat rapidly with anticipation.

"Turn left, oaf!" she demanded. "Then stop."

The carriage jerked to the left, nearly flipping over, its left wheels spinning in the air. Landing on the ground with a thud, it stopped abruptly. The quistrals breathed mightily, their muscles quivering. It was a miracle they were still standing.

The Queen of Hearts didn't even wait for the driver to let her out of the coach. She blew the door open with a sharp glance and tumbled out. Eying the slain jubjub bird but a moment, she walked briskly past it. Her blood red skirts swished wildly with every step she took. Her chest rose and fell quickly against her tight corset, dreading what she might discover in that shack.

A soldier on each side of the shabby door awaited her arrival. They bowed deeply as she approached, but she ignored them. The door burst open with a glance and the trapdoor flew open with a flick of the wrist. The Red Queen never faltered.

Full skirts flowing, she traveled quickly down the stairs, cards following her. Continuing on past the pedestals—though she could tell that the faulty heart still lay beating in the carved wooden box—she walked briskly and purposefully down the hallway of beating boxes.

Coming to the spot, she stopped. Helena knelt down, pushing aside dozens of other boxes ruthlessly. None of the hearts fell out, though a few lay exposed. She soon found what she was looking for.

The Red Queen stood with the old, dirty box in hand. Letting out a deep breath, relief flooded through her. *It's still there.*

Opening the box confidently, she nearly dropped it in shock. She stared down at the empty box with cold, dark eyes. *It's gone.* There was no doubt in her mind of who took it.

"Alice," she hissed coldly, her jaw clenched.

"What is it, Your Majesty?" asked a tentative card.

Head snapping back, the Queen of Hearts glared at him. She walked up to him purposefully, gaze cold as ice. Plunging her hand inside his chest, he gasped out in pain before she tore out his heart and thrust it into the empty box.

The Red Queen pierced her lips as she growled wickedly, "Off with your head."

His fellow soldier then took up his sword without hesitation and struck.

*****

Celeste awoke with a start. Her skin was damp, her hair sticking to her neck. Thoughts raced through her mind in a jumble. *She knows.* Helena knew they had Remus' heart. She knew Alice had returned. She knew they would come. Celeste hung her head, covering her face with her hands; her chest felt like her heart and lungs were filled with broken glass.

Their advantage of the element of surprise was shattered and gone.

Chapter Twenty
Snark for Battle

Alice watched on as the Dormouse proudly presented the blacksmiths to the group, trying to figure out what was wrong with Celeste. But the White Queen was busy observing the assortment of weapons the blacksmith displayed. The others seemed intrigued too, completely fascinated.

"As you can see, Your Majesty," a broad armed blacksmith with an aquamarine beard was saying. "We have created the finest swords in all of Wonderland. The only blade that could rival these would be the vorpal sword itself!"

"Yes, I do see that they are very fine," Celeste commented.

The blacksmith lifted a sword to show. Indeed a fine blade, it gleamed bright and its hilt was crafted to perfection. Kai took the sword to examine it better.

"Well balanced," he uttered, hefting it in his hand.

"Yes, the hilt is lined with lady's-slipper," the blacksmith boasted. "The leathery plant helps with the comfort and balance."

Kai stepped back to wave the sword around impressively. "Light and swift."

He nodded vigorously. "The blade was crafted from the finest diamonds in the Diamond Mountains."

"A *diamond* blade?" Jack gaped, astonished.

"Well, of course!" the blacksmith boomed. "They are the best for Wonderland swords! The lady's-slipper naturally clings to diamond. But, of course, it all depends on the skill of the blacksmith's hand for these to be the finest of blades. The swords that the Red Queen's cards use are not as skillfully handled. Their blacksmiths focus on speed, not perfection."

Kai placed the diamond sword on the table with the assortment of weaponry. "It's a fine sword."

"I take that compliment very highly," the blacksmith obliged. "I recognize a fine weapon critic when I see one."

Alice wondered how Kai developed such ease in handling weapons. It was as if he'd handled them for more than just fighting.

Doe gave a small cough, indicating for the blacksmith to move along.

"Oh, yes," he said, holding up a finger. "We have prepared many other weapons as well as swords. The enchanted daggers are a particular favorite, able to return to the one who last threw them with only a simple command."

He lifted a dagger, its blade diamond, and tossed it on the ground. With a simple bark, "Come," the blacksmith caught it as the dagger flew into his hand. He grinned proudly, especially when he saw Wendy's eyes widen.

"We also have bows and arrows carved from the wood of a tumtum tree—finest wood in Wonderland—and the arrowheads are of diamond as well," the blacksmith went on.

Red took up the bow, studying the craftsmanship. Balancing it in her hands, she inspected the aim and the tightness of the bowstring. She seemed much too comfortable with that weapon in her hands. But she smiled politely and laid the bow on the table once more.

"How many weapons have you forged?" the White Queen questioned, earning a curious look from Alice.

But the blacksmith grinned. "Come, I'll show you."

He led the group to a large shed on the other side of the workshop, opening the door to reveal the interior. The walls were lined with a large assortment of weaponry. Diamond blades and armor were stacked on tables. Barrels full of swords, bows, and quivers sat propped against the walls. Stray knives and arrows had fallen on the floor.

Everyone gaped at the numerous amounts of deadly objects. Doe looked on this with pride, as did the blacksmith.

"You've overdone yourselves!" Dum gawked.

A proud grin spread across the blacksmith's face. "If it's a war coming, we'll be ready."

Those words made Alice cringe. *That's exactly what I'm afraid of.*

"We've been preparing them for weeks, Your Majesty," the trainer explained, his arm spreading out toward his trainees practicing all different kinds of combat. "Every man, woman, and animal here is well prepared for a battle."

"Excellent," the White Queen said. "I trust your judgment and will put it to good account."

The trainer's face went scarlet. "Well, uh, thank you, Your Majesty."

Alice's arms were crossed, observing the scene with hesitation and almost apprehension. The idea was becoming clearer to her now, and it was no less frightening. Wonderland was ready for war.

"Right, well, now we've seen the training grounds," Doe squeaked from Dinah's back. "I think we should continue on. You may return to your trainees, sir."

As the group made to leave, Red called, "Come on, Jack."

She grabbed him by the wrist to pull him away from a duel he was about to get himself into if he wasn't careful. The woman who would've pounded him scowled at Jack as Red dragged him away.

"Must you always look for trouble?" Red muttered.

"What? She started it," Jack insisted.

"Yeah, sure she did."

Doe and Dinah led the crew through the camp, the mouse very excited about showing them their next stop. She bounced up and down with such anticipation that Dinah had to meow at her every once in a while to keep her from getting too rowdy. But Dinah didn't really seem to mind; she was obviously excited, too.

"Let's call it our *secret weapon*," the Dormouse said mysteriously as they approached a tent towering over every other.

She and Dinah took a while to move aside the tent flap, but they got it open just the same. Alice furrowed her brow, unsure of what she was seeing. Inside was a very peculiar, very *large* creature. Slightly bigger than a fully grown jubjub bird and definitely broader, this creature seemed to be a clash of all different animals. Its snout was small with a black nose and long whiskers, large brown eyes and two pointy ears completing its face. It had four legs and on each foot there were three toes in the front and one in the back, all with sharp claws. Large wings folded against its ribcage and a long tail with three spikes on each side moved slightly back and forth. Dark green feathers covered its body, perfect for camouflage in the woods.

Alice didn't know whether to be frightened or laugh, which made it even more terrifying.

"Doe," she asked, "what is that?"

"*That*," the Dormouse piped proudly, "is Boojum, the snark."

"A snark!" Celeste exclaimed, sounding just as shocked as Alice felt confused.

"It must've been very hard to catch," the White Rabbit commented, impressed. "How'd you find it?"

"Dinah found him." Doe smiled. "He followed her here!"

Dinah purred with pride.

"Hmm…" Dum cocked his head. "I've always pictured a snark as more of a bird."

"Well, as you can see," Doe said, "besides the wings, feathers, and feet, Boojum doesn't look anything like a bird."

Boojum was attached to a long chain that kept him within his boundaries. He stretched out his long wings, filling up the tent as he yawned, revealing numerous teeth and a long pink tongue.

Doe grinned. "Neat, huh?"

"Certainly impressive," Kai muttered.

"I for one wouldn't want to be on his bad side," Jack commented.

"Is he… tame?" Wendy asked.

"Who, Boojum?" Doe chuckled. "He's tame enough. Of course, he was pretty dangerous and nippy at first, but once he likes you, then he's the sweetest gigantic puppy you'll ever meet!"

Celeste walked up to the snark, inspecting him. Boojum sniffed at her before consenting in letting her continue, his cat eyes dilating. She laid a hand on his shoulder, though it was a bit high.

"Is he ready for battle?" she asked.

Alice frowned.

"Well, sure!" Doe assured. "We've been preparing for weeks on end, especially on this big guy. We don't want him going after the wrong soldiers."

Celeste nodded, continuing to inspect Boojum as he settled back down for a nap. His tail tapped the floor lightly as her hand passed over him.

"He's really taken a liking to Dinah," Doe went on. "It's like they're long lost siblings or something."

As if to prove her point, Dinah strolled up to Boojum and rubbed up against his chin affectionately. A deep rumbling noise echoed from inside the snark's chest, almost like a purr.

"Told you." Doe put her paws on her hips.

The White Queen mumbled, "Helena sure won't be expecting this."

A glassy look came over her eyes for a split second. It was like a sparkle or a gleam somewhere behind her pupils. It disappeared quickly, but it concerned Alice all the same.

Celeste turned away from Boojum and over to the Dormouse. "I'd like to see my father's sword."

Doe's brown eyes widened. "How'd you know we had it?"

"I know a lot of things you wouldn't expect," she said simply, adding under her breath, "That's one of the reasons why Helena wants me." Then, resolute, she stated, "Now, show me."

*****

Helena was writing a letter. Not very long, but it was what she felt she needed to do. She needed advice. She needed direction. She needed to know what the next move was, or if there even was one.

"Your Majesty?" Lana asked.

Lana was one of the only few who were somewhat close with the Queen of Hearts. Yes, she was very much terrified by her, that much was obvious, but though she was just a servant girl, Helena found her company comforting. Not that Lana was a friend per say, she was just one of the few who sympathized for her. Lana did not like the torture or the killing that Helena did, nor did she enjoy it when Helena was with her daughter, but she seemed to still not entirely *hate* the Red Queen.

Helena certainly enjoyed her company more than either the Duchess' or the Knave's.

"Yes?" Helena paused in her writing.

"I was only wondering…" Lana lingered a bit before continuing carefully, "Who do you write to?"

"Why, I write to a lot of people," the Queen of Hearts said.

"Well, yes," she chose her words cautiously. "But, you don't write many… personal letters often. You hardly do. But when you do, it's always to the same person. I was just wondering, who is it? Is it a secret love?"

"No," Helena spoke softly, wistfully. "No, any love I've had is long gone."

"Then who is it… Your Majesty?" she added the title after but a moment's hesitation.

Helena looked away. "Someone who helped me through something I'd never thought I would escape from."

Lana hesitated again before she spoke, "The other day you mentioned someone. You didn't say who it was directly. But I thought that maybe this person you write to and this certain someone is the same person. You speak of this person as *helping you through something*, like one would describe a friend. But the one you spoke of… didn't seem like that. Are they the same person?"

Helena sighed, "Yes, they are indeed the same."

"It seemed as though you were terrified by this someone."

Lana knew she should stop. She bowed her head and returned to her sewing. There were very few moments when the Red Queen was so open. She didn't want to push it, though she was afraid she'd already gone too far.

Helena looked back at Lana, eyes distant. "No, I'm not terrified. I simply don't wish to disappoint."

*****

"Now, just know that the vorpal sword is not how it once was," Doe cautioned.

"I know," Celeste said. "It was destroyed after Helena killed our father."

Doe looked in wonder up at her, probably wondering how she could possibly know that. She was a living mystery, Celeste was. She knew far more than she let on. She could see things, was plagued with visions and insights. She

232

inherited this trait from her mother, though very few knew it, and it was why she was not yet dead. The Queen of Hearts needed to know something only her big sissy knew.

"*Vorpal sword*," Red pondered aloud. "Isn't that the name of the sword in that song you sang last night?"

"Yep," Dum answered. "The vorpal sword is a sword of legend. It belonged to the King of Diamonds."

"It's the only sword that can penetrate the hide of a jabberwock with ease," the White Rabbit explained. "It is truly a marvelous specimen of early magic. Indeed a sharp blade, the spell cast upon it makes this sword unable to compare with any other."

"Yes, and I would very much like to see it, if you don't mind," Celeste snapped a little too anxiously.

Dum grabbed her hand, muttering, "Hey, what's wrong?"

"Nothing," she assured, squeezing his hand. "I just *need* to see my father's sword."

His green eyes searched her face. He knew something was wrong, that Celeste knew something more. But he also knew that she wouldn't tell anyone until the time was right.

"Alright," he whispered.

"In here," Doe announced.

The group entered a small tent. It was nearly empty but for the silver and gold draperies decorating the inside and a statue that stood in the center. The sculpture was made of white stone, hints of diamond embedded in the cracks. Carved in an incredibly detailed life-sized statue of the King of Diamonds, it even had the small twitch of a smile he'd worn during his life.

In the statue's outstretched hands was a stone platform holding the vorpal sword. It was broken, as expected. The hilt was still intact, a deep purple diamond gleaming at the top of the pommel. The blade itself was broken into five pieces.

The White Queen gingerly touched the hilt, her fingers tracing the words inscribed in it. It had been a long time since she'd been near that sword. She hadn't seen it since the King of Diamonds died, murdered by his daughter's own hand.

That glassy look came over her eyes again for the second time.

Alice noticed.

"Doe, would you mind maybe showing the others to the kitchens?" she asked. "I'd like to have a word with Celeste for a moment. We'll meet you there later."

"Sure thing!" the Dormouse said happily. Turning on her heal, she beckoned, "Come along, folks. Follow me!"

Tweedle-Dum cast a worried look at the White Queen, meeting Alice's eyes before leaving with the others. Immediately, the Dormouse began talking about the scrumptious foods the chefs had made, blabbering on about the special seasoning on the slithy toves meat. The White Rabbit began to protest on her detailed descriptions in disgust, and Jack was picking on him for being such a vegetarian when their voices became inaudible in the distance.

The two were alone, but Celeste still stared up into the statue's face. With a sigh, Alice moved to the other side of the statue. Celeste still didn't look at her.

"Celeste, what's going on?" Alice voiced at last. "What aren't you telling us? Why do you keep asking the same questions about battle preparations: is this ready, is that ready? Is there something we should know about? Is there something *I* should know about?"

Celeste sighed, finally turning to face her. "You're right. There's something I haven't told you... Helena knows that you're back, officially, and that we have Remus' heart. She knows that we'll be coming."

Alice shook her head, confused. "But, how?"

"Don't you remember those soldiers we left tied up in the Tulgey Wood? And the ones we passed by on the road?"

Alice's face fell.

Celeste nodded. "I suspect it wasn't hard putting two and two together. She went to the vault, found Remus' heart missing."

A knot formed in her throat. "It wasn't the one on the pedestal?"

"No. That was a trick, just as you suspected. You chose the right heart."

Alice's head spun as she tried to process all of this. Several emotions overwhelmed her: relief that she'd chosen the right heart, fear that the Red Queen knew they were coming, confusion over Celeste's keeping quiet, and anger that their plans for surprise were spoiled.

"How do you know all this?" she asked at last, feeling stupid once she said it.

Celeste smiled slightly. "You know my power, Alice, that I know more than I would like. It shouldn't be too hard for you to figure out."

She put a hand to her head, mind racing. "Borogove! There goes the element of surprise."

"I know. That's why we need to move quickly. Tomorrow would be best."

Her stomach flopped. "*Tomorrow?*"

"Yes. Our only advantage is that we're ready, that we're prepared to fight."

"The faster we attack," Alice muttered as if finally understanding, "the less prepared she is for it."

"Exactly! That's why I've been asking if everything is prepared for battle. That's why I needed to see my father's sword."

"Wait," she questioned, this being the confusing part for her, "why do you need to see the vorpal sword?"

Celeste spread her arms over the sword's pieces in growing excitement. "Just look at it! Don't you see? It's only broken into *five* pieces! It's still fixable."

"But, why do we need it?"

"Helena will pull every card she has. I know for a fact that she has a jabberwock she's raised since it was an egg. You heard White: this is the *only* blade able to penetrate the hide of a jabberwock. This is the *only* blade that can kill it!"

The gears in Alice's mind were spinning. "Alright, so once you have the vorpal sword, you can kill it and give us the advantage."

Celeste shook her head. "No, not me. *You* must kill the jabberwock."

"*Me?!*" Alice exclaimed. She could hardly take any more of this. It was too much. Celeste had to be joking. *How can I kill a jabberwock?* She was barely able to kill that jubjub bird, and then she had help.

"Yes, you, Alice! I know it must be you. I can feel it."

"But, it's *your* father's sword!"

"But it's also Wonderland's sword," the White Queen persisted. "And Wonderland needs you."

"But, I didn't mean to come to Wonderland," Alice insisted, that horrible feeling rising in her chest, the kind that came from learning that someone out there may have manipulated her entire world. "It was a mistake!"

"Yes, it was a mistake, and what a wonderful mistake it was!" Celeste took her hands and looked her full in the eye with such mad joy it was hard to imagine she was the White Queen. "You found a place to call home here, Alice. You found love, friendship, and family. You've changed all of us for the better. So many here love you, Alice. They love you so much that they undoubtingly make you our leader, and they're willing to risk their lives for you! And it's because you remind us of what Wonderland used to be, and will be again if we are only mad enough to fight for it." She pulled Alice in a full embrace. "And for that we are all grateful."

Alice bit back tears. But though she was touched by her friend's words, she was still unsure about facing a jabberwock. The sword winked at her as the light caught its broken blade. Was she ready to wield it?

The colors of dusk rained through the sky. As the rich hues of paint from the heavens touched the darkness of night, the sun began to disappear beyond the horizon. The sun still caught a glimpse of the crowd awaiting their queen to make her announcement.

Celeste stood on the podium, tall and regal. Her head held high, she looked over the people of Wonderland. No one could question the authority and royalty before them. Celeste had every look of a queen.

"My friends, I have something that I must share with you. I have knowledge that Hele—" She interrupted herself and took a deep breath. "The Queen of Hearts knows that we are planning an attack."

This brought on a wave of whispers through the crowd.

"Settle down, please. Settle down," Celeste beckoned.

All was quiet instantly. Everyone wanted to hear what she had to say next. She was, after all, their true queen.

The White Queen spoke strongly and clearly for all to hear, "This news is troublesome, I know. With this knowledge in mind, it has been decided that the day of attack will be pushed forward. Our best chance of victory is to move tomorrow."

More chatter rippled through the crowd. They quickly died away as the White Queen continued to speak.

"I know that this is unexpected," she went on, "but it is our only chance. If we wait any longer, the Queen of Hearts will have doubled or even tripled her resources, and we will have no chance of victory. I advise everyone here who is willing to fight to make preparations. My generals, Tweedle-Dum, the Dormouse, the White Rabbit, and Alice will explain the plan of attack with you later tonight. We move out at dawn and we attack tomorrow at dusk."

The crowd stirred, but was silent.

"I call upon the best of the blacksmiths to please meet with me at once. Everyone else is dismissed. Go. Prepare for battle!"

The crowd instantly obeyed the White Queen's wishes. As Celeste moved off the platform, she was met by the five top blacksmiths in Wonderland.

"You wished to speak with us?" one asked, inclining his head at her approach.

"Yes, for you five I have but one task," the White Queen said. "Re-forge the vorpal sword."

No sooner had these instructions left her mouth did the sun disappear behind the horizon in order to let the moon and stars shine in the night.

Chapter Twenty-One

Hatter to Rescue

Red moved silently through the night, the Wolf blending well into the shadows. Only the bright green of her eyes and the glint of sharp teeth showed in the darkness when the moon shone through. Her feet tread silently over twigs and dirt, her breath soft. She needed to be as quiet as possible if she was to take them by surprise.

A tinge of déjà vu swept over her, the memory of a time before the Wolf, before Fang was hunting her. But she'd been something entirely different then… She shook her head. That was the past, a subject she never liked to dwell on.

Approaching the castle walls, Red could hear the soldiers pacing, breathing, making their rounds along the castle walls. They'd all be upon her at once if she wasn't careful.

Crouching low to the ground, she slinked closer, watching. There were seven guards talking together, so close she could almost hear their hearts beating rhythmically, unsuspectingly. Red didn't process their words. She needed to focus. Her paws tread quietly, but because she put more weight on them to stay low, her footfalls were heavier.

One of the guards stopped midsentence and came to a halt. Red froze in complete standstill, her body pressed flat against the ground. She heard his heart change pace. The guard's eyes searched the area where she lay. It'd be difficult to find her since she blended so well in the shadows, but if a light shone, it wouldn't be hard to figure out where she was hidden.

Unfortunately, luck wasn't on her side. As the guard began to turn away, a cloud drifted away from the moon. Light poured down. Red's eyes gleamed in the moonlight, giving away her position.

She growled deeply, baring her teeth. The guards drew their swords, but not before she sprung.

*****

"Your Majesty! Your Majesty!"

His boots crashed against the floor, armor rattling as he ran. Though it was hard to run in full armor, he knew if he wasn't quick he'd be in trouble. He skidded to a halt before the Red Queen's chambers.

"Your Majesty," he gasped out heavily.

"*What?*" she snapped harshly.

The doors were open, but the Red Queen didn't turn from looking out at the quickly darkening sky. Her hand pressed against the window's cold glass. It had been only yesterday that she discovered her brother's heart missing.

"There's a creature, Your Majesty. I've never seen it before." The card's eyes were filled with fear. "It killed the main guards."

"Describe this creature," the Queen of Hearts ordered.

"Like a bandersnatch, but smaller, faster. Fur dark as night, wicked green eyes. I've never seen anything like it!"

The Duchess stood to the side of the door as if she'd stepped from the walls. She raised a thin eyebrow, trying to conceal the tarts in her mouth. But her yellow eyes revealed the truth: The Duchess had no clue what the monster was.

The card turned back to his queen. "Your Majesty, what strange evil is this?"

241

She needed only ponder his words a brief second. A smirk on her face, she turned to the fear stricken soldier. But it amused her to see the Duchess so unnerved over something that did not, in her mind, deserve such fear.

"That would be a wolf, *card*," she said as she strolled up to him. "It's not a creature of this world, but it is an *animal* no less."

She was so close that he could feel her breath on his face. The Duchess' reptilian eyes observed this silently. Grabbing him by the jaw unyieldingly, the Queen pushed him against the wall. The soldier's eyes bugged, choking from her hold, gripping her wrist in a failed attempt to force her to release him.

The Red Queen leaned closer, her deadly tone like ice, "One lone wolf, you say, has killed *all* of my cards guarding the castle walls?"

The soldier forced himself to nod despite the pressure she gave him. He sputtered nonsense, saliva flying from his mouth.

"And *you*," the Queen hissed between her teeth, "were the only one to live to tell the tale."

"Are you going to kill me?" he gasped out, lips puckered.

She stared into his very soul, eyes cold and dark. "Not today. I need every soldier at my disposal at the moment."

She released him and he collapsed to the floor, breathing mightily. The Duchess sighed, disappointed not to see a good murder.

The Queen of Hearts glared down at the soldier. "Next time you may not be so lucky."

The soldier twitched uncontrollably as he bowed. He sputtered nonsense again, trying to kiss her feet.

Helena turned away from him. "Now, go. Tell everyone to prepare for battle. NOW!"

She heard the clamber of armor as he scampered out of the room.

"You too, Duchess."

The Duchess coughed in her throat, stooped her head, and shuffled away.

Tracing her fingers along the glass, the Queen looked out the window with a new gleam in her eyes. She laughed softly to herself. "A *wolf*, sister? *That* is your secret weapon? You'll need to conjure up more than that to defeat me, Sissy. I expected more from you."

*****

A great howl echoed through the night. It reached their ears, sent a shiver down their spines even though they knew what it meant and who called it. The signal had been sounded.

It was time to move.

Thank you, Red, Alice thought in relief.

Turning to her team, she whispered affirmatively, "Let's go."

Alice leading, the group moved silently through the night. The moon shone brightly above them, only partially full, so the team stayed in the shadows. Approaching the castle walls, Alice slammed her back against the rock, her team following in suit. She let her breathing regulate again, waiting for Dum's signal. The minutes ticked by. Still, she heard nothing.

"What's taking them so long?" Wendy whispered beside her.

"I don't—" but her response cut short.

A sharp yip split through the air. Alice jumped. Then she calmed, reasoning, *Boojum must be growing impatient.* But the Snark wasn't even part of Dum's team... Hopefully the Red Queen's cards hadn't noticed.

"Was that the signal?" a fellow team member asked.

Fast footsteps sounded above as soldiers rushed to the upcoming trouble. Alice's team pressed flat against the wall, hiding in its vast shadow. The clanging footfalls subsided as the cards ran past.

Alice pointed up above them. "*That* was the signal."

She gave a nod to an older member who served under the King of Diamonds, Bill. The lizard nodded back, stepping away from the wall. Crossbow aimed perfectly, he fired an arrow at the top of the barricade. The point lodged itself in the molding between stone, a rope hanging down the wall's side. Bill tugged it to check for security.

"Ready to go, Miss Alice," he said nasally, eyes darkened under the shadow of his newsboy cap.

Alice nodded. "Alright; your go, Wendy."

Wendy took hold of the rope and climbed it quickly, her movements nimble. *How is she so good at that?* As Wendy disappeared over the top, Alice wondered if she'd done a lot of climbing back in Neverland before she could fly. Or maybe she could always fly...

A thicker rope than the first cascaded down the side of the wall. Quietly thanking Wendy's swiftness, Alice was the first to pull herself up. Halfway up, she heard a scuffle and clash of metal.

Wendy, she thought worriedly, scrambling up the rest of the way.

Falling over the ledge, Alice felt relief when she saw Wendy retrieving a dagger from a fallen soldier's ribcage.

Wendy caught her eye. "Passed out." She tapped the edge of the blade. "Poison."

"Fast work," Alice commented.

She shrugged. "I try."

"Remind me not to get on your bad side."

"Will do."

*****

"KNOCK IT OFF ITS HINGES!" Tweedle-Dum thundered, completely enthralled with mad excitement.

Obeying his orders, the petals of the giant wind-flower were wrenched opened. The army moved out of the way as mighty winds blasted out of the gigantic flower, pounding against the castle gates with a force stronger than any amount of man power could ever pull off. The noise reverberated off the wall in a deafening blare. Dum and his team stuffed cotton in their ears.

Jack laughed at the sight. It'd taken a while to get the wind-flower so big. At least Celeste had a lot of that growing potion left over. The airstream was so strong it was almost visible as the gates caved to its strength.

With an immense crash that rattled Jack's teeth, the gate fell right off its hinges. No longer having an obstacle blocking their escape, the gusts blew away and the wind-flower wilted.

Behind the fallen gates stood leagues of dumbfounded soldiers, stupid looks plastered on their faces.

The rebellion didn't attack yet. They waited anxiously for their general's orders.

Dum hefted his sword high in the air. "ATTACK!"

Crazed battle cries filled the air as Tweedle-Dum's army charged through the fallen entrance. The Queen's cards came to their senses at the last minute, but the rebellion already had the advantage.

"Brilliant plan, Dum," Jack laughed loudly. "Crazy, but brilliant."

"No, not crazy." Tweedle-Dum grinned. "It's bloody mad!"

He charged into battle atop his iquistral, bellowing at the top of his lungs. Jack laughed, caught up in the excitement. Following atop his aquistral, he joined the victorious cry of the mad rebellion.

*****

Alice heard the fighting at the main gate, the ruckus Dum's army was making. Smiling to herself, she continued her fast pace as the six ran along the castle halls. Fortunately, they didn't encounter any soldiers on the wall. It wasn't until they scaled the wall again, crossed a courtyard, and snuck into the castle that their luck ran out.

"Halt in the name of the Queen!"

Skidding to a halt, Alice drew the vorpal sword. The blade gleamed brilliantly, newly forged.

The head soldier drew his sword as well, seven others following suit. "I said *halt*!"

I don't take orders from you, she thought as she swung her sword. The vorpal sword broke through the card's blade easily.

Alice's team attacked.

The head soldier jabbed his broken sword at Alice like a knife. She raised her arm, the diamond vambrace protecting her forearm as she deflected his blow and sent the blade clattering to the floor. Knocking his arm aside, she ran her sword right through his breastplate. Heart pounding, she forced herself to tear her sword from his chest as he fell. The vorpal blade was completely clean.

Whipping around, she saw Wendy drop and kneel as two soldiers charged from either side. A dagger in each hand, her arms shot out so the blades hit each soldier in the soft spot under the hip. They staggered in pain, one swinging his sword aimlessly and barely missed Wendy. The other fell back in surprise as Wendy tore out her knife only to throw it back, letting the potion take effect. The first card knocked the other dagger out of her hand, pointing his sword at Wendy's throat. He only looked sleepy despite the poison in his blood.

Alice raced to step in, but Wendy barked, "Come!" and the dagger flew out of the unconscious soldier's hip barreling towards her. In one swift movement, Wendy caught it in midair and sliced the card's hand off. He yowled in pain as Wendy dropped her knife in shock. That hadn't been her target.

Her self-repulsion left her defenseless, but before the handless soldier could react, Alice jumped in and off his head.

Another soldier lay dead with an arrow in his chest, two more unconscious on the ground, and the remaining had their hands up in surrender.

"Please, don't hurt us," one pleaded.

Bill had his crossbow aimed at one's chest while another held his sword up to one's throat. Alice strolled up to

247

the soldiers who both gulped in unison. Drawing a pinch of pink powder from a pouch strapped to her belt, she blew it into both cards' faces. Their eyes rolled to the back of their heads, instantly falling over asleep.

"What'd you do to them?" asked a chartreuse haired team member.

With a shrug, Alice answered simply, "Sleeping powder."

*****

"Hurry up," Red sneered for the umpteenth time.

"I'm hurrying as fast as I can," the White Rabbit insisted.

"Well, hurry faster!"

"Miss Red, the healing tonic does wonders, but it takes time to do its job. Now, stop your fussing!"

His paws smothered the cream on her leg where a deep gash stung terribly. Red flinched. The bleeding wouldn't stop and dirt clung to the wound. *I should've seen the sword sooner!* she scolded herself. If she had, she could've jumped out of the way and wouldn't be stuck here.

"Ah, I know how you feel," Doe admitted, kicking her feet. "I want to get to battle just as much as you do! At least you can go as soon as you're healed up. I've got to stay here 'til later with reinforcements."

"You'll get plenty of fighting when we get there," White snapped. "Honestly, I don't know why you're both so anxious to go kill people."

"It's not the killing I'm anxious about," Red muttered, though she didn't mind the killing all that much.

"What else is there in a battle?"

She looked out over the scene of the castle waking up for a fight. "It's the protecting I'm more interested in."

Boojum yipped again, this one quieter than the last.

"Dinah," Doe pleaded. "Please tell Boojum to be quiet! He's going to give away our position."

Dinah commenced in a series of pats, rubs, and mews to Boojum. The Snark shifted a little, but settled down obediently, head resting between his claws.

The White Rabbit placed his paws on his hips. "Well, Miss Red, you are free to go if you wish. The wound healed up nicely, but do be more careful!"

Red looked briefly down at her newly healed leg. It still itched for some reason. Ignoring it, she shifted into the Wolf and bounded toward the battlegrounds.

*****

Alice inhaled deeply as her team entered the dungeons. It was cold and musty, just as she remembered it. They were far underground and could no longer hear the ruckus above. She didn't want to think about what could be happening in the battlefield.

"Alright, you all know the plan," Alice said quietly to the others. "You three, go right. Wendy, Bill, and I'll go left. Free everyone you can, then meet back here. When we've finished, we'll join the battle. Everyone got it?"

They nodded.

Splitting up, Wendy, Bill, and Alice walked quickly to the left, each holding a weapon at the ready. Memories of this place drifted past Alice's subconscious, but she ignored them. Of all the prisoners in these dungeons, she was probably the sanest of them all. That wouldn't have lasted long, though.

Many cells they passed contained only skeletons and piles of bones. One held a rotting corpse, flesh still clinging to its body. Alice held her breath upon passing it, trying not to vomit. Wendy, surprisingly, was the least repulsed by the sight. Again, Alice wondered what all she'd experienced in Neverland. The last cell they passed was empty of all but a pile of heavy chains and a few mome raths. Bill gulped at the sight, as if he could only imagine what it formerly imprisoned.

Quickening their pace, the dark eeriness around them seemed to swallow them whole. But Alice recognized the faint light at the end of the hall, heard the sound of metal armor rubbing together. She knew this place all too well. That was the cell where she'd been held prisoner.

Upon approaching the corner, they stopped. Wendy peeked around it, quickly jumping back. By her expression, Alice knew it wasn't fear that made her jump, only caution.

"How many?" she asked.

"About fifteen, maybe twenty," Wendy responded.

"And prisoners?" Bill asked.

"One."

"Twenty guards for *one* prisoner." Bill gaped, looking to his general. "Is it worth it?"

Alice gulped. She snuck a look around the corner. Her heart pounded in her ears. When she looked back at Bill still waiting for an order, she yearned to say *yes*… but this wasn't the mission. It might've been why she came, but it wasn't why they had.

Alice sighed, deciding to be honest. "I understand it's a risk, so I'm leaving it up to you on whether to join or not.

But that's Remus in there. I'm going to get the Hatter... or die trying."

Wendy nodded gravely, but didn't hesitate. "So am I."

Relief washed through her despite everything. She couldn't find the right words to express how grateful she really was to have a friend like Wendy.

But Wendy just smiled softly. "You'd do the same for me."

Bill hefted his crossbow and secured his cap. "We lessen the risk with three. Let's blast this tea party and go kick some cards' buns!"

With that, they braced themselves—Alice steadied her breathing—and attacked at once. Bill stayed behind, taking aim and shooting from a distance, laughing manically. Wendy threw knife after knife, each returning to her outstretched hand when called. Alice was aware of their actions even as she struck fatal blows of her own.

The cards hustled into counterattack.

Wendy dodged a sweeping sword, taking the opportunity to stab a dagger in the man's knee as she ducked. It was then easy to lodge another in between his ribs as he doubled over in pain, the poison working fast.

Alice turned from felling one opponent and took a hit to the face from an armor clad fist. Her cheek throbbed terribly, but she snatched his arm and twisted it into a painful position as she flung herself on his shoulders. Using her legs to hold the soldier, she forced him to fall back, twisting to get atop him and not be crushed. He fell with a crash. Alice used her weight to keep him in place, grasping the back of his neck with all her strength until he slipped out of consciousness.

As Wendy was occupied in heavy combat, Alice unleashed a handful of sleeping powder on the next wave of soldiers. Six fell instantly, snoring and drooling in forced dreams. As Alice went to relieve Wendy of some opponents, she leapt back as arrows zipped by her, launched into unsuspecting soldiers in uncomfortable places. She nodded in thanks to Bill, who reloaded his crossbow with the speed of a lizard.

Soon the cards lay scattered over the ground unconscious, dead, or asleep.

During this whole scene, Remus just sat there, humming, swaying. Droplets of blood from the battle outside his cell stuck to his face, but he didn't flinch. Though he never rose or shouted, he did watch. His gaze was indifferent, never focusing, never hoping.

"Stand back," Alice warned Wendy, wiping blood off her cheek.

Catching her breath, she swung her sword and sliced through the lock easily. The door swung open. Alice rushed inside. Remus looked at her curiously, solemnly. Hands trembling, she took his hands and helped him to stand. He allowed her to, but it was like a puppet: not willing, yet not resisting.

"Come on, Remus," Alice whimpered, as if that would change anything. "It's going to be alright."

He moved like the ghost of the man he used to be. Light blue eyes shown like glass, as if his soul were somewhere far away.

"You remind me of someone I used to know," he muttered so softly she almost missed it. "Curiouser and curiouser… On the brink of madness. Careful not to cross it too much. Only just enough…"

She bit her lip to keep back stinging tears. "Who would that be?"

He closed his eyes as if trying to remember. Then in all seriousness, he whispered, "Myself."

She tried unsuccessfully to swallow the lump in her throat. Reaching into an armored pouch on her belt, she drew out the beating heart. It was warm thumping against her palm. She dropped the vorpal sword, the sound echoing off the walls.

Alice looked up at Remus' face again. He looked at her as if trying to remember a dream. But his eyes were still so ghostly that it was hard to remember he was still breathing, still alive.

But he isn't alive, Alice thought. *To live without a heart, to live without love, that couldn't be living.*

The Hatter's gaze fell to the heart in her hand. He murmured to himself, "Mine…? M-missing…?"

She gulped, trying to calm down, trying not to think about those blank eyes, trying not to recall the fight awaiting them above. Closing her eyes, thoughts of Remus flooded through her mind. But she couldn't do it. The heart throbbed in her hand, his lifeless eyes bore through her. Every time she thought of it all, her stomach knotted up.

If this really is just a story, she thought, *now's the time to wake up, Alice.*

But Alice didn't wake up. Lorna didn't brush the leaves off her face and take her home to tea. A white rabbit with pink eyes didn't come up to take her away to a better place at a better time. Because this wasn't a dream. Lorna was gone. Her childhood home wouldn't welcome her. The pink eyed rabbit was a lie. And nothing could save her now... except her.

"Alice," Remus sighed, brushing past her thoughts. "Brave, impossible Alice..."

Brave, impossible Alice, she thought with a smile. *Stop being so sensible.*

She thrust the heart into his chest.

Pain seized her heart in a squeezing fist. Remus yelled out agonizingly, and Alice's cry joined. Tears slipped down her cheeks as she buckled over, hand still holding the heart in place. With her free hand she clutched at her own chest, screaming.

"Alice!" Wendy's exclamation broke through, but wisely she didn't rush to her friend's aid.

Remus grabbed Alice's shoulder, his grip strong. Their screams filled the air. All she felt was burning, suffocating pain.

But somewhere in the back of her head she knew she had to let go or else they'd both die. Forcing her stiff fingers to release the heart, she tore her hand away.

Pain and screams instantly stopped, leaving a ringing silence. Alice gasped for breath, hand on Remus' chest where she could feel his heartbeat under her palm. Gripping her shoulder, he too struggled for air, his breathing purposeful for the first time in months. But it was all they could do not to fall into each other.

Remus was first to move, pressing his forehead to hers. "Alice."

She couldn't hold back the tears anymore. His sky blue eyes were his again. Breathing heavily, she managed, "Hatter."

He grinned, and that too was at last his own.

A cough behind them turned their heads. "Uh, I don't mean to interrupt the happy reunion, but we've got a schedule to keep."

Wendy elbowed Bill in annoyance.

"What?" He raised his long hands. "There's a war up there we need to get to!"

Wendy rolled her eyes.

Remus laughed, a pleasant sound in that dark scene. They stepped out of the cell hand in hand to follow the other two down the hall. It was in that moment that Alice noticed how their hearts beat as one.

Chapter Twenty-Two

War of Wonderland

"Remus! Alice!" exclaimed the large brown rabbit, his worn vest a dirty orange with purple polka dots. Bonier and messier than his cousin, the March Hare's twitchy ears seemed bare without the lime green hat Alice was used to seeing him in. None the less, it was good to see the March Hare again, even with straw on his head.

The man beside the Hare looked over with excitement, then confusion. "Alice, how did you get here?" He looked completely identical to Dum, except for a few key traits of shabbiness and malnutrition. Not to mention the new scars on his face: four lines running diagonally from eyebrow to chin.

"It's a long story," Alice said. "Good to see you, Dee."

Tweedle-Dee grinned as if the whole matter were forgotten. "You too, Alice."

Unfortunately, the reunion was cut short. The other members of Alice's team just arrived, followed by thirty other newly released prisoners.

Bill pointed out their need for urgency, "We need to get going. There's a war going on!"

Alice led her team and the escaped prisoners quickly to the battle. It wasn't too hard to find it. All she had to do was follow the noise.

They entered the Great Hall where the battle loomed before them. Alice blinked aside the flashback of the last time she'd been there. So much had changed since then…

But this wasn't that battle. It had been strictly and only a rescue mission.

This was a war.

Alice took in the sight quickly, the variety of creatures on their side, the swarms of cards and monsters on the other. It was all a confused mess of violence. She caught a glimpse of Celeste blinding soldiers with flashes of light, using exploding potions when she could. The Cheshire Cat was an easy find as he hovered over the battleground, dropping things on heads and also distracting annoyed soldiers. Tweedle-Dum was a fighting maniac, Kai and Jack close by. Just as she thought about it, she saw the Wolf streak by to wrestle with the bandersnatch.

Alice looked away from the scene, meeting Remus' gaze as he smiled briefly. He squeezed her hand assuredly before turning back toward the battle and raising his sword.

"FOR WONDERLAND!" the Mad Hatter bellowed.

"FOR WONDERLAND!" the freed prisoners echoed in extreme, maddening enthusiasm.

They charged into battle.

Alice ran headlong into it, wounding as many cards as she could with the vorpal sword. The floor was slick with blood. The enemy advanced in a fury.

She saw the charging soldier before Celeste did. Racing up to them, Alice swung her sword at the attacker. The blade went right through him, his body severed in two. She gaped at the fallen soldier in shock.

Celeste looked at what would've been her undoing. "Thanks."

Alice didn't respond, but she turned from the corpse to continue fighting.

Out of nowhere, Remus barreled through the chaos to envelope his big sister in a hug.

"I'm so glad you're alright," Celeste whispered, planting a kiss on his cheek.

Remus only faltered a moment to jab a soldier in the nose before responding, "You too, Sis."

Alice unintentionally reminded them of the battle when she killed a bandersnatch right in between the two. That got the fire to rage in them again and immediately they returned to the battle.

A streak of black fur zipped by as Red bounded up and snapped the neck of a nearby soldier. In the same moment, she took the chance to slice open a bandersnatch with her sharp claws. Red didn't stay long, soon jumping on to her next victim.

She gave a yelp when something nipped her tail, turning to find that she'd grabbed the attention of a jubjub bird. Its huge wings knocked her over as she transformed, and she landed hard on the floor. Left vulnerable, Red cried out as the bird lunged.

Blood sprayed. Its head landed at her feet, Jack looking triumphantly at the bird's headless body.

"What were you thinking?" Jack exclaimed. "Don't you know better than to pick a fight with a tub-tub bird alone?"

"I'll try to remember that next time," she said as Jack helped her to her feet. "And, it's *jubjub*."

Jack grinned. "I know."

Kai's blade clashed against another, sweeping it aside to strike his opponent's shoulder before finishing him off. Another soldier ran toward him, sword raised as he gave a great yell. Kai stepped aside and knocked the card on the head. The soldier fell unconscious.

He saw Wendy out of the corner of his eye, knife poised for the toss, looking right at him. Kai didn't have time to react before she threw it, blade headed straight for him. It flew right past his ear and lodged into a soldier's throat just behind him. The soldier's sword raised as if to strike Kai, but it fell from his hands as he dropped dead.

When Kai turned back to find Wendy, she already disappeared.

*****

"Mock Turtle, we need to hurry," the Dormouse exclaimed. "The moon's rising and Boojum is getting antsy."

She spoke truth. The snark wiggled and twitched around uncontrollably. It was all Dinah could do to keep him quiet. The battle could be heard from their standpoint and it was making them all feel the way Boojum acted.

The White Rabbit looked up at the sky. "You're right. I suppose it's time for us to get going."

Doe raised her paws in silent triumph. She turned to the awaiting reinforcements. All were quiet, ready for orders.

"It is time!" Doe's squeak was surprisingly loud. "Prepare to charge!"

The crowd of armed rebels cheered.

White sheathed his short sword. "You'd better saddle up, Miss Doe."

She scampered up onto Boojum's back alongside Dinah. Boojum could sense the excitement, trembling all over with anticipation. He was a whimpering maniac.

Doe cried excitedly, "Release the Snark!"

*****

Across the room, Dum fought three soldiers at once with expert swordsmanship, blade clanging against their swords in a series of sweeps and thrashes. He lunged unexpectedly, now only fighting two. One card thrust his rapier at him, missing by a hand's width. Dum took the opportunity to jab the hilt of his sword against the back of the bent soldier's neck, and the man fell to the floor.

The last one was difficult. Dum was almost backed up to the wall. He continued to swing his sword at his opponent's, but it soon clattered out of his hand.

The soldier held the sword up to his throat. "Any last words?"

Tweedle-Dum grinned madly. "Drop dead, bloody borogove."

The soldier scowled at the insult. With the shriek of metal, a blade sprouted from his chest. The soldier gave a gargled gasp, looking blankly at Dum in horrified shock. Confused at the turn of events, Dum watched as the blade was yanked out and the soldier fell over dead.

There stood a grinning Tweedle-Dee.

"Honestly, Dum," Dee exclaimed, "must you always get into trouble?"

"*I'm* not the one who's been in prison," Dum quipped, sharing the same grin that Dee had.

Dee laughed.

Dum casually kicked his sword up from the ground and caught it in midair before running it through an approaching bandersnatch. He turned back to his brother as if nothing happened.

He looked his twin over. "Cabbages and kings, mate! You look terrible!"

"You're one to talk," Dee said, punching a soldier in the nose before resuming conversation. "You sound just like Mother."

"No, Mother would add, '*Have you eaten?*' And that, my good brother, I did not say."

They laughed crazily, no difference between them. A soldier came rushing up to them with his sword raised. Dee struck the blade and launched into combat. Dum sat back, crossed his arms, and watched as the duel went on.

"You're a bit rusty, mate," he critiqued as the duel went on.

Dee smiled, parrying an attack. "I can still beat you any day."

The card tried to make a move, but Dee wasn't as distracted as he'd thought. Dee sidestepped him with a scoff.

"Excuse me," Dee criticized in annoyance. "I am *trying* to have a conversation with my brother, thank you very much!"

With the card temporarily confused, Dee took the opportunity to run his sword through his stomach.

Resuming conversation, Dum asked, "Seriously, though. What happened to your face?"

Dee raised an eyebrow. "Cat fight with the Red Queen."

"Did you give her worse scars?"

"Oh, I gave her scars alright, but they're not the physical kind."

Dum understood immediately. They laughed together once more over the old joke they shared since childhood. Never could anyone leave more scars on the soul than the Brothers Tweedle. It could be frightening.

Secret weapon in mind, they resumed the fighting.

Alice froze in terror as a great banging caused the wall to shudder, the noise echoing over the battlegrounds. It cracked and crumbled with each deafening blow. The fighting seemed to still as they all waited to see what monstrous horror would emerge. In an explosion of stone and debris, a huge creature bounded out into the war zone.

Alice smiled at the sight.

"Callooh! Callay!" the Dormouse squealed from her perch. "You get them, Boojum!"

Remus questioned beside her, "Are Dinah and the Dormouse riding a… *snark?*"

"Yes," Alice answered, laughing in spite of herself. "Yes, they are."

"Woo-hoo!" Doe screamed as Boojum leaped around, chirping with excitement.

Dinah gave a yowl and Boojum set to work attacking soldier, jubjub bird, and bandersnatch alike. Following the snark through the broken wall came a flood of rebel reinforcements led by none other than the White Rabbit.

"White!" the March Hare exclaimed, hopping from Alice's side to his cousin.

"March, old chap!" White proclaimed. "Sorry, can't talk now. We've got a kingdom to reclaim!"

"Tea Time to that!" March shouted, fighting for Wonderland alongside him.

Alice laughed before rejoining the battle also. The vorpal sword was serving her well. It was light and had good movement, able to penetrate anything she wished. It also became blunt when she was about to accidently wound an ally, which was very convenient.

"You know," Remus said, "we might actually win this thing!"

He finished off his opponent and moved onto the next awaiting victim.

"Did you ever doubt we would?" she asked, giving a blow to the leg and another to the head of her opponent.

He grinned at her.

A sword flashed

"Look out!" Alice warned.

Remus dodged the blade, but it grazed his arm. A sharp pain burned and Alice called out in shock. Nothing touched her. Nothing pierced her skin. But she still felt the stinging pain as Remus finished off his attacker, blood seeping through his sleeve.

"What happened?" he asked, concerned.

"Nothing." Alice smiled weakly. "Just try to be more careful. I'll explain later."

Remus was confused, but resumed attack.

Alice gritted her teeth and took up her sword again. She knew what had happened. The side effects had kicked in. Now, she felt the pain he felt, which meant he could feel hers. She'd nearly forgotten about the price she'd paid.

Taking up her sword for this particular fight, Wendy was in the middle of dueling with a very determined soldier. Unfortunately, her skill didn't match his with a sword. What could she say? It'd been a long time since she'd used one. Besides, she was used to cutlasses.

There was an evil gleam in the soldier's eye, one she knew all too well in the eyes of certain pirates. He was determined, his mind set on winning this. Such confidence was dangerous to fight against, especially since she couldn't match it.

A vase fell and shattered on his head.

That left the soldier in shock for a moment. Wendy was as surprised as he was. Then, a large chunk of the broken wall crushed his skull and he dropped, knocked out. She looked up to make sure she wasn't the next victim of falling knickknacks.

The Cheshire Cat smiled down at her, clucking his tongue. "Naughty little card. Should've known better than to try and hurt Wendy."

Her heart leapt. "You got my name right."

"Hmm… I suppose I did." Chess' smile widened before he disappeared.

Celeste saw the bandersnatch out of the corner of her eye. It leaped through the air, aimed to land on her. Before she could move aside, Boojum came out of nowhere and grabbed the bandersnatch in midair. The snark shook the beast in his mouth like a giant toy, sinking his teeth into his victim.

"All good, Celeste?" the Dormouse shouted from the snark's back.

"Yes, thank you!" Celeste shouted back, waving.

Boojum dropped the dead bandersnatch on top of a card before bounding after an unsuspecting jubjub bird. Celeste heard Doe and Dinah scream and meow encouragement. She smiled, shaking her head.

It hit her like a blow to the head.

What is it now? She thought in a panic, *What's wrong?*

Everything around her was a blur. Then it all became clear again just as suddenly as it blurred. But now, she knew. Celeste knew she was coming.

The doors burst open. Everything stopped. Time itself seemed to stop. They expected this would happen, but it was different to expect it than to experience it. Their chances of victory seemed to teeter dangerously off balance.

There, in all her splendor and horror, stood the Queen of Hearts.

Chapter Twenty-Three
Jabberwock

"You call this a battle?" the Red Queen mocked, no surprise in her tone.

Dressed in black with dark scarlet embroidery along the edge, she wore onyx leather boots, her outfit sleek and precise. Her long, dark brown hair encircled her scalp in a roll of braids, but she wore no crown. It was as if it was implied, as if there was no need for a crown to prove who she was.

"A *battle*…? Well, I must admit you all are maddeningly brave to rise against me," she continued, her voice traveling through a silent room. "But there comes a point when bravery easily turns to stupidity. You all have fought valiantly; a fact I've not overlooked. So I am willing to make you a deal."

The crowd of rebels shifted uneasily. But Alice stood still, waiting with the Hatter to hear what Helena had to say. The Queen of Hearts was prone to violence. To see her so calm, so *willing* to make any sort of deal was… unsettling. It either meant she was afraid to lose, or confident to win.

The Red Queen smiled dangerously. "If you give me what I want, then I'll let you leave this palace unharmed. You can go back to your own little towns and resume your ordinary lives. We'll forget this little incident ever happened. However, if you don't accept… I can assure you it won't be pretty. It won't end well for you at all. I have my own surprises up my sleeve. And trust me, my surprises are leagues more *deadly* than your measly little snark."

Alice's ears pricked as Boojum growled, baring his teeth. Dinah and the Dormouse had to restrain him from doing anything stupid.

"To avoid more turmoil and destruction, all you have to do is give me my sister, the White *Queen*—"

"No!" Tweedle-Dum's sharp protest resonated over the battlefield.

"Please, Tweedle, I wasn't finished." The Queen of Hearts continued, "I wish simply for the White Queen *and* Alice."

Remus wrapped his arms protectively around Alice. She leaned in, trying to hide in his arms. Everyone was silent.

The Red Queen kept talking after a moment's silence, "Come now, I'm not going to *kill* them! Surely, Alice, Sissy, you wouldn't ask all these innocent people here to die for you? I'll have you both either way. At least this way there's less bloodshed."

Still, everyone was silent. Alice swallowed hard, listening to the beat of Remus' heart. *What will we do if...* but Alice didn't dare let her thoughts wander so far. She didn't want anyone to die for her. But she knew that these people of Wonderland—a *better* Wonderland—were counting on her. She couldn't give up now.

The Queen of Hearts shrugged. "No? What a shame. I suppose I'll just have to take the alternative." She smiled cruelly. "Allow me to show you what a *war* looks like."

Instantly jubjub birds, bandersnatch, and cards poured in behind her. The rebels shifted back at the sight. Alice's heart pounded. Somehow she had a feeling what was coming.

None of the reinforcements attacked yet, though.

She thought she saw those dark eyes look directly at her as the Red Queen yelled, "RELEASE THE JABBERWOCK!"

The castle shuddered. Debris fell from the rafters. The crowd around them surged back in panic. But Alice stayed put, frozen as Remus' arms squeezed tighter around her. The horror was coming.

The jabberwock emerged from the great doors, more terrible than any dragon in all of the fairytales. Deep purple scales plated its body like armor, bulging fiery eyes struck fear to those that dared to look in them. A webbed crown enclosed the back of its cranium. Two great leathery wings were folded to its sides and four legs ended in jagged claws. Four long venomous canines stuck out of the front of its tubular snout, many other sharp tiny teeth crammed into its maw in rows. Its long forked tongue flicked out of its mouth like a snake, tasting the air.

"RUN!" Remus bellowed.

"ATTACK!" roared his cruel sister.

Everyone rushed in an uncontrollable current to get out of the castle. Alice held tight to Remus' hand, but looked back just as the jabberwock let loose a stream of indigo lightning off its tongue. The electricity struck everything closest to it, frying rebels, cards, bandersnatch, and jubjub birds alike as they fled for their lives. The smell of fried meat and burnt flesh mixed with the smell of blood. Alice's heart dropped.

It doesn't care whether it kills friend or foe.

Turning away again, she ran hand in hand with Remus, following the multitude. A crash sounded behind them, indicating the jabberwock knocked over another wall.

The crowd pushed hard against them as chunks of stone and debris fell from the ceiling. Screams split the air. Before she knew it, the masses pulled her apart from Remus.

"Alice!" she heard him shout

"Remus!" Alice shrieked, "*Remus!*"

But Remus had been taken away by the flow of the crowd.

"Remus!"

With a thud, Alice was knocked to the floor, feet passing all around her. She heard a clang as diamond clattered against stone. Looking up, she saw the vorpal sword lying on the ground before her. In a panic, she reached and grasped the hilt. A squawk sounded too close for comfort; she rolled over to avoid a tramping jubjub bird's feet. Gasping for breath, she stood with sword in hand.

Alice knew it was time.

She turned and surged against the flow, entering the Great Hall once more and breaking free from the crowds.

The Red Queen wasn't there. Only the jabberwock with eyes of flame remained inside. It had slipped on fallen rock and was picking itself up. It might've been dangerous, but it was also clumsy, she observed.

"Hey!" Alice shouted, realizing how mad she was.

The jabberwock's head snapped around to her, holding her gaze. Its fiery eyes seemed to melt through her very soul. She didn't like what she saw in those eyes: pure cruelty and everything that made up hatred and wickedness. It was hard to explain, but staring into those malevolent eyes made her burn as if she were on fire. Not even the evilest of people could possibly bear to look into the eyes of a jabberwock.

Alice ran, sprinting for the open doorway the Red Queen had previously emerged from. The jabberwock was on its feet in an instant. It spat out magenta lightening, sparks flying from its tongue, but Alice was too fast. She reached the doorway quickly, out of range from the electric stream.

"Over here, you oversized lizard!" she taunted.

The jabberwock's eyes flicked to the sword, the purple diamond on the pommel, the same color as its scales. In a flash, such severe loathing came over its eyes that even Alice could see it. All jabberwocks loathed that sword, as well as any of its wielders. The jabberwock with eyes of flame came whiffling through the rubble, bounding after Alice.

*****

The battle continued outside in the castle courtyard. The rebels soon realized that the jabberwock no longer pursued them, so they turned again on their enemy in fierce attack. The rose trees were soon splattered with blood of the slain, white petals stained red.

Jack was a bit preoccupied at the moment, battling a very large group of opponents. Unfortunately, he hadn't realized that he'd ventured into a swarm of enemies. He almost regretted his mistake… Almost.

Fortunately, Jack's talent of aggravating anyone he met came to his advantage. The more his opponents despised him, the more they were distracted, the easier it was to defeat them. For once, his cocky comebacks ended up saving his life instead of endangering it.

"Look how light you are on your feet," Jack observed while dueling a card. "Have you been taking ballet lately?"

The soldier growled, "I'd keep my mouth shut if I were you."

"Well, if you were me," he quipped, "I'd be hideous!"

Out of annoyance, the soldier tried a thrust at his arm, but Jack stepped out of the way easily. The soldier missed a step and stumbled, enough for Jack to kick him in the shin and strike him in the shoulder.

He cocked his head. "Maybe you aren't so light on your feet."

The soldier was knocked unconscious, a growing bump on his head.

A nasty snarl caught his attention. He turned to find a massive bandersnatch bounding towards him, teeth bared and drool foaming. Its yellow teeth gleamed in the moonlight. As it prepared to pounce him, Jack stuck out his sword so the blade sank into the bandersnatch's head. It slumped over dead, his blade still deep in the skull.

Jack gripped the hilt. "You should've picked on someone your own size."

He tugged, but the sword didn't budge. His heart flopped. Trying again, Jack put one hand on the bloody head and pushed. Still, it didn't move.

Soldiers and rebels scampered away quickly. Jack turned his head to see what everyone wanted to avoid.

He thought, *Is it that jabber-what's-it again?*

But when he found it, his stomach tightened. The Queen of Hearts was walking his way, dark eyes fixed on him.

Blast it!

Jack frantically tugged at his sword, trying desperately to get it free. He didn't want to face a foe like that without a weapon in hand. The Red Queen was approaching quickly. Jack grasped the hilt with both hands, putting his foot upon the bandersnatch's head, and pulled as hard as he could.

"Come on," he hissed. "*Come on!*"

The blade finally slipped free of the beast's brow and Jack held his sword up in triumph. Before he could get away, it flew out of his hands. Whirling around, he found himself looking into those dark deadly eyes of the Red Queen.

Gasping in spite of himself, he tried to run, but his feet betrayed him. They were like heavy stones stuck to the ground. He couldn't run, couldn't escape.

The Queen of Hearts looked over him briefly, her gaze sending icy fingers up his spine. He swallowed the lump in his throat. It was as if she were trying to find the best way to kill him.

Jack mustered the best grin he could. "Hi."

The Red Queen raised an eyebrow. Her smile was wicked. "*Hi.*"

He rubbed the back of his neck. "Uh, can we talk about this?"

"What's there to talk about? You've killed many of my numbers. It seems to me my only way to solve this problem is to… dispose of it."

"Well, maybe, but I think you may feel differently if, you know, we just talked this through, get to know each other a bit—"

"You talk too much."

"—Let's just start over; um, I'm Jack." He stuck out his hand, trying not to tremble.

Her eyes flared, but her hand touched her belly subconsciously. "I had a son named Jack…"

Before he could figure out how to respond, her hand jerked up and dug right into his chest. Unbearable pain exploded, shooting through his nerves. He cried out in agony, muscles seizing as he felt her fingers clutch his racing heart.

Darkness swam over Jack's eyes. The Red Queen tightened her grip, sending another jolt of pain coursing through his body. He cried out again. Tears welled up in his eyes. He never thought it would end like this.

A black blur flew past him. Instantaneously, he felt the release on his heart as the hand yanked back. A jolt jabbed his shoulder. Jack took great gulps of air as he fell back, heart pounding rapidly. His vision slowly cleared, but it took time for him to comprehend the scene.

Red transformed back to her human form, her stance dangerously poised. Her sword raised, she stood protectively over him. The Queen glared at her, gripping her arm where claw marks still bled steadily.

"Get away from him," Red hissed.

"So, you're the Wolf that strikes terror into my cards." The Queen of Hearts smirked as the marks on her arm glowed scarlet before healing themselves. "I must say, I'm quite surprised."

"Yeah, well get used to it," Red shot. Jack kind of liked it when she used that tone, as long as it wasn't directed at him.

"Oh, it'll take a whole lot more than a mere Wolf to cause me to drop to my knees fear," the Queen of Hearts laughed. "You shouldn't test me."

"I've faced worse demons than you before."

The Queen sneered. Sparks flew off her fingers before the lightning streamed directly for Red. But her sword shot up and met the electricity, the diamond blade deflecting it from hitting her and Jack. The lightning subsided. The two women stared at each other.

Jack blinked away more fuzziness in his head.

Red advanced, bashing aside lightning streaks with her sword. The Queen retreated a little at a time, though she didn't look in the least like giving up. Each flash was blinding, but Red didn't seem fazed.

A blast fried a spot of grass just beside Jack. He jerked back, regretting it instantly as pain shot down his dislocated shoulder. But he couldn't tear his eyes from the scene. Red was one fluid motion of ferocity, a fire blazing in her eyes that could match the Queen's in intensity. It kind of scared him.

Because of her advance in combat, Red seemed to be winning the duel. But then magic came into play. The sword melted in her hands, the dripping diamond searing her palm and burning her flesh. Red cried out in pain, burnt hand dropping the melted sword.

The Queen of Hearts flicked her wrist and Red was knocked off her feet, landing hard on the floor. As she stood, thorn branches extended from the rose trees, binding her limbs in place. Red couldn't move.

"I told you," the Queen scolded in amusement. "You shouldn't have tried me."

Red spat at her feet. The Queen raised her arms, bolts of lightning flicking off her fingers. Red's expression showed no fear as she prepared to face her death. Jack called out, trying to stand but couldn't; the pain in his chest and shoulder was too much.

A bolt of white wind shot past, blasting the Queen of Hearts to the side. She landed hard fifty paces away, searching for her attacker. At the garden's end stood the White Queen.

Celeste waved her hand, the thorn branches turning to brittle twigs. Red easily snapped them and freed herself. Jack sighed in relief as she turned to his aid, clutching her burnt hand.

Helena and Celeste locked eyes, frozen. It had been a long time since they'd seen each other face to face. Rage bubbled up inside Helena once again as her senses returned, and Celeste knew it. The White Queen turned and ran, determined to keep her sister distracted. The Red Queen screamed as she followed in pursuit.

*****

Alice sprinted down the hallway, the jabberwock hurtling after her. Its great wings crashed against the walls. Breathing heavily, she made a sharp turn up a flight of stairs. A sound like fingernails scratching chalkboard resonated as the jabberwock slipped and slid past the opening. Alice heard a loud crash below, thinking it must've rammed into a wall.

She climbed the stairs in a rush. The staircase was long and winding. Stomach tightening, she had a sickening feeling that she was ascending a tower. *Just don't think about it*, she thought desperately. But it didn't matter. Climbing a tower was not the best thing a girl afraid of heights should do.

The silence unnerved her with the jabberwock's disappearance. It didn't help with the hollow pit in her stomach.

A screaming far below pricked her ears.

The wall exploded directly behind her. Thrown to the stairs, Alice screamed. Exposed, a blaze of razzmatazz lightning came flashing towards her. Instinctively, she raised her sword like a shield. The vorpal sword glowed a brilliant purple.

Prying her eyes open, Alice found the electricity blocked by a violet force field cast by the blade. The jabberwock's lightning could not touch the vorpal sword… or Alice. She stared at it in shock. But the jabberwock flying outside the tower was furious.

She snapped out of her stupor, scrambled to her feet, and ran up the stairs. The fear of being burned to a crisp overwhelmed her fear of heights.

She could hear the great crash of flapping wings as the jabberwock flew up, trying to get her from the outside of the tower. Its tail crashed against the stone wall and her step faltered. Recovering her footing quickly, Alice continued on.

Keep breathing, Alice. Don't stop.

Giant claws made a grab for her through an opening in the wall. Her heart skipped as it barely missed her, and she jumped over the scaly foot.

The steps ended, a door standing in the way. Alice kicked it open, bursting into an empty room. She tried to catch her breath, her heart aflutter. The mighty gusts of the jabberwock's wings pounded her eardrums.

I need to go higher, she knew, though her stomach disapproved the idea. But if this was to work, she had to ignore fear.

Rushing to the window, she dared not look down. Her eyes looked toward the sky as she began to climb out, but that was almost worse. She crawled half way out the window without falling—a great success in her mind.

Alice heard the jabberwock circling the tower, drawing nearer. She froze stock still, legs dangling inside, body clinging to the window frame outside. Thankfully, she was poised under the roof's shadow. The jabberwock came into view. Alice held her breath, her heart thumping in her ears and her stomach doing flips. But the jabberwock didn't see her, and resumed circling the tower.

Letting out a small sigh, Alice quickly scrambled out the window, back pressed against the wall. Fear gripped her. She was aware of everything. The wind blew around her in cold gusts. Her heart seemed to plummet when she even snuck a peak down. Alice took a deep breath, swallowing the lump in her throat.

This is the only way, she told herself. *I can't compete with it on ground level. Don't be sensible, just be mad.*

The roof's edge loomed above her head, a ledge able to hold her. Alice shakily sheathed the vorpal sword so as not to lose it. Before she overthought it, before doubts could stop her, she jumped. Her hands grabbed the ledge. She suppressed a scream as she found herself dangling far, far above the ground. It didn't help that her palms were sweaty.

She had to move quickly before the jabberwock found her or she fell to her ultimate doom. Able to hoist herself up onto the tower roof, she crouched panting on the tile. The moon's rays fell upon her, making her visible to everyone.

Keep moving, she prodded, though every muscle protested.

Shakily, she drew the vorpal sword and crawled up the cone roof. It couldn't be long before the jabberwock found her. And if she slipped and couldn't stop, then... She swallowed, trying not to think of how far *down* she'd fall before hitting the ground.

At that moment she slipped. A squeal escaped her throat as her foot caught a stray tile and she stopped abruptly. Emerald lightning struck right above her head, leaving the shingles black and smoking. She cried out again in shock. The jabberwock had found her.

Hurrying now, she sped up her work, nearing the tip of the cone. The jabberwock scratched its claws on the roof in a failed attempt to grab Alice. Shingles fell. The tower jostled. Alice flattened herself to roof to keep from falling. The jabberwock landed heavily behind her.

Approaching the top, Alice scrambled to her feet, sword in hand. Clinging desperately to the flagpole, she turned to face the jabberwock as it crawled after her. She took a deep breath. There was no going back now. She had to do this.

The jabberwock started for her, feet and claws ripping the roof. It struck out, jaw snapping at her toes.

Alice jumped.

She stepped on it right between the eyes, using that to launch into the air and land with sword raised on the jabberwock's back. Before she could topple, she plunged the vorpal sword between its shoulder blades and held on tight.

The jabberwock threw its head back, giving an earsplitting screech as orange blood oozed from its wound. Alice grit her teeth, locking her grasp on the lodged hilt in its back. The jabberwock jerked to the side, thrown off balance. It groped at the tower roof before plummeting down.

Alice screamed, her insides rising, knuckles white.

The jabberwock tried to extend its wings, but it was so painful that they only partially opened as gravity pulled it down. The ground was approaching rapidly, and both enemy and rebel alike were scattering out of the way.

The impact rattled the earth. Alice was flown off from the intensity, sword still in hand. She landed painfully, the vorpal sword flying from her grip and clanging to the ground.

Stars specked her vision. Every muscle ached, bones sensitive, skin scraped and bruised. She trembled uncontrollably, as if the rush was only just catching up to her. But she sighed, thankful to be back on solid ground. Perhaps no one would mind if she just lay there for a while…

Then she heard the sound of scales scraping against each other, and her heart fell. The manxome jabberwock was still alive. The shouts and clashing of diamond and metal filled the air as the battle raged on around her. But there was only one foe for her now. Alice reached for her sword, grasping its hilt in a tight fist.

She stood slowly, achingly. Blowing wisps of hair from her face, she turned to the jabberwock.

Her breath caught in her chest, pressure crushing her ribcage and squeezing her lungs. She gasped for air, feeling as if she were drowning, suffocating. More stars swam before her eyes, dark spots threatening to consume her.

Fighting it back, she couldn't find out what was happening. No one choked her. Nothing hit her. But the pain felt as if she were being squished, crushed, suffocated...

Her vision tunneled and she saw the jabberwock standing with the Mad Hatter pinned under its foot, claws keeping him in a secure hold. Remus groped for the fallen sword just out of his reach, staring into the jabberwock's eyes of flame.

Panic hit her with more intensity than the heavy pressure in her body. Alice already lost Remus once; she was not going to lose him again.

She ran at the jabberwock, vorpal sword raised to her shoulder, the pain like a lash of fire surging through her core. It was like running through water, but she fought it with every ounce of strength she had. The jabberwock opened its maw, long fangs mere breaths away from Remus' face. Venom dripped. Neither saw Alice until the last second.

Alice gave a tremendous cry in pain and fury as she plunged the vorpal sword through the jabberwock's neck, slicing through thick hide and tearing through spine. Orange blood sprayed everywhere. The jabberwock barely had a chance to scream. The head landed to the side, fiery liquid pooling. The giant body fell sideways, releasing Remus from its hold, the bone crushing pressure diminishing.

The vorpal sword slid out of her fingers. Remus scrambled to his feet and let Alice fall into his arms in exhaustion. The truth settled down on the battlefield around them despite the desperate fighting: Alice had slain the jabberwock. The battle was as good as won.

Chapter Twenty-Four

Beginning's End

Helena was frantic. Scrambling around madly, she tossed vials and boxes into her bottomless purse. She was completely mortified that she'd lost the battle—or at least, almost. But the rebel's troops outnumbered her own now, and some of her own cards had the audacity to turn on her. She needed to act quickly.

The Queen of Hearts flew out of her closet and into her chambers. Flinging her bag over her shoulder, she snatched the crystal letter opener and put it in too. Picking up the box lying on her desk, she'd just taken out the crystal and tossed the container aside when she was interrupted.

"Helena, stop."

She froze, staring at her sister. The pale crystal was in her hand. The White Queen stood before her, having just stepped out of the doorway. The Red Queen's eyes darted from Celeste to the crystal, then back to her sister again.

"It's over," Celeste said calmly.

But those words didn't strike fear into her, nor did they make her nervous. Instead, Helena felt a surge of rebellious pride.

"Now, that's where your wrong, Sissy. This is far from over." Helena cocked her head. "And I think you know that."

Before Celeste could stop her, she threw the crystal at her feet. It broke to pieces and a bright light filled the room as the air crystalized. Celeste had to shield her eyes against the brightness of it. In an instant, the light diminished and Helena was gone.

Celeste stared blankly at the spot where her sister disappeared. If she wasn't in such shock, she would have wept. That's how she was on the inside. But instead of weeping, she didn't move. She didn't react in any way. She just stood there, calm as could be.

*****

"Hatter, my fellow lover of hats," the March Hare proclaimed upon seeing them.

"Old Mock Turtle, Hare!" Remus exclaimed when they neared. "You look worse than after that brawl between the Lion and the Unicorn!"

"*Really?*" the Hare gawked. "*That* bad?"

Alice nodded, taking in the full sight of the March Hare. His right ear was torn, his tail ripped out, and a toe on his left paw was missing. Brown fur matted with blood, a deep gash sliced through his left shoulder.

A fair haired young woman with hazel eyes tended to his shoulder. Her face was pale, but not because she was shy of blood. Stitching up the wound as carefully and tenderly as she could; the healing tonic could only do so much.

"Anyway, you should've seen the other guy. He's right over there." March tried to point, but found it difficult with a missing toe. He winced slightly as the woman tightened another set of stitches. "Borogove!" he mumbled. "This missing toe will take some getting used to."

"Would you please hold still?" the woman pleaded.

"My apologies, Miss Lana."

"You're alright, then?" Remus asked.

282

The March Hare grinned, revealing a missing tooth. "It'll take more than a jabberwock to kill this rabbit!"

"That's a relief," he sighed. "It would've been maddening to find a replacement business partner. It's so hard to find good help these days."

Alice elbowed Remus in the arm while the March Hare laughed hysterically. Lana tried her best to get the March Hare to be still.

"Speaking of hats…" Remus said, "Here's yours."

He produced a lime green top hat from behind his back and placed it atop the March Hare's head. Long ears stuck out the top where two holes were made especially for them to stick through.

"Thanks, Hatter!"

"You're quite welcome, Hare."

Alice looked around nervously, afraid of who else may be in the makeshift infirmary. Healing tonic was being hastily produced to one side by a long stream of rebels and castle servants. The able bodied ran bandages from one side of the room to the other. Experienced and amateur doctors barked orders. The injured cried or screamed in agony. Friends only able to stand by and watch murmured desperate prayers or wept mournfully.

So this is what the end of a war looks like, Alice thought, even though she had the sneaking sense that this couldn't be the end of it.

Her gaze fell on a friend and her heart dropped. She made out Wendy's form by his side. Anxious, Alice pulled Remus behind her as she made her way toward them.

Kai lay there unconscious, blood trickling from a stitched up gash on his head. Someone had removed his shirt to reveal a bruised body and a deep sever in his side. But it was his left leg that didn't appear normal at all. A broken branch seemed to have lodged itself inside his shin, blood soaking it, Wendy trying to stem the bleeding. Alice's stomach flopped, finding it hard to imagine the branch as bone. Unfortunately, however, it was his broken tibia that stuck out of his leg so splintered and bloody.

Wendy looked up teary eyed and white as a ghost. She didn't pull away, even though it didn't seem like her attempts were working. Blood stained her hands up to the elbows. But she herself wasn't hurt but for scratches and bruises.

Alice was speechless in shock, face turning cold.

But Wendy didn't need a verbal question to explain shakily, "He… he was fighting the Knave of Hearts when a bandersnatch snuck up on him and snapped his leg. The Knave struck him when he was injured, hit him on the head… I found him, killed the Knave, tried to stop bleeding…"

Wendy's voice broke as she took in a shaky breath as if trying to keep back a flood of tears. Remus approached to examine Kai's wounds grimly. Gently, he pulled Wendy's hands away from the protruding bone, she being in such shock that she didn't resist. Feeling useless, Alice pulled Wendy close and held her. She'd never realized how small her friend was until then. It only made her seem stronger.

Remus regarded the hollow faced man stitching up Kai's side. "Why aren't you tending his leg?"

The man looked up solemnly. "I treat cuts, stitch them up. I can't do anything about the leg until the White Queen gets here."

Wendy started mumbling again as if to herself, "It's happening again. When the Lost Boys returned from a pirate attack... a tribesmen ambush..." Tears fell freely now. "I couldn't save them."

She squeezed her eyes shut, sobbing quietly, trembling, as if the dam of shock would only let a trickle of sorrow leak through. Alice bit her lip, almost wishing she wasn't so thankful not to know such pain. Her own was burdensome, but not nearly so close to Wendy's.

Remus turned and met Alice's eyes, a knowing look passing between them. He set his jaw, reaching a decision.

"Well, we can't wait for my sister," he spoke to the man. "Get up and help me."

"What are you going to do?" Alice questioned.

"We have to align the bone," Remus muttered. "That'll make it easier for Celeste to heal it."

The skinny man seemed apprehensive, but one look at Remus made him comply instantly. No matter how much Remus tried to ignore it, he was still a prince. When he was serious, a prince was exactly what he looked like.

Remus turned to Alice grimly, a warning in his eyes. She understood. Pressing her brow against Wendy's head, she shut her eyes for good measure. Just when she was beginning to wonder if Wendy was still looking, the terrible crack split the air. She cringed. The bone had been realigned.

Instantly, an agonizing cry made both girls jump as Kai jerked awake. Alice still didn't look, afraid of what she might see. Wendy clutched her arm.

She heard Remus as he tried to keep Kai still. Alice bit her lip so hard it began to bleed. The pain she'd felt with Remus when the jabberwock's foot crushed him and nearly broke his ribs seemed nothing compared to the pain Kai must've felt.

"What happened?"

The sound of Celeste's voice made Alice look up, vaguely wondering how she'd arrived so quickly.

The sight made her gut churn. The bone no longer stuck out of Kai's leg, but it bled profusely. The color had drained from Kai's face as pain overwhelmed him. His breathing rapid, his cries were enough to draw the attention of everyone around them. The stitches on his side stretched to their limit.

"What happened?" the White Queen questioned again, right at Kai's side. "What'd you do? How long has he been like this? What caused this?"

Remus' face was pale, but he answered quickly, "Bandersnatch broke his shin; the Knave of Hearts split his side and knocked him on the head. We aligned the bone so it'd be easier for you to mend. He just woke up. You came just in time."

Celeste was already examining Kai's leg. She placed her hands on the gash, earning another yell from Kai. Alice winced. But Celeste didn't hesitate to look closely at the wound, eyes darting everywhere.

Her arm shot out, hand hovering over Kai's head. She closed her eyes, muttered a few words. The tension in his face eased out, his eyes closing, his breathing regulating.

Once done, Celeste returned her focus on his leg, taking a deep breath in preparation. Placing her hands over the wound, she began to whisper so softly Alice couldn't make out what she was saying.

Despite whatever she'd done to numb the pain or relax him, Kai hollered out in deafening anguish. Eyes squeezed tight, head wrenched back, his body craned in a gruesome position. Celeste continued her incantations with uncanny tranquility, a white glow lining the wound's edges and growing ever brighter.

Kai's muscles tensed so much the veins up his arms and those in his neck stuck out plain and visible. His screams were agonizing, worse than before. Alice wanted nothing more than to look away, but her eyes were fixed on the sight.

"What's going on?" Jack rushed up to them with Red at his side.

Prying her gaze away, she took in the sight of the two. Jack's left arm was in a sling, and Red had a bandaged hand and split lip. Alice felt like hugging them both, thankful they were both safe, but Wendy clutched her arms too tightly.

"What's she doing to him?" Red asked in extreme concern.

"She's helping him," Alice tried to explain.

"You call this helping?" she shrieked. "He's in pain!"

"And he'll be in even more pain if Celeste stops," Remus stated over his shoulder.

He and the other man tried their best to keep Kai still. The light around his wound glowed brighter. Celeste's eyes were shut tight. Beads of sweat formed along her brow. She was putting much energy into this spell, more than she'd ever care to admit.

Perspiration coated Kai's skin, jaw locked open, screams hoarse. The stitches along his side popped off from the strain. Celeste's hands trembled slightly. The light grew so bright that it was hard to look at. Jack and Red shielded their eyes. Alice buried her face in Wendy's hair.

In an instant, the light vanished and Kai's shouts quieted. Alice dared to look up. Celeste stood with her hands still on Kai's shin. His wound was healed without even a scar. The gash at his side was mended. Even the cut on his temple had healed, the stitches falling out.

Breathing heavily, Kai opened his blue eyes and looked around like he didn't know where he was. Remembrance filled his expression as his gaze flicked from face to face. He sat up slowly.

"Did we win?" he asked, voice gravellier than usual.

Wendy burst out of Alice's arms and rushed up to him, nearly knocking him over as she threw her arms around him.

"You'll be sore for a few days," the White Queen said. "Try to stay off that leg as much as you can, but it should be fine."

Kai looked at her gratefully, obviously still trying to piece together what had happened since his duel with the Knave. "Thank you."

"It was the least I could do." She smiled. "Now, I have some work to do. Your friends will catch you up on recent events."

After the dead were buried and the injured were tended to, Alice met the others in the White Queen's old chambers. The room was fine, though very unkempt with cobwebs hanging and dust clinging to everything. She looked at each of her friends, grateful to still have them, unsure what she would do if she lost them. But even with her relief, she couldn't help but feel so strange.

It doesn't feel right, she thought. *This can't be over. There are too many loose ends, too many questions.*

She couldn't stop herself from asking the obvious, "Where'd she go?"

The Knave of Hearts was dead. The Duchess was imprisoned. The only one unaccounted for was the Queen of Hearts.

But Celeste didn't answer, her distant eyes staring out the musty window. Remus laid a hand on his sister's shoulder in silent encouragement.

When she spoke, it as if she didn't quite know what she was saying, "Helena has flown to her master. She's gone to another world far beyond the borders of Wonderland."

"*Master?*" the White Rabbit muttered, as if this didn't make any sense.

"Yes."

"So, the Queen of Hearts is just a pawn in this game?" Dee queried.

"I would say she's more of a bishop," Dum commented.

"No, too saintly. She's more like a rook."

"True."

"So, there's someone out there *worse* than the Red Queen?" the Dormouse proclaimed, swinging her feet off the edge of a table.

"Yes, there is," Celeste said, still not turning to them. "That's why she wanted me... alive. I have the ability to know the fate of her master, the ingredients to gain her power." She sighed, narrowing her eyes. "It's becoming clearer to me now."

"What's her master's fate?" Jack asked, cringing as he moved his shoulder slightly.

"It's uncertain, but even if it was, I wouldn't tell you. It's… too dangerous to know." She cringed, squeezing her eyes. "… But what I can say is that it includes the five of you."

"The five of who?" the March Hare asked.

"Whoooo," the Cheshire Cat pondered absentmindedly. "Whoooo arrrre yoooou?"

"Wendy, Jack," Celeste answered without turning, "Red, Kai, and Alice."

"Why us?" Kai asked, rubbing his scar.

"Because this *master* is the one who wants us," Wendy whispered.

Alice turned to her, wondering how she hadn't thought about that. The idea settled in her mind with all the dread of facing the jabberwock.

"That's it, isn't it?" Wendy inquired the White Queen. "The Red Queen's master is the one who wants us."

Celeste's shoulders slumped slightly. Her head nodded, affirming the statement. Alice gulped; Remus squeezed her hand tightly.

What happens now? Alice thought.

Red spoke up, "Who is this master?"

The White Queen sighed, looking back at them at last. "I don't know."

"How do we know which world we go to?" Wendy asked.

Alice chewed her lip. After a thorough search through the Red Queen's chambers, the White Rabbit was finally reunited with his pocket watch. He was preparing to part with it again, unsure when next he'd see it. The pocket watch was silver with a pearly face, a diamond button in its center. Instead of numbers, ticking hands pointed to stars of rainbow gems.

"Oh, you don't know which world you go to," the White Rabbit assured. "The watch is strange that way. It's in control and decides which world to go to. You have no say in the matter."

Remus took Alice aside, looking her in the eye. "Are you sure about this?"

"Yes, I'm sure," she assured. "I have to go."

"Then let me come with you."

Everything in her wanted to say *yes*. But she shoved that aside. "No. Five already pushes the pocket watch's limit. Besides, you have to stay here."

He took her hands in his. "What I *need* is to be with you, keep you safe."

"You don't need to keep me safe," she insisted, looking back at her fellow Facility escapees. "We'll keep each other safe."

Remus scowled. "I hate this."

"I know…"

"This is maddening."

Alice sighed. "Remus, you have to stay here, help restore Wonderland. It's your duty. I know you don't want to be a king, but it's time for you to step up and be the prince that you are."

He looked at the floor sheepishly. "I know."

291

She tried for a smile, lifting his chin up. "Hey, don't worry about me. I'll be back." She kissed him gingerly.

Turning, she joined the others in saying their goodbyes. Over the course of their adventures, they'd all become closer. That didn't make this any easier. Well, everyone except for Jack and White, whose annoyance with each other still held fast.

"Bye, Tiny." The Dormouse punched Jack in the shin playfully. "Good luck out there."

"Bye, Mousy." Jack saluted her; and Doe saluted back.

The Cheshire Cat appeared out of nowhere in a cloud of mist. "Goodbye, Ruby."

Red sighed in annoyance. "I told you, it's…"

He waited expectantly, multicolored eyes shining, grin widening.

"Never mind. Goodbye, Chess."

Tweedle-Dum stuck out a hand to Kai. "It's been nice meeting you, mate. Take care of that leg of yours. And, uh, sorry about the whole *Si* thing. Sometimes things just come out of my mouth before they've registered in my brain."

Kai shook his hand. "That's alright, Thrush."

Dum grinned, probably realizing Kai wouldn't stop calling him *Thrush* just for payback.

Dinah rubbed up against Wendy's leg, purring loudly. She scratched Dinah's ears.

After giving the Brothers Tweedle hugs, Alice turned to Celeste, whose eyes shone. She pulled her into an embrace, holding each other for what seemed too short a time.

"Be careful," Celeste whispered.

"I'll try."

When they pulled away, both had tears hanging off their eyelashes. Swallowing the lump in her throat, Alice went to join the other four around the watch.

"Alice!"

She turned around, instantly enfolded in Remus' arms, his mouth pressed to hers. There were tears on her cheeks that weren't hers.

Their lips broke apart a moment for Remus to whisper, "Hurry back."

"I will," Alice promised, kissing him one last time.

She squeezed his hand before releasing it and joining the others in holding the pocket watch.

"Just one more thing," Celeste warned. "Wherever you end up, be cautious. There's a war coming. Nothing could've prepared any of you for what lies ahead."

Alice and the others nodded in understanding. But she was too distressed to worry or question. Alice was leaving Wonderland again, and this time it was by choice.

What are you getting yourself into this time, Alice?

"It's time," the White Rabbit said solemnly. "Don't forget, do not lose that watch. That is your ticket home, whichever world you call home."

"Goodbye," Alice whispered, "White Rabbit."

His black eyes looked up at her, the same sadness in them. "Goodbye, Miss Alice."

Alice, Wendy, Red, Jack, and Kai held tightly to the watch. Alice looked back at Remus, his tears still glistening on her cheek. As Wendy pushed the diamond button, the Mad Hatter's smile was the last thing Alice saw before they left Wonderland.

Chapter Twenty-Five

New World

The Queen of Hearts walked briskly down the hall. The grand doors opened at her approach and she walked in. Black boots clicked with each footfall. She stopped just short of the platform.

"What news have you brought me?" the voice was cruel and cold.

"There was a… *situation* back in Wonderland," the Red Queen stuttered only slightly.

"What kind of situation?"

"It was just a measly old battle. Isn't that typically the case?"

"Did you take care of it?"

She hesitated but a split second. "No, not exactly."

"Did you obtain the information I need from your sister?"

"No, but I know something better." Helena smiled.

"Yes?"

"I know that the five you seek are now working together."

Her master said nothing.

"Yes, they were together," the Red Queen continued on with a smirk, "in Wonderland."

"Do they know?"

"No, I'm certain Sissy wouldn't have told them. She'd think it too *dangerous*."

Her master relaxed a bit, taking a thoughtful pause. "They're in Wonderland, you say?"

"I said they *were* in Wonderland," she corrected, "but I highly doubt they're still there."

The Master pondered a moment more. "Thank you for this information."

The Queen of Hearts inclined her head, smiling. "My pleasure."

"Since you cannot return to Wonderland, I assume you have brought the necessities?"

The Red Queen patted her bag. "I did, indeed. I will begin preparations presently."

"And your associates?"

"The Knave is dead." She shrugged. "And it's not worth it to waste resources retrieving the Duchess. She can rot in her cell for all I care."

"So be it. Get to your preparations then." The Master's eyes gleamed two different colors. "We must rely on the others to do their job."

The Red Queen smiled and bowed her head slightly before strutting away, walking confidently. She hadn't disappointed her master. Her chest swelled with pride.

She said to herself, "Those kids don't know what they're in for."

*****

They were thrust into a world of colors, flying, spinning. All hands were glued to the watch as the golden needles whirled round and round, faster and faster. Alice joined the others in screaming, yelling, and shouting from the excitement and fear pulsing through them. Ticking echoed around them, filling her ears achingly. Alice watched the clock's face, the hands spinning wildly around. It made her dizzy.

The arrows froze, pointing to a single jewel star. Colors melted away. The ticking ceased.

They landed with a thud on the ground, each falling in a different direction. Alice lay sprawled on the grass, heart racing, trying to catch her breath. She held the pocket watch tightly in her hand.

Wendy was first to get up. Alice sighed, slipping the watch's chain around her neck and tucking it under her shirt for safe keeping. She stood, observing their surroundings. They were in a forest by the looks of it, high up near the edge of a cliff. A mountainside, maybe? Alice joined Wendy in looking over the scenery. The height on which she stood made her head spin, but the view was admittedly incredible.

Jack rubbed the back of his head. "You'd think Long Ears would've given us a warning that we'd be crash landing…"

"Where are we?" Red groaned as she got to her feet.

Wendy was smiling, happiness and tears dancing in her eyes. "Neverland."

Acknowledgements

First and foremost, I want to thank my family for their unwavering support and love. I wouldn't be the person I am today if it weren't for them. And as a girl who isn't quite as witty as I'd like to be, it's always a blessing to have such sarcastic jokesters around the house who can help fuel my writerly wittiness.

To my old friends from the West Coast, my new friends on the East Coast, and friends everywhere in between, thank you so much for being part of my life in such various ways. God has blessed me in knowing each and every one of you when I needed you most. I couldn't be more grateful for your friendship.

I want to acknowledge the wonderful works of Lewis Carrol, J. M. Barrie, and Hans Christian Andersen, as well as the tales of "Little Red Riding Hood" and "Jack and the Beanstalk." Without these marvelous stories and glorious characters, this book wouldn't be a possibility. It has been a joy and a privilege to use these tales and give them a new light, though I will always adore the originals.

For additional, less obvious acknowledgements, I wanted to tip my hat to "Goldilocks and the Three Bears"—which was a cool little subplot to include—and the renowned nonsense poem, "Jabberwocky" by Lewis Carrol, which was incredibly fun making Tweedle-Dum lead in song.

Thank you to Aleshyn_Andrei and Sergey Novikov for the gorgeous images that make up this cover, and to Derek Murphy with his extremely helpful tips on creating beautiful book covers. And thank you to the people who have shown support and enthusiasm for this book. It's your excitement that makes me overflow with enthusiasm to share this book with all of you!

And lastly, thank you to my Lord God, who has given me this talent and passion, and who has been with me through everything. I don't know where I'd be without Him.

Get ready for the next adventure...

The Realms Series

Book Two
NEVERLAND

Emory R. Frie

...Coming 2017

Emory R. Frie is the author of debut novel, *Heart of a Lion*, and her new fairytale rewrite, *Wonderland*, the first instalment in The Realms Series. Emory will be attending Berry College this fall to further pursue her writing craft. Raised in Oregon, Emory now lives in South Carolina with her family, Scottie dog, and retired barn cat.

www.ingramcontent.com/pod-product-compliance
Lightning Source LLC
Chambersburg PA
CBHW020237180626
46810CB00006B/2233

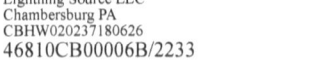